I0635719

For permissions, contact:

Crown Cipher Publishing

crowncipherpublishing.com

First Edition: 2025

Cover design by Crown Cipher Publishing

Interior design by Crown Cipher Publishing

A Crown Cipher Publishing Release

We protect this Fucking House

No, Not This Email

SECOND THOUGHT SERIES: FIRST THOUGHT · BOOK 1

JAMES E. LORRAINE

No, Not This Email

Publisher: Crown Cipher Publishing

www.crowncipherpublishing.com

Printed in the United States of America

Table of Contents

Dedication

For the ones who laugh through their love stories,
even while holding hands with the trauma.

Because we don't always heal before we connect—
sometimes we're still limping when we finally get chosen.

This is for the ones who woke up one day and said,
"I will not perform for love today. I will be seen in full."

For every person who dared to be soft,
even when softness wasn't safe.
For those who gave themselves room to be
messy, magnificent, and still worthy of being wanted.

I dedicate this to the pain,
the pleasure,
and the persistence—
because that's what it takes,
every single damn day,
to choose yourself
while making space for people
you grow to care for,
love for,
and live for.

To the group chats that kept you alive,
to the crushes that had no sense of timing,
and to the drafts you never sent—
not because you were scared,
but because for once,
you knew better.

And finally,
to everyone who's ever whispered:
"I'm ready now. Just… don't make me say it first."

I see you.
I got you.
I laugh with you—

because if you don't,
you'll cry and text somebody you swore you blocked.

James E. Lorraine

Chapter 1: Happy Hour. Hot Mess.

Jean's martini was already waiting when she walked in. She didn't even sit yet— caught Jordan's eye from the front of the bar and raised two fingers with the grace that made you think this was her place. It wasn't. She moved like it.

Velour Social had only been open four months, but Jean already had her spot—center bar, left of the flower wall, facing the entry so she could clock everyone who walked in and make a clean exit if the vibes turned weird. Not that they ever did. Not here. Not with Asha running the floor like Beyoncé's meaner little cousin.

"Lychee martini, extra cold, splash of elderflower," Jordan said, sliding the glass across as Jean settled into the velvet-backed stool. "Was about to text you."

"You're cute, but I'm not a text-me-when-you're-thinking-about-me kinda girl," she smiled. "I'm more of a pull-up-on-you-when-I'm-in-the-mood type. That."

Jordan grinned, polished and unbothered. "Duly noted."

Jean looked around. Thursday crowd. Light but pretty. All linen and ankles. The people who said things like "vibes only" and meant it. The playlist was floating somewhere between Ari Lennox and old-school Brandy—mid-tempo soul with enough bass to remind you why you shaved above the knee.

She adjusted her top, a deep plum satin wrap blouse that whispered money, and crossed one leg over the other. The gold cuff on her ankle caught the low bar light. She didn't come to be seen, but she damn sure came correct.

Asha clocked her from the other end of the bar and walked over grinning. "Lord. She done pulled out the 'I—got-a-promotion' blouse."

Jean smirked. "You're not wrong."

"You ain't even let me finish saying congratulations on the last one."

"Still working for James King," Jean said with a shrug. "Different battles, same bullshit. new heels."

Asha cackled. "I live. Who you waiting on?"

"Danielle. "
Asha's eyes widened. "Ooooh. Therapist Danielle or 'I'm not your therapist but I'll make you cry' Danielle?"

"Both. Depends on how much she's had to drink."

Asha nodded like she understood and she did. "Want me to line her up?"

"She takes her martinis dirty. Blue cheese olives. She classy-nasty."

"Say less."

Jean turned her attention to her phone and pretended to scroll, but she was watching the door. Danielle wasn't late, just dramatic. The woman who waited until she knew you were seated, relaxed, and halfway through your first drink before walking in and changing the temperature of the whole room.

And like that, the temperature changed. Danielle walked in like a goddamn HBO season finale. Not the girl you rooted for, the one you feared. Slim-cut black pants, sharp as a promise, and a sleeveless halter top that said 'I'm free now.' Her curls were in a loose updo, enough neck to stir something in the weak, and her lip was blood red.

Jean didn't turn around, but she felt her.

Danielle slid onto the stool next to her like it had been reserved. "Here's to your promotion."
Jean clinked her glass against Danielle's dirty martini and said without missing a beat, "Still working for Ellie Sinclair. Not answering emails after 6."

They sipped like grown women do when they've lived long enough to stop lying to themselves and are now learning how to lie better to other people.

"You ever think," Danielle said, "how different we'd be if we hadn't met that first day of orientation?"

"Girl, if I hadn't met you, I'd probably still be fake-happy with Marcus and pretending I like sweet wine."

"Shut up. You used to love Moscato."

"I used to love a lot of shit that gave me headaches."

Asha, now eavesdropping while pretending to polish glassware, choked on her gum.

Danielle glanced sideways. "How long before Kiki and Ramon show up?"

"Give it twenty. Ramon's gonna act like it was Kiki who took too long to get dressed, but we all know his beard takes more maintenance than her whole body."

"Mmm. Velour's finest sugar swirl." They paused. Watched the door.

Sure enough—Kiki and Ramon, hand in hand, arguing in that flirty way that only couples with good sex and therapy can. Kiki waved like a Black auntie at a concert. Ramon winked at Danielle and Jean as they walked in.

Danielle turned her body toward Jean, away from the door. "So. Real talk. What's going on with Tyrone?"

Jean's brow arched. "Who?"

"Who … Church Candy. All that ass and all that attitude."
"Stop."

"Did he not wear a silver mesh tank top and a floor-length duster to the last R&B night, looking like he moonlights as a Marvel villain?"

Jean laughed loud—sharp and unfiltered. "You are so inappropriate."

"I'm also right."

Jean leaned in. "He's a sweetheart. finished his PhD in something weird. Folklore and mythology."

"Of course he did."

"He's starting a podcast."

"Of course he is."

"He calls it Let That Church Candy Testify. I swear to God."

Danielle laid her head on the bar. "We are not gonna make it as a species."

Then, the door opened again. Tyrone, aka Church Candy (CC for short) entered in a silk kimono, sunglasses, and what looked like leather joggers. He blew a kiss at Asha, bowed at Jordan, and floated toward the back lounge like he had ancestors watching.

Danielle watched him pass. "And yet… I'm weirdly proud."

"Don't be," Jean said, sipping. "He tried to quote Audre Lorde at brunch last Sunday and ended with a Maya Angelou line. I almost threw my mimosa."

They both paused. Looked around. Laughed. It felt good to laugh.

Real good. Like they hadn't done it in a minute. Like the world outside wasn't chaotic and crumbling. Like they hadn't each cried at least three times in the last ten days alone over men who wouldn't know accountability if it called them collect.

Jean took another sip. Slower this time. Danielle watched her. "You okay, though?"

Jean nodded. Then stopped nodding. "You ever realize you finally got the life you wanted, and now you gotta figure out if you want it?"

Danielle didn't answer right away. She lifted her glass and let it sit at her lips. "I think we confuse what we wanted with what we survived," she said finally. "And now that we're safe, we don't know what to do with peace."

Jean swallowed something heavier than vodka.

The music shifted. Ari into SZA. The lights dimmed a little. Jordan leaned in to whisper to Asha, who nodded, then disappeared into the back.

Danielle swirled her glass. "It's okay to change your mind,. Even about things you prayed for."

Jean turned to face her fully. "Even about people?"

Danielle's eyes didn't flinch. "Especially about people."

Their silence wasn't awkward. It was honest. One of those moments that happens between friends who know each other too well to lie, too proud to cry in public, and too tired to keep pretending that being strong didn't cost them something.

Jean wiped the edge of her glass with her napkin. "Anyway. I'm thinking of gonna Paris next month."

Danielle blinked. "Alone?"

"Yeah."

"Girl, you hate flying."

"I also hate being this version of myself and she lives here."

Danielle let the words land. "Take me with you."

Jean tilted her head.

"Fuck it," Danielle said. "I'm not joking. I got a passport and PTO. I'll even let you pick the hotel."

Jean looked at her. "Fine," she said. "But you're not allowed to psychoanalyze me until at least the second croissant."

Danielle smiled. "Deal."

They clinked glasses again. Slower this time. Like they knew they'd decided something they couldn't take back. And like that, they were off on a new chapter, a new trip, maybe even a new version of themselves. But for now… the martinis were cold, the bar was warm, and the night was getting started.

Jean had barely taken a sip when a voice cut through the music. "Oh, so you can answer his texts but not mine?"

She turned, slow and deliberate. "Lord, give me the strength… or give him the sense to walk away."

It was That Guy—a two-date wonder she'd filed under "Do Not Resuscitate." He was grinning, but it was the kind of grin you put on when you're about to throw a drink.

"Guess I wasn't exotic enough for the throne," he said louder, catching the attention of half the bar.

Jean leaned back on her stool. "Sweetheart, the problem wasn't that you weren't exotic. It's that you were exhausting."

The Velour Veterans hollered. Asha actually dropped her bar towel. CC stood up, ready to escort, but the man muttered something and bolted.

Jean sipped her drink like nothing happened. "Some people don't understand the concept of a clean exit."

Danielle was halfway through her second martini when she spotted the trouble. It wasn't loud. Not yet. Trouble rarely is when it walks in wearing three-inch heels and a chin held too high. This trouble came with a designer clutch, visible side-eye, and a tight smile that only opened around men and money.

"Don't look now," Danielle said without looking up. "But here comes somebody who swears y'all are best friends because y'all exchanged skincare tips once in a bathroom."

Jean didn't flinch. She sipped. Danielle sipped. They didn't have to look. They knew.

"Brittany," Jean said under her breath like it was a codeword for 'duck and roll.'

"Mm-hmm," Danielle replied. "Brittany with a 'y' and unnecessary energy."

Brittany had the pretty that made insecure men misbehave and confident women tired. Not because she was a problem, but because she made everything a performance. If she complimented you, it was followed by a story of how she did it first, better, or in Paris.

"JEANNNNN!" Brittany squealed, arms out like she'd spotted a war hero.

Jean turned in time to receive a half-hug and a cheek-air-kiss combo that smelled like Chanel and audacity.

"Look at you! Giving finance baddie tonight!"

Jean smiled politely. "Hi, Brittany."

"And Danielle," Brittany added, dragging the name out like it had too many syllables. "You still doing that therapy thing?"

Danielle blinked once. Sipped slower. "Every damn day." Brittany laughed like she got the joke but didn't.

Jean leaned in. "What brings you to Velour, Britt?"

"Oh … got done with a little strategy session. Couple of my clients were in town. Tech bros. Boring but rich, so." She shrugged like her moral compass was in storage.

"Mm," Jean replied. "Can't beat boring with a budget."

Before Brittany could reply, Asha appeared like a Black girl guardian angel. "Excuse me, Brittany, right?" she asked, professional but lethal.

Brittany turned, smile flickering.

"Your table's ready. You're in Ramon and Kiki's section. Follow me."
"Oh, I'm not dining tonight. Just wanted to say hi to the girls," she said, gesturing toward Jean and Danielle like they were on display.

Asha didn't blink. "Then let's get you a bar tab so Jordan knows not to comp anything."

That did it. Brittany hesitated, adjusted her clutch, and finally walked away—but not without tossing a final glance over her shoulder that screamed, 'I'm relevant, dammit!'

When she was gone, Asha exhaled. "You're welcome," she said, sliding a fresh napkin across the bar.

Danielle reached for a cashew. "She said 'tech bros' like that was a flex "

Jean chuckled. "She's been trying to get invited to the Women Who Win Brunch for three years. Wore the same Fendi belt two seasons in a row and blamed it on her assistant."

"Wait," Danielle said, sitting up straighter. "Is she the one who claimed her man invented a crypto coin that turned out to be points on a coffee app?"

"The very one."

Danielle howled. Jordan, overhearing, leaned in. "Y'all need your own talk show. I'd tune in for the outfits and the drag."

Jean winked. "Call it Therapy and Throat Punches."

Danielle nodded. "Subtitle: She Can Heal You or End You. Choose Wisely."

They were still laughing when Kiki and Ramon finally made their way over, drinks in hand. Kiki was in a green halter jumpsuit that made her look like money and chaos. Ramon's shirt was open enough to show chest but not enough to get banned from brunch spots.

"You bitches look expensive," Kiki said, kissing the air near both their cheeks. "Danielle, your lip says don't try me, and Jean—whew—your aura got me ovulating."

"Thank you, sis," Jean replied. "I call it 'glow-up with a side of leave me the fuck alone'."

Ramon dapped Jean and hugged Danielle like siblings who used to fight but now share playlists.

They pulled up extra stools, and like that, the table expanded. So did the energy. Velour had a way of doing that. People came as couples or solos, but somewhere between cocktail two and playlist shift three, whole tribes would form like jazz bands—freestyle, unscripted, alive.

Danielle leaned over to Kiki. "You ever feel like we're all about one spilled secret away from a soft launch meltdown?"

Kiki nodded dramatically. "Girl. I'm one late period and one group chat leak away from moving to Mexico."

Jean sipped her third martini and leaned in. "Not Mexico. Tulum."

"Facts," Kiki said. "White girl reset vibes."

Ramon raised his glass. "To emotional fugitives."

They all clinked.

The door swung open again. Everyone glanced, out of instinct. A tall, clean-cut man in a steel-gray suit walked in, alone. He was the kind of fine that didn't announce itself. The kind that grew louder the longer you looked. Dark skin. Trim beard. Walked like he knew exactly how much rent he paid and how much peace it cost him.

Jean saw Danielle see him. Danielle looked away, then back again. Slower this time.

"Oh no," Kiki whispered. "I know that look."

Danielle exhaled. "That's—"

"Don't," Jean interrupted. "Don't give him a name. Once they have names, they get plotlines."

"Too late," Danielle said. "He was a plotline."

Jean turned fully toward her. "Was?"

Danielle nodded, eyes still locked on the man as he approached the bar. "We went out once. Good date. Great kisser. Terrible communication. Said he wasn't ready for anything serious. And then popped up a week later in a brunch photo with a whole girlfriend."

Kiki leaned back. "Oop."

Ramon let out a low whistle.

"He see you?" Jean asked.

Danielle nodded. "He did the 'pretend you don't see her, then double-take and half-smile' maneuver."

Jean rolled her eyes. "Classic coward formation."

Danielle swirled her martini. "You ever wonder if they know what they're missing or if they assume we never felt it?"

"I stopped wondering," Jean said. "Started assuming they do

know. But knowing ain't the same as being man enough to say it."

Danielle glanced back at the man, who was now pretending not to be scanning the room every thirty seconds. "Anyway," she said. "He's somebody else's problem now."

Jean raised her glass. "To offloading emotional debt." They clinked again. Louder this time. No one smiled.

The martinis were gone. Then came the espresso martinis. Then came the fries "for the table," which meant "for Jean, who needed a buffer between her last sip and her next mistake."

Kiki had moved to a lower lounge seat, heels off and legs curled under her like a threat.

Ramon was DJ-adjacent, arguing with Jordan about the merits of mixing Burna Boy with Anita Baker.

Church Candy reappeared from the back like a cartoon reveal, this time with glitter on his cheekbone and a feather in his hair. "Don't ask," he said before anyone could, sliding into the seat next to Danielle.

"I wasn't gonna," Danielle replied. "But Reason #655 I don't date men anymore: glitter without context."

Church Candy gasped. "Excuse me?"

Danielle sipped. "You heard me."

Jean leaned over, laughing. "Wait, how high do the reasons go?"

"I stopped numbering after Reason #481. That one was about a man who believed almond milk came from almond cows."

The table cackled. Even Ramon, mid-playlist debate, shook his head. "Nah, that's bad."

"That's tragic," Jean added.

"Don't worry," Danielle said. "I've healed. I'm happy now. Fully recovered and gay."

Church Candy raised a glass. "To recovery." They clinked again. Church Candy sipped like it was communion.

Jordan slid two fresh drinks across the bar. "From the gentleman over there."

Jean and Danielle turned slightly. The man was already watching. Ashy elbows. Smug smile. Button-down shirt that needed starch and prayers.

Jean downed hers instantly. Danielle blinked. Made a face. Whispered behind her hand: "Oof. No."

He started walking over. Ashy arms. Mismatched energy. Not a single molecule aligned with the vibe. Jean shook her head.

"Don't get me wrong," she said loud enough for only their section to hear. "I could use some dick—but if his arms are ashy? I guarantee his whole body's ashy. Last thing I need is a dusty Black ass walking away thinking he did me a favor."

He reached them with a half-smile. "… I saw you drink it…"

Jean didn't even blink. "I didn't say I didn't drink it. I said I didn't invite your unmoisturized ass over here."

The man blinked, stood there a beat too long, then slinked off without another word.

Asha, watching the whole thing from behind the bar, gave Jean a silent fist bump. They all laughed. Loud and layered. One of those laughs that comes from survival. From knowing you're not the one to play with.

That's when Jean's phone buzzed. She glanced down and instantly stilled. Danielle, mid-sip, noticed.

"You good?"

Jean didn't answer right away.

Danielle leaned over. "Who is it "

Jean tapped the screen off and placed the phone facedown. "Nobody."

"That 'nobody' usually has you checking flight prices at 2 a. m."

Jean's jaw flexed. "It's him."

Danielle nodded slowly. "Of course it is."

"You ever think a man leaves enough room for you to miss him on purpose?"

"All the time," Danielle replied. "Then I remember that Reason #118 was me crying on the floor while he posted gym selfies."

Kiki whistled low. "Whew."

Jean looked toward the door. She wasn't expecting him, but that didn't stop her body from tensing like she might have to pivot, hide, or throw something.
"He said he was proud of me," she said quietly. "Said he saw my name come up in a Forbes article and smiled."

Danielle's laugh was soft. "The ones who made you question your worth love to compliment it when they can't afford it anymore."

Jean stared at the marble of the bar.

"Don't text him back," Danielle said.

"I wasn't gonna."

"You already unlocked the phone."

Jean sighed. "It's muscle memory."

Danielle reached across and turned the phone over again. "Break the habit before it breaks you."

Jean looked up at her. That same softness she rarely let anyone see crept into her eyes. Danielle didn't flinch. "He doesn't get to take up space here. Not tonight." Jean nodded.

They let the silence settle. But it wasn't heavy. It was a hug with no arms. A moment between friends that didn't need fixing, witnessing.

Church Candy, sensing the vibe shift, slid his glass down the bar and whispered, "Y'all need shots or silence?"

Jean smiled. "Both."

Danielle raised her hand. "Tequila. No lime. No chaser. I got shit to forget too."

Jordan lined them up like an exorcism.

They each took one. Danielle hissed. Jean exhaled. Kiki moaned. Ramon coughed. Church Candy blessed himself.

Jordan raised a brow. "Y'all good?"

Danielle wiped her mouth and said, "We stay good."

Jean nodded. "And when we're not, we get better."

Church Candy whispered, "And when we're petty, we get louder."

The music switched again—Rihanna this time. "Desperado." Slow, sharp, unapologetic.
Kiki stood up, arm in the air. "This my song!"

Everyone else laughed. Even Jean, even after the text, even after the ghost of a man tried to claw his way back into her peace. Danielle leaned over again. "You sure you're okay?"

Jean turned to her, face warm. "I am." And she meant it. Because she was surrounded by good drinks, good energy, and the people who didn't need an invitation to show up for her. She was allowed to be soft here. Allowed to be angry. Allowed to be healing.

Velour wasn't a bar. It was a confessional. A battlefield. A girls' locker room after the championship game. It was where they laughed, cried, lied, and told the truth before they were ready.

And tonight? Tonight, it was where they reminded each other that survival wasn't enough anymore. They were here to live.

Chapter 2: Revenge, Rotisserie, and Red Flags
Group Chat: Velour Veterans (Muted □)

CC: Can someone explain why I woke up with glitter in my belly button and a receipt for 3 tequila shots I didn't order?

Asha: Because you're loud and God is fair. Also, that feather you were wearing? Still in my purse.

Kiki: LMAOOOOOO. I'm crying. Not the feather.

Danielle: If you find my silk scarf in there too, return them. Thanks.

Jean: Don't y'all have jobs? Or is it me clocked in and pretending not to smell like liquor and lies?

Ramon: Some of us are working. I'm on a Zoom.

CC: And yet… you're in here.

Asha: Lmfaooooo busted.

Jean dropped her phone on her desk and leaned back in the chair, trying to remember if she'd taken Tylenol or thought about taking Tylenol. Her head wasn't pounding, but it was giving "Don't try me."

Her heels were expensive and unnecessarily high. Her inbox was already out of pocket. And her calendar? Insulting.

Budget meetings. Partner updates. That one finance VP who always asked questions with no actual curiosity. All before noon.

She closed her eyes and exhaled. She was 38 years old, C-suite, still flawless—and yet she was one espresso shot away from telling someone to circle back and get the hell out her face.

Her phone buzzed again.

Danielle: Tell me why I walked in late, hair still damp, and somehow got complimented for "being early for once."

Jean: Because people don't know how lesbians work. You were late on purpose. It's your right.

Danielle: Exactly. I don't dream of labor or morning meetings.

Jean: "Dream of labor" is going on a tote bag.

Danielle: Put it next to "Reason #717 I'm gay now: less explaining."

Jean smiled. Danielle always made her laugh, even on mornings like this. Especially on mornings like this. And somehow, always when Jean needed to be reminded she wasn't crazy— surrounded by the wrong energy too damn often.

Her email chimed.

Subject: "Quick question (won't take long)"

She didn't open it. That subject line had never told the truth.

Meanwhile, across town, Danielle was stirring oat milk into her coffee like she was plotting its downfall. Her office was quiet, clean, full of plants that thrived in indirect light and petty gossip. Her assistant had left a neatly stacked folder on her desk with the Post-It: "FYI—resched'd w/Dr. Whitmore. New client at 1p.m. is the trauma doula."

She didn't know what that meant. And she wasn't ready to find out. Danielle took a sip, slid into her chair, and opened her notes app to update her affirmations list.

1. I'm not going back.
2. I'm allowed to leave what doesn't feel safe.
3. I don't need closure from people who lose access.
She paused, then added:
4. If they lie in your face and call it love, it's a scam.

She set the phone down and laughed to herself. "That's gotta be Reason #744."

A knock at the door. Her assistant peeked in. "Danielle, your 9:30's running late. Want me to push your noon call back in case?"

Danielle smiled. "Yes, please. And remind me—who's the new client again?"

"The trauma doula."

Danielle blinked. "Still not clear on what that is."

The assistant grinned. "Me neither, but she's paying full rate."

Danielle raised her mug. "Amen."

Asha: Why this man walk into my bar now wearing a T-shirt that said "Alpha Energy, Beta Problems?"

Kiki: Screaming

CC: Block him. Preemptively. Off the shirt.

Jean: Was he ashy?

Asha: Jean. He had crust in the corner of his MOUTH.

Danielle: Y'all gonna make me quit my job and open a bar that screens people at the door like TSA.

CC: If they can't explain who Audre Lorde is, they don't get in.

Ramon: Half y'all didn't know who she was till last year.

Jean: And yet here we are—educated and exfoliated.

Danielle: And unbothered.

Danielle: Girl. My 1:00 told me she found her self-worth in a sound bath and lost it again at brunch. I can't do this today.

Jean: Tell her to schedule an appointment with God. You charge by the hour.

Danielle: And by the nerve.

Jean smirked. Her office was an 11th floor icebox with views of the skyline and zero tolerance for bullshit. The door was closed, the staff was scared, and her inbox was acting like it didn't know who she was.

Subject line: " wanted to circle back □" Circle back where? To what? For who? Jean didn't reply. That email could rot.

Instead, she turned to her phone and opened the group thread she kept muted for her own mental health.

CC: I need y'all to be so serious. This man asked me to be his platonic Valentine.

Kiki: Excuse me?

Asha: That's a hate crime.

Ramon: … did he say "platonic" with his whole chest?

CC: Yes. Platonic. As in "no penetration but you can pick the playlist."

Jean: Was he at least tall?
CC: 6'2 with anxiety and a birth chart that screamed "I cry after head."

Danielle: Bitch, I'm white people confused.

Kiki: OH MY GODDDD 😂😂😂

Asha: Danielle that's your new tagline.

CC: Put it on a hoodie.

Danielle: Put it on a PTO request.

Across town, Danielle was sipping her third peppermint tea of the day and wondering if it was illegal to charge extra when a client cried before they sat down.

Her 2:00 had texted to reschedule because "Mercury was acting funny ". Danielle muttered, "So was your boyfriend but you didn't reschedule him."

She texted Jean again:

Danielle: How do I tell my clients I'm not God, Oprah, or their mother? Just a girl with a license and a low tolerance for delusion.

Jean: Say it with your chest. Or a rate increase.

Danielle: Tempting.

She sighed and glanced at the orchid on her desk. It was fake, like half the stories she heard weekly.

Meanwhile, Jean's phone rang. She didn't recognize the number.

She stared at it like it owed her money.

It stopped. Then buzzed. Unknown Number: "Hey stranger □ thinking about you…"

Jean stared. She hadn't saved his number—but her trauma had.

Jean to Danielle: Somebody's son, somewhere lying.

Danielle: I laughed like I wasn't two seconds from spiraling. Say it louder for the inbox.

Jean: These men be emailing my soul like it's Gmail. No subject line. No greeting. trauma, sent at 2:36 PM.

Kiki: Quick poll: Tonight… are we doing email reconciliation or not?

Asha: Define reconciliation.

CC: By dick type, dating app, or sexual preference?

Ramon: Wait, what the hell is email reconciliation?

Danielle: It's when you go back through your emotional inbox and try to see which men you need to delete, archive, block, or report as spam.

CC: Not report as spam 😩😩😩

Jean: If he starts texts with "wyd," he's a phishing scam.

Asha: If his name is Tyler and he's 32, he is spam.

Kiki: If he's Latin and says "I'm different," he's got a baby mama, a tattoo of prayer hands, and a cousin who DJs quinceañeras.

Ramon: HEY.

Danielle: She didn't say your name, Ramon.

CC: Yet.

Danielle's next client walked in wearing a mesh top and an emotional support dog in a baby sling.

She smiled, took a deep breath, and reminded herself that professionalism had a price—and she charged it hourly.

Across town, Jean was now sitting through a financial update Zoom where one White guy kept using "synergy" like it was a safe word and another kept saying "I'll defer to Jean" like he wasn't scared of her.

She texted Danielle under the table:

Jean: If one more mediocre man defers to me like it's polite and not cowardice, I'm flipping this table.

Danielle: If one more woman tells me "her truth" is different than "the truth," I'm switching to OnlyFans.

Jean: You could make bank. Therapist with soft hands and trauma eyes?

Danielle: You've thought about this.

Jean: I have spreadsheets.

Velour Veterans

CC: Someone's ex liked 3 of my thirst traps in a row. Should I respond with a heart emoji or a photo of his man?

Kiki: Do both. But add a Bible verse.

Ramon: Isn't this illegal?

Asha: Nope. This is gay law. CC has jurisdiction.

Danielle: I'm logging off. Y'all not about to drag me into sin during office hours.

CC: Too late. You're complicit now.

Jean: I already packed a go-bag in case this thread gets subpoenaed.

Danielle set her phone down and looked out her office window. Somewhere out there was a woman who would get her jokes, remember her coffee order, and eat her out without asking if she had any healing left to do.

That's all she wanted. Well… that and decent salmon.

Across the city, Jean closed her laptop and exhaled. There was a man out there who still had her name saved under "Don't." And she meant to keep it that way.

There are many ways to fall in love. But in this friend group, falling came with disclaimers, background checks, and backup plans. Because love didn't come with risk—it came with receipts.

Email reconciliation: It started as a joke. A tipsy group chat thread one night after too many lemon drops and a man named DeMarcus who swore he didn't have kids—plural—then posted his daughter on IG with the caption "My twin ☺".

Since then, every Friday, like clockwork, Jean, Danielle, and whoever else survived the week would do a full emotional audit.

No one gave out numbers anymore. That was dangerous. Too accessible. Too permanent.
Burner Gmail accounts. Work throwaways. Jean had so many she lost count—half of them were created mid-drink order.

Danielle, of course, had hers categorized: Work safe. Weekend safe. Post-therapy safe. One labeled "DO NOT ENGAGE UNLESS DICK EXCEPTIONAL."

It was clinical. Strategic. And necessary in a dating pool that had turned into an unchlorinated hot tub of half-healed men and bad decisions.

Friday. 5:42 PM. Jean's office looked like Restoration Hardware and Liberace had a threesome with a Black art dealer. There was a velvet chaise no one sat on, two crystal decanters (one held whiskey, the other judgment), and a gold-framed quote above her desk that said: "Don't invite me to the table if you're scared I'll flip it."

She was typing—well, pretending to—when the door opened without a knock. James King.
Clean suit. No tie. Smile too charming for HR. The CEO of the firm and the only man alive who could walk into her office like the bill collector knew his name. (Technically, he did.)

He held up a folder. "Request denied."

Jean didn't even look up. "What request?"

"For your corporate card increase. You already have two."

"One is for food. One is for decor."

"Jean, you ordered a marble desk clock shaped like a twerking unicorn."

"It's a conversation starter."

James walked to the door, paused, and tossed back, "Answer your emails. Pretty please and thank you."

Jean finally looked up. "As the heart and soul of this company— the reason you're even with the love of your life—you deny my request for discretionary spending and expect me to answer petty emails?"

James grinned. "Umm… fuck yes. And you don't need two assistants."

"Then fire one."

"Don't tempt me." He opened the door. "And don't make me move you back across the hall so I can babysit you."

Jean raised her glass. "You'd be lucky."

Velour Veterans

CC: Roll call. Who's bringing the trauma tonight?

Danielle: I'm in. Got three new emails this week and one of them included a dick pic with a filter.

Asha: A filter?

Danielle: Valencia. Why would I wanna see an aesthetically warm dick?

Jean: They don't want healing. They want angles.

Ramon: I swear y'all attract the weirdest men.

Kiki: Nah, men are the weirdest men.

CC: I once got a video of a man jacking off in church parking lot.

Danielle: Was he moaning or praying?

CC: BOTH.

Jean: And yet… you didn't block him.

CC: No, I added him to my "Hinge But Make It Holy" folder.

Danielle: God is so tired of us.

Asha: Not more tired than we are of His sons.

Later that night, the crew gathered at Velour Social like they always did when the week had been too long and the inboxes too full.

Jean wore all black and earrings that could wound.

Danielle was in wide-leg slacks and soft lips.

Church Candy wore a sheer button-down and eye glitter.

Kiki brought snacks. Ramon brought nothing but vibes. Asha was behind the bar like a sexy oracle.

Drinks were ordered. Trauma was unpacked. And the first round of emails was pulled up.
They each had one.

Jean's: "Hey stranger… I know I messed up, but I've changed."

Church Candy read it aloud in a dramatic voice. "I know I messed up, but I've changed… and I still live with my ex but we're roommates."

Jean rolled her eyes. "I gave him the burner with numbers in it. That should've been the red flag."

Danielle scrolled through hers. "I got one that said: 'I feel like you misunderstood my intentions when I ghosted you.'"

Kiki spat her drink. "BITCH, WHAT?!"

Danielle nodded. "Apparently, he ghosted me intentionally so I could 'process my feelings'."

Jean was cackling. "What is this, emotional fasting?"

Church Candy jumped in. "He intermittent ghosted you. For clarity."

They were in tears.

By 10 p. m., they had deleted six emails, flagged three red flags, added two new emails to their tracking sheet, and agreed that one guy with a neck tattoo and a motorcycle deserved one chance if he sent photos with good lighting.

Asha refilled their glasses. Jean leaned back, looking around the table. They were beautiful. Messy. Healing. Loud. And together. That was all that mattered.

Danielle raised her glass. "To soft boundaries and hard lessons."

Church Candy added, "To dick filtered in Valencia."

Jean clinked her glass last. "To the inbox. May it be lighter next week."

Chapter 3: Shit We Said We'd Never Do

Danielle was already two drinks in when she walked in. Not Jean. Not Asha. Her. The woman who looked like she belonged in a dream or a delusion. Thighs like rebellion. Skin like almond milk with trauma. A twist-out so perfect it had to be done by a woman with healed parents.

She was wearing leather pants, a white tank top with no bra, and eyes like she'd choke you then journal about it. Danielle blinked.

Asha noticed first. "Girl. You good?"

Danielle nodded slowly, sipping her dirty martini like it was communion. "I'm…. fine. I'm —bitch, that woman got me feeling spiritually bisexual again."

Asha leaned over the bar. "She walked in with a water and made it sexy. That's dangerous."

Jean slid in next to her. "Who we objectifying?"

Danielle didn't answer. She adjusted her top, grabbed a napkin, and scribbled down her "polite burner"—the email she used for maybe-worthy women who gave enough dyke energy without being full chaos.

Burner: note: try not to fall in love again. you don't even know her trauma score.

Jean peeped the handwriting. "Oh, it's serious. You using lowercase letters."

Danielle got up, walked over like it wasn't her first queer rodeo, and came back five minutes later glowing.

Kiki looked up. "And?"

Danielle exhaled. "Name's Selena. Jamaican and Dominican. Drives a hybrid and owns a strap collection."

CC gasped. "A hybrid and a harness? God do got favorites."

Danielle whispered, eyes wide, "She smells like palo santo and revenge sex."

Jean shook her head. "So… you're in love."

Danielle clinked her glass. "Pending trauma report, yes."

Later that night, Jean was leaning against the bar with CC when a man walked by—and her whole face changed. CC clocked it immediately. "Is that a 'we used to fuck' face or a 'we shouldn't have fucked' face?"

Jean sighed. "Both. That's Nate. One-and-done. Like a Costco sample that tasted great but didn't come in bulk."

CC turned, eyed him from the back. "Mm. He cute in a 'do you have a job or good dick' way."

Jean nodded. "Dick was good. He ate pussy like a starving hostage tasting food for the first time since captivity."

CC fanned himself. "That's a vivid mental image. I approve."

Jean lowered her voice. "But he had a turtleneck."

CC froze. "Not the Adole sausage with the skin on it."

Jean: "Yes. And when I went to give him head? Bitch. The breeze shifted and something lethal hit me."

CC's eyes widened. "Oh no…"

Jean continued, deadpan: "Like shit."

CC clutched his chest. "Oh bitch, it sounds to me like you got some dick with a bit of booty on it."

The whole crew howled. Asha almost dropped a shaker. Jean put her hand up. "No, CC. It wasn't that. But when I saw his underwear, it looked like he went to Hershey Park and stayed too long."

Kiki gagged. Ramon damn near left the table. Asha wiped her eyes. "Wait. Wait. Wait. So despite all that—you still fucked?"

Danielle leaned in, eyebrow raised. Jean slowly put on her oversized sunglasses. Indoors.
And whispered: "Don't judge me."

That's when things shifted. Because Danielle got a message—one of those messages.

Not a text. Not a DM. An email.

Subject: "Hey…. I'm in town." From: Kathy Sent: Friday 9:08 PM "Hey. I know it's been a minute. But I'll be in town for a few days and I'd love to see you. I've been thinking about you. Hope you're good."

Danielle stared at the screen. Her face shifted. Energy shifted. The whole room didn't know it yet—but shit was about to change.

Jean caught it. She always did. "D? You good?"

Danielle nodded, closed her phone, and swallowed what was left of her martini. "Yeah. … old ghosts."

But this wasn't an ex. This was the one who broke her when she still believed people were good because they loved her out loud. The woman who held you while plotting your downfall. Kissed your back while texting someone else. Said "I'm figuring things out" after figuring her fingers out with a new girl's whole spirit.

And CC said, "Whatever it is… I got holy water and a blunt."

Velour Social was full. Not crowded. Full. With energy. With recklessness. With the heat that said somebody was gonna kiss someone they shouldn't by last call.

Danielle was mid-pour when he walked in. Blonde. Blue-eyed. Built like a retired lacrosse player turned barista. Black tee. Skinny jeans. A single gold chain that didn't belong to him but absolutely lived on his neck.

"Ayyyyyy," he said, arms outstretched like he walked in from Wakanda.

CC turned around slow. "Jesus take the flavor."

Jean sighed. "Here come this white boy again."

David—but he refused to answer to it. "It's Jamal," he reminded them for the thousandth time. "Juh. Like journey. Mal like—"

Kiki cut in. "Like 'malpractice,' which is exactly what your name is."

"Damn," Ramon laughed.

But Jamal didn't break stride. He dropped down into the booth like the bill collector knew his name on it. "I brought wine," he grinned, holding up a bottle like it was a peace offering.

Asha squinted. "That's a gas station rosé."

"Imported," he said proudly. "From Jersey."

CC crossed his legs and leaned back. "Imported like your entire identity, colonizer."

Jean was already done. "Why are you here?"

Jamal shrugged. "Because I love y'all. And Black women. And truth. And oxtails."

Danielle, who had been distracted by That Email, finally glanced up. Jamal saw her face. "Yo… who hurt you? I'll fight him."

Jean whispered, "It's a her."

Jamal nodded seriously. "I'll fight her, too. In a respectful, gender-equal way. Like a poem with fists." They let it slide. Because for all his nonsense, Jamal was family. Broke. Always dating Black women and quoting Erykah Badu like scripture.

But family. He meant well. He … also wore Malcolm X socks and once got kicked out of a cookout for bringing walnut infused potato salad.

Tonight, he was mid-rant. "I'm saying," Jamal insisted, pointing at his own eyeballs. "There's a tribe in Africa—deep in Sudan or Chad or somewhere—Black as hell, blue eyes like mine. Google it."

CC didn't blink. "Oh, you mean the Wodaabe? Yeah, boo. That's 'cause your great-great-great-granddaddy went on an expedition and left more than a thank-you note."

Kiki choked. Ramon spit out his drink.

Jamal threw his head back and laughed. "You ain't shit."

CC grinned. "And yet? Still Blacker than you, sweetie."

Danielle wasn't laughing. She was scrolling. That email still open. That name still floating. That ache in her chest still waiting to be processed. She sipped her drink like it might tell her something.

Like it might dull the echo of betrayal still reverberating in her body.

Jean noticed. "You good?"

Danielle looked up. Swallowed. Forced a smile. "I'm alright. … deciding which burner to use."

Kiki smirked. "Oh, it's like that?"

Danielle: "If I use my Wednesday email, I might kiss her. If I use my Sunday email, I might forgive her."

Ramon leaned in. "What's the Sunday one?"

Danielle: "It's the one I used to give people I hoped would change."

The table went quiet. Then CC said, gently: "You're not still hoping, are you?"

Danielle didn't answer. Instead, she scrolled. The photo was still there. The two of them. Smiling. Before the crash. Before the lie. Before she learned that women cheat with the same slickness as men but cut deeper because they know exactly how to hide it.

Meanwhile, Jean was texting someone whose name she hadn't said out loud in weeks. Not an ex. More like… a relapse.

CC peeped the screen. "Oh no, ma'am. Not him. Didn't he say he don't eat pussy anymore because he's 'preserving his energy'?"

Jean sighed. "I was bored."

"Girl, boredom should not be a dick trigger."

"Tell my hormones that."

Kiki raised her glass. "To poor decisions. May they at least come with orgasms."

Asha toasted. "And may they leave quietly after."

Jamal returned from the bar with a tequila shot and a sense of purpose. "I've decided," he announced, "to only date women who can quote Toni Morrison and hold a plank for more than 60 seconds."

CC blinked. "So basically you're gonna be single forever."

Jean cackled. "You can't even hold a conversation for 60 seconds without saying 'the culture'."

Danielle was quiet. Then, suddenly: "I emailed her back."

The table stopped. No one said anything. Danielle set her phone down like it was evidence, looked at everyone, then downed the rest of her drink. "I told her I'm free tomorrow. But I didn't say which burner to use."

CC whispered, "Bitch, that's... romantic chaos."

Danielle: "That's foreplay with a safety net."

Jean leaned over. "You sure about this?"

Danielle nodded.

"No. But I'm tired of wondering who I'd be if I never asked."

They were one espresso martini away from disrespect at Velour Social. The booth was loud. Laughter rolling like thunder. Asha behind the bar, humming something sexy. CC fanning himself dramatically. Danielle staring into her cocktail like it held her past, present, and future.

Then it happened. The door opened. And Asha, without looking up, muttered above a whisper— "This motherfucker here…"

Jamal, of course, heard it. "What's what's going on?" he said, sitting up. "We got a problem? You want me to handle this motherfucker or something?"

Everyone turned to look. The man walking in was… colossal. Tall. Built like a linebacker that prayed before games and kept his baby mamas in rotation. Skin smooth. Beard shaped. Smile that could melt ice off a Range Rover.

But CC squinted. Something was off. CC leaned over to Jean, eyes narrowing. "That man could beat all our asses in under 20 seconds, starting with Jamal's fake Black ass."

Jamal blinked. "What I do?"

CC held up a finger. "First of all, you brought gas station rosé and tried to make it fashion."

But then his eyes dropped to the man's feet. The sneakers. Size 15. Bright. Clean. But… strangely long. Like unnecessarily so.

CC made a face. "Oh hell no. Not this again."

Ramon asked, "What?"

CC sighed. "The big foot myth. I swear for God, I've been on the bad end of that joke more times than I care to admit. Bent over. Candle lit. Ready to bite the pillow like it owed me money—only to find out they done already finished and jumped in the shower."

Jean spit out her drink. Danielle choked. Kiki slid her wine glass away like she needed both hands to clutch her pearls.

Asha, still behind the bar, wiped her hands dry and walked over. "You wanna know what makes that even funnier?" she said casually, leaning one elbow on the table.

"Because you've experienced it too?" Jean grinned.

Asha shook her head. "Because that man? Destroyed me."

CC clutched his chest. "Come again?"

Asha nodded slowly, "Don't get me wrong. He fine. Body crazy. Cocky in a way that made my ovaries text each other to make a decision."

Jamal was wide-eyed. "Damn. That strong?"

CC gasped. "Like a panty dropper but.... meth-level damage?"

Asha nodded. "Exactly. I was walking funny for a week and a half. Like my hips went on strike. But he's permanently on my do-not-call list."

Jean leaned in, lips parted. "Wait wait wait... after all that? Why?"

Asha took a deep breath. "I spent five hundred dollars on these Egyptian cotton sheets. Had them for one night. One. This motherfucker's toenails—"

CC: "Oh God."

Asha: "—looked like he'd been climbing cliffs with no shoes since birth. Straight Freddy Krueger claws."

CC slapped his napkin to his forehead. "I'm sweating. I'm genuinely sweating."

Danielle burst out laughing. "Stop—no, for real."

Asha threw her hands up. "I'm not exaggerating. His Eagle claws sliced through the sheets like he was tap dancing through a nightmare. The sex was amazing. The feet? Trauma."

Kiki shook her head. "And you still let him hit?"

Asha didn't flinch. "Hell yes. But as soon as he left, I threw out the sheets and his number."

Jean raised her glass. "Amen, sis."

Ramon toasted. "To the toxic ones with strong thighs and terrible hygiene."

The laughter felt like a release. But for Danielle, the ache never left. It shifted. From her throat to her chest.

She was back on her phone. Reading that same email. Again.

"I'm in town. I'd love to see you. I've been thinking about you."

Jean saw it. Didn't even need to ask. She slid over, their knees touching, and whispered, "You don't owe her a damn thing."

Danielle replied without looking up. "I know."

But she didn't delete it. She didn't mute the thread. She didn't even breathe different. Because some ghosts don't haunt. They linger. In the hair. In the inbox. In the silence that comes after someone says your name with all the history still in it.

Danielle stood. "I need air." They let her go.

Outside, the night was humid. Loud. Alive. Cars rolled by like background music. Her heels clicked against the pavement like punctuation.

She didn't cry. Didn't smoke. Didn't call Selena. She stood there. Remembering.

All the ways love had entered. All the ways it had left.

Inside, Jean sat alone for a second. Jamal was rambling about reparations again. CC was mid-monologue about someone who wore leather pants with no ass to support it.

But Jean's mind was elsewhere. Because her phone buzzed. And the name on the screen was one she shouldn't have saved. HIM. The man who didn't deserve her time. Didn't deserve her body. But somehow kept finding ways to sneak into her thoughts like a virus.

She looked at the message: "You up?"

Jean whispered to herself, "Don't be that bitch." Then she opened her messages and replied. Because some silences say more than the people who leave them: "Not for you."

Back outside, Danielle opened her Notes app. She didn't know why. But she typed. "Sometimes the problem isn't that people leave. The problem is they remember you once you've healed."

She didn't send it. Didn't post it. She saved it under a folder called: "NO! Not That Email."

Danielle was halfway through her second protein bar and still starving. Her lunch break had been hijacked by a last-minute intake—some high-functioning CEO who "felt like a creative empath but also maybe on the spectrum" because he didn't like loud music and had recently dumped his Scorpio girlfriend via Google Doc.

So when Ellie Sinclair herself came strolling into Danielle's office without knocking—oversized sunglasses, a green smoothie, and a vibe like she was halfway between fabulous and feral—Danielle didn't flinch.

"Don't sit," she said flatly. "You're not on the calendar."

Ellie dropped onto the couch anyway, crossed her legs like a retired heiress, and took a dramatic sip. "I'm not here for therapy. I'm here for gossip and validation."

Danielle kept typing. "And a reminder you're the boss "

Ellie smirked. "Don't get it twisted, bitch—my name is still on the building "

Danielle leaned back in her chair. "Only because I saved your kingdom. And I'm never letting you live down when you told me you'd be forever in my debt. You're still in the negative "

Ellie pointed at her smoothie. "This is why I love you."

Danielle smirked. "You can't afford to fire me."

Ellie adjusted her sunglasses. "So. Who is she?"

Danielle didn't blink. "Nobody."

"That's not the energy you're giving. You've got the glow."

Danielle paused, then exhaled. "Met her this weekend. I gave her a burner."

Ellie gasped. "The burner? You're protecting yourself. I respect that."

"But…"

Ellie sat up. "Oooooh bitch."

Danielle nodded. "She might be the type I regret not regretting."

"You're in trouble."

"Not yet."

Ellie stood, tossed the empty smoothie cup in Danielle's trash. "Well, keep me posted. And for the record—yes, I'm in love with James, but I'm still a horny bisexual bitch in recovery."

Danielle cracked a smile. "You need a sponsor."

"I am the sponsor," Ellie winked. "And the addiction is still fine as hell."

Same Day—Outside Velour Social, 7:46 PM

Jean was stepping out of her Uber when she saw him. Tall. Smooth. Chocolate with a tight beard and the eyes that made promises his hygiene couldn't keep.

She turned quickly, heading inside before he could make contact.

Inside, CC was already posted at the bar with Kiki and Ramon, sipping on a lychee margarita and talking trash about someone's ex that hadn't even walked in yet.

The moment Jean slid into her seat, CC leaned forward. "Girl."

Jean held up her hand. "Nope."

"You saw him, didn't you?"

Jean pulled off her coat slowly. "Why the fuck is that man still allowed in public?"

Kiki covered her mouth, laughing. "Wait—is that the turtleneck?"

Jean nodded solemnly. "He's still alive. Somehow."

Ramon winced. "Did he speak?"

"Almost," Jean said. "But I think the Lord held my ankles in place and whispered, 'Don't do it, bitch'."

Danielle walked up mid-convo. "Who's got ankles in a chokehold?"

Jean waved her off. "Nobody… a ghost from the sausage graveyard."

CC gasped. "Not sausage turtleneck making a comeback tour!"

"Boy, if you don't—"

They all cracked up, the name alone now iconic.

Later that night at her apartment, Danielle sat on her bed with her laptop open, staring at a blank message. "Hey… I know this is weird. But I keep thinking about you." She deleted it. Typed again. "Hi. It's Danielle. I don't usually send second emails unless it's to cancel someone. But you might be the exception."

She hovered over the send button. Then closed the laptop. Checked her phone. Still no reply. Nothing in the burner inbox either. She laid back, arms crossed, heart annoyed at itself. Because somehow, the silence felt personal.

Group Chat—"Burner Reconciliation Bitches □□"

Jean: Tonight's agenda: Email reconciliation. Ho phase edition. Filters: dating app, dick type, or sexual preference. Choose your fighter.

Danielle: Sexual preference. I got a new burner making my gay heart nervous.

CC (Church Candy): I volunteer as tribute. For cults, coochie, or communion. give me snacks and themed robes.

Kiki: My husband's sitting right here so I'm participating via emoji only.

Jean: Girl, he knew what he married. You locked him down before Apple started asking apps not to track.

Ramon: This convo is above my tax bracket. I'm gonna refill Kiki's wine and act like I don't hear shit.

Jamal (David): This thread is why I can't date Black women. Y'all too bold.

Danielle: That's because none of us are dating you, David.

Jamal: It's Jamal. Respect the tribal lineage.

CC: Your lineage includes banana pudding and gentrification. Sit down, DNA test.

Velour Social –
The booth was loud. Velvet-curved and story-slick. Jean had one leg cocked high like she was daring her credit score to drop. CC was mid-monologue. Danielle was rereading a text she'd never respond to.

"I got one," CC announced, fanning dramatically. "This one's called The Eyes Betrayed Me."

Everyone perked up. CC leaned in. "So. I match with this dude on Hinge. Fine. Glasses. Reading a book in every photo. Gave good dick with a purpose energy."

Danielle sipped. "We love a librarian with stamina."

"Girl, I met him at this wine bar," CC said, eyes wide. "He walked in with that walk. Confident. That 'I still talk to my grandmother' confidence." The group nodded.

"He smelled like sandalwood and second chances. We vibed. Talked about Toni Morrison and toe-curling. He laughed. I laughed. It was giving Black love and pelvic alignment."

Ramon clapped. "C'mon, alignment!"

"But then…" CC paused. "We get back to his place. Lights low. Tension high. He takes off his glasses—and bitch…" Everyone leaned in.

"…his eyes damn near crossed like he was searching for two different answers."

Jean choked on her drink.

"I said, 'Wait, what's going on?' and he said, 'Oh, I'm blind without my glasses.' But the man looked like Mr. Magoo trying to smolder. Squinting. Lips puckered like a confused duck. I thought he was blowing a kiss—I said, 'You got asthma, baby'?"

The table roared.

"I tried to push through," CC continued. "I thought, maybe he's a grower—not in the dick department, but in facial symmetry."

Ramon wiped tears. "Was he?"

"HELL no," CC said. "Every time he came toward me, it looked like he was navigating with sonar. Like a sexy bat. And not the good kind—the kind that ruins brunch."

Danielle held her chest, wheezing.

"But I had shaved. I had marinated. I wasn't backing out now." CC said. "So I took one for the team. A blackout sex session with a man who couldn't see and couldn't find the beat. I spent more time adjusting his trajectory than enjoying the damn moment. Bitch was thrusting diagonally."

Jean slapped the table. "THRUSTING. DIAGONALLY."

"I felt like I was being attacked by an aggressive Roomba."

A lull hit the booth. Danielle was staring at her phone again. Jean clocked it.

"You still checking for that email?"

Danielle nodded. "She said she'd write me back. It's been three days."

CC leaned over. "Real inbox or burner?"

"Real."

"Girl…" they groaned in unison.

"She had an energy." Danielle said quietly. "Like someone I could let in without giving directions."

Jean softened. "That's rare."

Danielle nodded again. "That's the problem."

"Okay, my turn," Jean said. "Y'all remember Sausage Turtleneck." The table collectively gasped.

"Yes," CC said. "The man with the scenic underwear and the hostage head game." Danielle nearly snorted her martini.

"Well," Jean said, sunglasses already sliding on, "guess who I saw in Whole Foods by the plant-based chicken?"

"No," Danielle whispered.

"Yes," Jean confirmed. "Same sweatpants. Same turtleneck dick swinging in 4K. He saw me and smiled like a rerun."

"Did he say anything?" Kiki asked.

"He opened his mouth and the breeze hit me. I grabbed a basil plant and walked off like my ancestors sent me."

"You didn't even say hi " Ramon asked.

Jean leaned forward slowly. "Ramon. I want better for you."

"Okay, but question," Jamal said, cutting in. "Why y'all so hung up on these failed situations? block and move on."
Danielle gave him a look. "Because women don't date bodies. We date hope. We date potential. We date the version of you we imagined before you opened your damn mouth."
Jean added, "And if you're fine, it's harder to let go. Fine dudes be the biggest liabilities with the best strokes."

"Y'all too emotional," Jamal muttered.

"Which is why your relationships last as long as microwave popcorn," CC said. "All that heat and no substance."

The table fell quiet again. Danielle said softly, "When I first came out, I thought dating women would be easier." Everyone turned to her. "But it's not. It's messier. Deeper. More intense. The threads are tighter. And when they break, they don't snap—they unravel."

Jean took her hand under the table. Danielle smiled weakly. "Sometimes I don't know if I'm lonely or in detox from the fantasy."

Jean raised her glass. "To all the burned burners." Danielle clinked.

"To the ones who got the real inbox. And still fumbled." CC toasted.

"To email reconciliation—because not every thread deserves a reply."

They all said it together, through grins and grimaces: "No. Not That Email."

Velour Social—One Week Later

Life had been… life-ing.

A week had passed since the group's last full night out. Work had been demanding. Emotions had been chaotic. Jean had three missed therapy appointments, Danielle had almost sent a "checking in" text to her ex, and CC had nearly texted a man back after seeing he posted a Blue Lives Matter meme.

So yeah—progress, but with detours.

Velour felt different tonight. Still rich with music and mischief, but the energy was stretched thin—like everyone was laughing through something they didn't wanna name. Then the door opened.

And in walked her—skin deep and golden, with natural curls bouncing and a smile that looked expensive. She walked straight to the bar and kissed the White bartender goodbye. Not a peck. A whole-ass kiss. Confident. Familiar. Confirmed.

Jordan grinned and kept polishing glasses like he didn't break a few hearts. The group saw it and immediately went quiet. Kiki blinked. "Wait… is that his girlfriend?"

Jean squinted. "That man got kissed like his dick, knows her love language, and loads the dishwasher correctly."

CC leaned over. "And his dick knows CPR."

Danielle raised a brow. "Also, her skin? It's giving almond butter and privilege."

Ramon nodded. "That's a high-value kiss."

Then Jamal appeared, cheesin' like he landed a contract with BET. "Okay y'all, guess who got a date tonight?"

Jean didn't look up. "Somebody desperate with bad taste?"

Jamal flipped his phone around. "Boom." The picture was a Black woman—beautiful, glowing, waist snatched, curls coiled, and edges looking like they got baptized twice.

CC blinked. "Ain't no way." He leaned in. "Didn't you say—and I quote—'I don't date Black women because they don't like me like that'?"

Jamal shrugged. "I only said that to make y'all feel better. All I date is Black women. I'm a Black king. … God forgot to put the melanin in my final formula."

Kiki squinted. "Bitch, we've seen your parents. Both white. Real estate white. Subaru white."

CC sipped his drink. "Shut the fuck up and go on your date so you can hurry up and disappoint, and get back."

Unbothered, Jamal kissed the air twice and walked out like a vanilla-coated Kendrick Lamar.

As soon as the door shut, CC exhaled. "Damn. I wasn't gonna say anything, but now I feel guilty."

Ramon turned. "Guilty about what?"

CC sighed dramatically. "Her dick is bigger than mine and the velociraptor with the Eagle Claws that Asha dated."

Kiki gagged. "Oh NO."

CC choked on his drink. "Not the Freddy Krueger foot flashbacks —please God, no." He threw his napkin in the air. "Fine. Let me text him and save his life. And his ass."

Everyone wheezed. Then everything changed. Danielle's phone lit up. She saw it. Read it. Locked the screen. Said nothing.

Jean caught the hesitation. "News?"

Danielle shook her head. "Not the kind I'm ready to speak out loud." Jean nodded. Nothing else needed to be said.

Then Jean's phone buzzed. Once. Twice. Three times. She didn't flinch. She declined it. All three times.

CC blinked. "Who keeps blowing up your line like you late to work?"

Jean finally let the screen face up on the table. One name: Khalil. The table went silent.

Kiki whispered, "Don't say his name again. Y'all know the rule."

Ramon made the sign of the cross with two mozzarella sticks.

Danielle closed her eyes. "That man has a hex attached."

Jean whispered, "It's him."

CC reached out instantly. "Give me the phone."

Jean yanked it back. Protective. Raw. The table said in unison:

"Bitch. Don't answer."

Jean didn't speak. She started typing. When she looked up, her eyes were glassy. Lined with tears she refused to let fall. "I gotta go," she said, standing. Nobody stopped her. She left like she always did—loud heels, quiet storm.

And then…Danielle picked up her phone. "Fuck it."

CC blinked. "Bitch… fuck it, like… you texting the ghost?"

Danielle shook her head. "No. I'm raising the dead." She hit CALL. The line rang once. Twice.
Then—"Hey!" Danielle froze. The voice was… warm. Excited.

"Oh my God, I've been hoping you'd call," the woman said. "I lost your info. I went back to that same bar twice hoping to run into you."

Danielle laughed, stunned. "I figured you disappeared. I thought I got ghosted with a smile."

"Never," the woman said. "You've been in my head. I was hoping it wasn't too late."

They talked. And it was easy. Light. Full of things unsaid but felt. When they hung up, Danielle sat still, smiling into the silence. Then her phone buzzed again. A photo. Her. The woman. Perfect lips. Perfect skin. And below that—two beautiful breasts, soft and unapologetic.

CC screamed. "Titties!"

Danielle held up her phone.

Kiki whispered, "God took his time with her."

CC stared. "I'm gay and I'm still jealous. Is that… natural light? Or glory?"

Ramon toasted. "To second chances and first looks." The table laughed. But there was weight in the joy. Because even on the days that tried to bury them, they still rose.

Danielle sipped her drink and whispered, "Resurrection. On a Friday."

Outside, Jean sat in her car. One unsent text glowing on her screen.
She didn't need to send it.
She needed to remember who she was before Khalil fractured her.
She hit delete. Then whispered, "Not today." And drove off.

Chapter 4: Who TF Is This?

Jean had everything. The apartment with skyline views. The custom furniture in rich, unapologetic colors. The walk-in closet that felt like a boutique for bad bitches. She had peace, success, freedom—and if you asked her, she'd tell you she was good. Better than good. Unbothered with receipts.

Monet and Danielle had only exchanged a couple messages since that first night—slow burn, but it stayed on her mind.

But on nights like this, even with a fresh twist-out and the scent of fig and amber dancing through the room, she couldn't lie to herself. She didn't need love. But dammit, she wanted it.

And she refused to believe that the motherfucker named Love wasn't on its way. Late, maybe. But coming.

"Bitch, is this couch velvet or Egyptian royalty?" CC called out from the living room, half-sinking into the buttery emerald sectional like it was made just for him.

Jean rolled her eyes. "That pillow cost more than your entire outfit. Keep your elbows off it."

"I'll keep my elbows off when Love keeps his dick in his pants," CC said, sipping something golden and probably stolen from Jean's bar cart.

Ramon and Kiki strolled in together, hand in hand, looking smug as hell.

Kiki didn't even sit before launching into it. "Okay, y'all. We got a story."

"We?" Ramon asked, instantly betrayed.

Kiki waved him off. "Let me paint the picture. We went to a swingers club."

The room went full-blink.

Danielle damn near dropped her drink. "Wait, what?"

"Not to swing! To peep," Kiki clarified. "I was feelin' spicy, thought we could watch. Be grown, voyeur style."

CC perked up. "I know that style."

Jean raised a brow. "And?"

"And child… it was not giving Eyes Wide Shut. It was giving—what's that gym with the purple machines?"

"Planet Fitness," Danielle muttered, bracing herself.

"Exactly. With diabetic tension and ankle monitors. I saw one woman with a titty so low, it hit her thigh when she bent over. And not in a cute way."

Ramon sighed, sipping his drink. "I told her it was a bad idea."

"You was feelin' yourself," Kiki shot back. "Some of them men were feelin' you too."

Ramon grinned. "They know premium cut when they see it."

Kiki nodded slowly. "Not the women, babe. The men."

The room screamed. Jean choked on a grape. CC started coughing and waving a napkin like he caught the Holy Ghost.

"They was watchin' him like he was the bottom bunk at summer camp," Kiki said. "One man walked up and said—and I quote —'You look like you could handle two at once'."

Ramon blinked. "I thought he meant... like tequila shots."

"He didn't," Kiki deadpanned.

Danielle was wheezing. "Y'all stayed?"

"We left and watched a Hitler documentary in the car to feel normal again." Kiki said.

CC wiped tears from his eyes. "I used to go to swingers clubs too," he said, sitting up. "Back when I was a little younger and a lot more reckless."

Everyone turned. "I stopped when I realized I was breaking up marriages," he said matter-of-factly. "Too many wives standing there smiling one minute—then crying in the car when they realized their husbands were out here bent over like a yoga instructor in a thunderstorm. I said nope. I'm done. I can't be part of the heartbreak ministry."

"Not the heartbreak ministry," Asha said, walking in with a drink and a fresh set of press-ons.

"Couldn't do it," CC shrugged. "If your husband takes more dick than you can deliver, baby, that ain't on me. That's on the vows."

Danielle was quiet, smiling into her phone. She tried to hide it, but CC already clocked it.

"That ain't a group chat smirk. That's a coochie connection."

Danielle flipped her screen enough to show the message: a picture of a rooftop lounge reservation, and a text that read "Wear red. You'll make the whole room stop."

"Awww shit," Kiki said, already invested. "It's the titty-text girl, ain't it?"

Danielle nodded. "We've been talking since she found my info again," she said softly. "It's been… consistent. Fun. She's not doing too much, but she's present."

Jean looked up from her wine. "I'm happy for you."

"I'm not doing cartwheels yet," Danielle said, "but I like the way she sees me. She listens."

Asha raised a brow. "Make sure she's not out here manifesting your chakras while secretly selling waist beads for $111. 11."

"Girl," CC said, "Danielle likes smart pussy. She'll be fine."

Jean set her wine down and leaned on the island. "I met someone too."

Everyone turned.

"Wait, what?" Kiki said.

"Yeah. But I'm not saying shit until I run his name through the system at work. Background check first, feelings later."

Danielle burst out laughing. "I respect the hell outta that."

"Protect your peace, boo," CC added. "Love out here playing dress-up. Make sure that dick ain't in disguise."

Jean smirked but didn't deny it. Then her phone buzzed. She glanced. Froze. The room felt it.

"Who is it?" Danielle asked gently.

Jean didn't answer. She opened her email. A single message sat in her "Mail" folder—Khalil.
She opened it. Two words. "I'm sorry."

Her jaw clenched. Her thumb hovered over the screen. "I'm tired," she whispered. "Tired of this recycled-ass dick showing up like a lost sock."

"Girl—" CC started.

"I blocked him before," Jean continued, "but that was spiritual. This time, it's through Gmail and AT&T "

With one tap, she deleted the email. With the next, she blocked the number. "Goodbye forever, you regretful son of a bitch," she said calmly, then exhaled.

CC raised his glass in a silent toast.

They were still absorbing that when Jamal walked in like a man who had seen hell, barely survived, and was now willing to testify. He didn't limp. But his spirit did.

"Look who finally showing his face," Kiki said.

"I had to let the swelling go down," Jamal muttered, collapsing into a chair. "Y'all… I'm traumatized."

Everyone leaned in like it was storytime at the sex AA meeting.

"I met her at the bar," he began. "Black dress. Skin flawless. Waist snatched like a corset commercial. Makeup beat to God's own playlist."

"So what went wrong?" Asha asked.

CC raised a finger. "Before he answers—I called him, okay? I told him that was a man. I said, 'That's a dude, baby. Trust me'."

Jamal rolled his eyes. "And I thought you was hatin'. Always calling out my dates, being extra."

CC crossed his legs and took a sip. "Bitch, I was being prophetic."

"So I ignored him," Jamal continued. "We go back to her place. Candles. Music. Couch. We're kissing. It's hot. She goes down on me... I ain't gon' lie—I finished too fast."

"Typical," Danielle muttered, sipping.

"Then," Jamal said, his face going pale, "she stands up. Drops her panties. And boom—there it is. Dick. Hard. Bigger than mine. Looking at me like it had a grudge."

Everyone froze.

"She looked me in the eye and said, 'I'm a woman—I have a dick too. I sucked yours. You definitely gonna suck mine or we gonna have a problem'."

CC SCREAMED. Danielle spat her drink out. Asha fanned herself with a throw pillow.

"I panicked," Jamal said. "Tried to fake a seizure or something. She grabbed my shoulder and said, 'Don't embarrass us.' I broke free, ran to the door—bitch had deadbolts!"

"Oh nooo," Kiki whispered, clutching Ramon.

"I finally get it open, stumble down the hall, and right as I hit the lobby—bam. She caught up. And let me tell you, that dick might've been pretty, but those hands were trained. I didn't leave untouched, let's say that."

"Wait—you got your ass beat after getting your dick sucked?" CC gasped.

Jamal nodded solemnly. "I came in... and went out."

The room fell apart. Jean wiped tears from her eyes. "Jamal. That's not a date. That's a Netflix documentary."

"I almost filed a police report, but I didn't even know what box to check," he groaned. "Assault... by misdirection."

CC howled. "The dick had hands and hands had choreography!"

"His bulge had a five-year plan," Jamal added grimly.

The room finally exhaled from all the wheezing and laughter.

Danielle's phone buzzed again. Another message. A picture of the dress the woman suggested she wear. Red, like the text said. Compliment included. She smiled without thinking.

Jean noticed. "If this one's real," she said quietly, sliding next to her on the couch, "let her be good to you. Don't waste time proving you're strong enough to survive the wrong one."
Danielle nodded, eyes soft. "Same for you." They clinked glasses.

CC stood, hand on chest like he was hosting a drag church revival.

"Whew," he said. "Between surprise gay husbands, haunted dicks, and deleting dumbass exes... I don't know what this is, but it's giving growth and genital tingles." He raised his glass. "To fresh starts—and background checks."

Chapter 5: Hope, Hair, and Holy Shit—It's a Real Date

Life wasn't calm, exactly. But it had leveled.

Velour Social had thinned out a bit—fewer last calls, fewer exes in the inbox. The group still gathered, still roasted each other in the group chat, still unpacked their traumas like party favors—but there was a gentler rhythm now.

Growth was happening, quietly and with sass. Kiki and Ramon were trying Pilates. Jean hadn't responded to a text that didn't include "reservation confirmed" in days. CC claimed he was celibate "by choice and divine restraint," but everyone suspected it was a scheduling issue. And Danielle—Danielle had a date tonight.

A real one. Not a "pull up and let's pretend to be friends" situation. Not a "maybe we kiss if the vibe is right" stroll. This was an actual date. Reservation. Time stamp. Dress code. And a woman who'd told her—straight up—"Wear red. You'll make the whole room stop."

She'd shared it with the group earlier in the week, complete with the screenshot and a dramatic caption: "God, if you send this woman to ruin me, say that."

They'd gone wild. But she'd made one thing clear in her follow-up: "Also, I didn't shave. If I end up doing anything tonight, it's God's will, not mine."

So the sabotage was preloaded. Legs a little fuzzy, lady bits a little less than runway-ready. Cinnamon Toast, as she affectionately called her box, was safely swaddled and slightly neglected—enough to prevent betrayal.

Now, standing in front of her mirror, Danielle adjusted the hem of her red halter dress and whispered to herself, "You are not gonna act like a middle schooler in heat. Breathe. Blink. And don't hump the booth seat."

She wasn't nervous. Except she definitely was.

The restaurant was dim, elegant, and humming with jazz and low laughter. Selena was already there when she arrived—seated in a corner booth like she'd been poured into the space.

She stood when she saw Danielle. "You look…" Selena paused. "Damn."

Danielle smiled, lips painted and nerves tucked under heels. "You clean up alright yourself "

Selena stepped forward and hugged her—firm, full, soft perfume lingering on Danielle's collarbone—and kissed her on the cheek like it was second nature. Not forward. intentional.

Danielle blinked. She wasn't used to that warmth that didn't ask for something in return.
Selena motioned to the wine menu. "I waited to order a bottle. Didn't wanna pair you with the wrong vibe."

Danielle slid into the booth. "Thank you. That's either romantic or extremely Virgo of you."

"Why not both?"

The conversation was easy—like they'd already done the awkward phase in a dream somewhere. They talked food, family, exes without bitterness, intimacy without shame. Selena told stories about growing up with two cultures and one very opinionated abuela who still mailed her Catholic guilt in handwritten letters.

Danielle shared enough—her job, her clients, her belief that therapy worked only when people stopped lying to themselves and their providers.

Selena listened. It was disarming. No power play. No peacocking. No performative flirting to fill space. Presence.

Midway through the main course, Danielle realized she'd been smiling for too long. Her cheeks were sore. Her inner thighs were… aware. And Cinnamon Toast was doing cartwheels with a hint of defiance.

"Ma'am," Danielle thought to herself, shifting in her seat. "Don't start nothing you can't shave for."

Selena said something—something funny, something clever—and Danielle laughed harder than she meant to.

Selena smiled. "You're cute when you try to stay composed."

Danielle lifted her glass, sipping to distract from the warm throb low in her belly. "And you're dangerous when you speak in subtitles."

"Subtitles are how do it," Selena replied.

Danielle didn't flinch. "Good. I read fast."

The night ended the way grown-woman dates should: No pressure. No messy lean-in. Just another cheek kiss, another soft smile, and Selena whispering, "Text me when you're home, okay?"

Danielle nodded. "I will."

Selena started to walk away, then turned back. "When's the next time you're free?"

Danielle's whole body smiled. "I'll let tomorrow." And she meant it.

By the time she got home, heels off and Cinnamon Toast safely tucked into sleep-mode, Danielle was grinning at her own reflection. Not because she'd "scored." Not because she'd proved anything.

But because she'd been seen—and still felt like herself.

She grabbed her phone and immediately got hit with it:

Velour Veterans ☐☐14 new messages.

She braced herself.

CC: If she didn't at least graze your thigh, I'm filing a civil complaint.

Kiki: So you shaved or nah?

Jean:Check the mirror, not the inbox. If your smile is stupid, we win.

Asha: If she wore real perfume and not body spray, you in trouble.

Ramon: I feel like I shouldn't be reading this.

Jamal:This thread makes me question my life.

CC: Also… I thought I had a date. This motherfucker stood me up. I shaved for no reason. Now I got smooth thighs and no dick. Jesus be a Tinder refund.

Danielle laughed. Full-out, alone in her robe.

Then she texted:
Danielle: Y'all are clowns. But I love you. Now please shut the hell up.

She muted the thread, locked the phone, and tossed it across the bed like it carried temptation.

She wasn't letting this night be meme-ified. This one? This one she was keeping for herself.

Shortly after her phone rang.

Danielle answered on the second ring, FaceTime angled enough to show perfect cheekbone lighting but hide the clutter behind her.

Jean didn't waste a second. "Spill it."

Danielle blinked. "Spill what?"

"What. The date. The vibe. The moisture. Start at A and work your way to Z, bitch."

Danielle smirked. "I'm not giving you anything."

"Because it was mid?"

"No," Danielle said, adjusting her ponytail, "because it was good. And I don't wanna ruin it by dissecting it with someone who would absolutely yell out a red flag because she doesn't like the way a bitch eats oysters."

Jean held up a finger. "Okay, first of all—slurping is a sin. I stand by that. Second, that sounds like glowing. You're glowing." Danielle blinked at herself in the corner of the screen. "Maybe I am."

"Uh huh." Jean leaned back against her headboard, bare-faced and beautiful. "You going Kiki and Ramon's later?"

Danielle shook her head. "Nah. I already told them I'm laying low this weekend. Catching up on notes and avoiding tequila decisions."

Jean nodded, casually. "Same. I got some stuff to catch up on. I'll see you next week?"

"For sure." The call ended. And Jean didn't move. She sat still for a minute, thumb hovering over her messages like a snake about to strike.

Then finally, she typed: "So, how's that energy coming along?" No overthinking. No praying on a reply. She tossed the phone on the bed and walked to the kitchen.

It dinged before she made it to the fridge. She blinked. Turned back. The screen lit up with one clean sentence: "Find out for yourself. Let me know where to pick you up."

Jean snorted. Typed back: "Pick me up? I don't know if you some serial killer. Give me a spot—I'll meet you there."

A moment passed, then— "Fair. I'll send a location. Dress like you look good."

Jean: "I was born dressed like that. 8 works."

She wore black. Not a dress—too obvious—but high-waisted wide-leg trousers, a barely-there top, and a cropped jacket that said "I'm fine, and I know it." Makeup sharp, hair laid, nails clean. No perfume— expensive body oil with a hint of danger.

The spot he picked was lowkey—Black-owned jazz lounge tucked between two boutiques in a part of town Jean only visited for candle stores and back-alley dumplings.

She parked herself, walked in alone—heels steady, vibe sharper than her liner.

He was already at the bar, posture casual, phone facedown. Not as tall as she normally went for. Definitely fine. Sloppy haircut— whoever faded him stopped at almost. Beard tight, though. Fit like he jogged to clear his head. Skin like green smoothies and daily SPF. Eyes that looked through people.

He stood when he saw her. Didn't reach. nodded once and said, "Jean."

She smiled. "Still might be a serial killer, but at least you've got taste."

They got a table near the stage— far enough to hear each other but close enough to let the bass flirt in the background.

He let her pick the drinks. She ordered mezcal with orange bitters. No sugar. No fruit. No flair.

"Straightforward and smoky," he said. "Like you?"

Jean raised a brow. "Don't get cute too early. I haven't decided if I like you yet."

He smiled. "Fair. But you will."

Jean blinked. "Okay."

They talked. Work, politics, art, therapy, sex—but not performatively. He didn't perform intelligence. He had it. And when she dragged his haircut—"It's giving pandemic barbershop apprentice"—he grinned and said, "That's fair. But you'll be the last woman to see it like this. My next cut will be with you in mind."

Jean sipped. "You're smooth."

"Only when it works."

She wasn't used to this. The balance. The back-and-forth that didn't feel like verbal combat. He listened without interrupting. Flirted without pressuring. And when she caught herself laughing —actual laughing, not the performative kind she gave mediocre men—she almost got mad about it. Almost.

Two drinks. No pressure. No reach. No suggestion of more.

When the bill came, he paid it with the grace that didn't need to be announced. Just folded the leather check holder closed and moved on like that was always the plan.

They stepped out into the warm night. Jean walked slowly. Let herself feel it.

He walked her to her car. Not too close. But enough to be seen.

Jean turned. "This has been refreshingly un-chaotic."

"I try."

She waited. Braced for the lean-in. The hover. The hand on her lower back. Instead, he extended his hand.

Jean raised a brow. "You gonna spin me next?"

He took her hand, kissed it—light, real, confident. And when she thought that was it, he leaned in enough to press a soft kiss to her lips.

No tongue. No hunger. … hello. Then he stepped back. "Text me when you get home."

Jean got in her car, hands light on the wheel, smile already creeping across her face.

He didn't press. Didn't grope. Didn't fumble the landing.

That man kissed her hand like he respected the pussy he wasn't gonna get. She drove off—badly. Almost clipped a planter on her way out of the lot. But she didn't care.

By the time she pulled into her garage, she knew. She opened her phone. Typed. Sent her real number. No burner. No backup. Because whatever this was? It didn't deserve a fake inbox. Not yet. Not this time.

Danielle didn't open the blinds. It was Saturday, and her apartment smelled like mint tea and restraint. She sat cross-legged on the couch in an oversized hoodie, laptop open, but no real intention of working.

The night replayed in soft loops. Selena's smile when she caught the check before Danielle could argue. The curve of her wrist as she swirled her drink. That half-second when their knees touched and neither of them pulled away.

Danielle sipped her tea, lips twitching. She wasn't a blusher. Not anymore. But something about the ease of it—the balance—had her nervous in all the right ways. Not butterflies.
More like… butterflies in hoodies. Calm, but plotting.

She opened her Notes app and scrolled to her affirmations. Read the old ones, then added a new line: "Desire doesn't always mean danger." She stared at it for a beat, then added: "You're allowed to want things that feel good and still feel safe."

A notification flashed—group thread.

Muted.

She didn't open it. Instead, she opened her texts. Hovered. Typed: "Last night felt easy. Hope your morning's the same." She stared at it. Paused. Deleted it. Typed again. Same message. No emoji. No overthinking.

She hit send. Set the phone down. Didn't look at it again. Not yet.

Jean was still in bed. She'd slept in the way only a woman with a good night behind her and no trauma in her immediate inbox could.

The room was quiet. No playlist. No clinking glass. Just light filtering through linen curtains and the scent of vanilla body oil lingering from the night before.

She stretched, then reached for her phone. Nothing dramatic. No long message. No missed call. But there it was: "You still owe me a proper insult for the haircut. Don't use your real number to block me."

Jean laughed out loud— once. Low and private. She typed back: "That depends on whether you get a real haircut next time."

A beat later: "Deal. But only if I get a second date."

She didn't respond right away. She read it three times. There was no pressure in it. presence. Confidence. He didn't ask for more. He stated his intention.

Jean opened her camera and looked at herself. Bonnet, bare face, last night's lashes barely clinging. Still fine. She grinned. Typed:
"Don't make me regret giving up the burner.
And make the next place quiet. No jazz this time." Sent.

Then tossed her phone gently to the other side of the bed like she was done playing with it.

Danielle lit a candle she didn't need. Scrolled Instagram, barely looking. Refused to check her phone, even though she absolutely heard it buzz five minutes ago.

Her stomach flipped. once. Don't do it, she told herself. She did it anyway.

Selena: "It was easy. You felt like peace. Let me know when

you're ready for round two.
Danielle melted into the couch like her bones didn't work anymore. She didn't even reply. smiled. Out loud.

Jean didn't tell anyone. Not yet. She saw the group thread buzzing about who left fries in the bottom of Kiki's Range Rover and who owed money from brunch, but she didn't open it.
Not because she didn't care. But because… for once, she wanted to feel something before she offered it up for commentary.

She wasn't hiding. She was protecting. She lay back in bed, staring at the ceiling. This one could still go wrong. He could still fumble the next call, say something stupid, mispronounce Sade, or quote Kevin Samuels.

But last night? Last night was right. She wasn't gonna taint it by needing too much too fast.

Danielle opened her phone again. Typed: "I'm free Thursday night. no surprise strap reveals on date two. I'm tender."

Selena replied instantly: "I'm respectful. But bring extra panties, in case you disappoint yourself."

Danielle screamed. Alone. Out loud. Into the void. Cinnamon Toast twitched in the background like 'bitch, I told you.'

She didn't say anything else. set the phone down, face up this time. Let the glow have its space.

Jean poured herself a glass of orange juice like it was champagne and sat on the edge of her kitchen island. She looked down at her phone one more time.

No regrets. Not today. No fake numbers. No fallback plans. She'd already given him the real one. And for once, she didn't feel like protecting the door... maybe just unlocking it a little to see what came in."

—

That afternoon, they both ran errands.

Danielle at Whole Foods, buying overpriced tea and texting nobody.

Jean at West Elm, looking at throw pillows she didn't need, wondering if his apartment had color or if she was gonna have to fix it.

They didn't tell anyone. They didn't post. They didn't groupchat the details or offer up screenshots for approval. Not because they were hiding. But because it felt sacred.

And both of them had learned what happened when you handed something fragile to a room full of people too busy laughing to hold it gently.

Danielle sat on her balcony that night, tea in hand, phone upside down.

Jean curled up in her reading chair with no book, no bra, and a head full of possibilities.

They didn't say it out loud. Didn't text it to each other. But they were thinking the same thing: "If this is gonna be different...I have to be different too."

And for the first time in a long time? That didn't scare them. It thrilled them.

Chapter 6: Back Rubs, Boundaries & Man Pussy

Danielle's phone was upside down again.

Not because she needed focus, but because she didn't wanna catch herself looking too fast. It had been two days since the rooftop text from Selena, and they'd been in a steady, sexy rhythm—funny messages, not too many, not too few. She wasn't spiraling.

Yet.

The group chat had gone off three times that morning. She hadn't opened it.

Her work inbox was full. She hadn't opened that either.

Instead, she sat with a client—tech founder, mid-thirties, swore he was "in touch with his inner feminine," which meant he cried after cheating and wanted applause for not doing it again.

She was nodding, taking notes, actively disassociating. Until her phone buzzed again.

This time, not the group. Not work. It was an email. Subject line: "Hey."

Danielle stared at the name. She didn't move. Didn't open it. Didn't need to.

There was only one woman whose subject lines were that lazy and still managed to carry emotional C4. She locked her phone. Forced her attention back to the session. Smiled.

Asked her client, "Do you think it's possible your version of healing only works when no one holds you accountable?"

The client blinked. "What do you mean?"

Danielle smiled again. Sharper. "Something to journal about."

Jean was in her closet, cussing at her hangers.

She had a second date with Green Smoothie, and somehow nothing in her closet said, "I like you but don't need you," without also saying, "Please disappoint me quickly so I can get this over with."

She grabbed a sleek black blouse and her wide-leg gray trousers. Classy. Soft. Slight threat. Perfect. She was halfway to the door when her doorman called out, "You've got a delivery."

She blinked. "What?" He handed her a cream envelope. Postmarked three weeks ago. The handwriting was familiar.

Her gut said: Don't. But she opened it anyway. Inside: a birthday card. Simple. Plain. Not cute. Inside the card, one sentence: "Didn't know what to write, so I figured I'd say I remember."

No name. No apology. No call to action. Presence. Uninvited and still too loud. Jean's jaw tightened. She tossed the card in her purse like it was poison, slammed the car door, and headed to the date. Already annoyed.

Group Chat: Velour Veterans □□

Asha:Y'ALL. Oh my God. Has anyone ever been on a date with someone so fine you're ready to sin... but then he took off his shoes... and the feet smell SO FUCKING BAD you wanna throw him in the shower like an exorcism?

CC: Bitch. I don't care how fine he is. If his feet stink, his dick does too. Tell him to wash his damn soul.

Asha: He had NO CHANCE. The moment those funky-ass corn chip toes hit the air, my pussy sealed shut like a bank vault in a blackout.

Kiki:I'm wheezing 😩😩😩

Ramon: Funky corn chip toes is WILD.

Jean: Nope. This one getting named. Immediately.

CC: Funky Corn Chip Feet™. His name is what I say it is.

Asha: I'm tossing this one up to the stinky gods. That man was too fine to smell like Frito regret.

Danielle cracked a smile when she finally opened the thread. But she didn't comment. She muted the thread again and tossed her phone to the side.

It buzzed again. Not the chat. Not Selena. The email. Still unopened. Still staring.

She got up and walked to the kitchen, hands shaking enough to remind her she wasn't as done as she claimed.

Healing is funny—it never warns you when it's about to be interrupted.

Jean walked into the lounge. She looked good—full glam, scent light and expensive, lips like they knew things and wouldn't tell. Green Smoothie stood when he saw her.

Smiled. Didn't hug her. waited. She appreciated that.

They ordered drinks, but Jean was off. She didn't want to be. But that damn card had settled into her system like dust.

He noticed. "You okay?"

Jean waved a hand. "Long day. Nothing a good drink won't fix."

He nodded. "Fair. But if it doesn't fix it… don't let it make you forget who you are."

Jean blinked. What? He didn't say more. took a sip. Didn't push.

She watched him for a beat. Realized she was waiting for him to be dumb. To ruin it. To remind her why she didn't date anymore.

He didn't. So she adjusted. Loosened up. But not all the way.

Mid-conversation, she cracked a joke that deflected something honest he'd said. A compliment, subtle, but clear. And instead of taking it, she dodged. Changed the subject. Smirked her way out of the moment.

He clocked it. Let it sit for a beat. Then leaned in, not closer— emotionally closer.

"Listen," he said. "I like you. And I'm in no rush. So take your time."

Jean tilted her head, halfway between skeptical and curious.

"It's okay to like me too," he continued. "And to like me on your terms. At your pace. I'll meet you there."

She blinked.

"You don't have to snap hard. You don't have to sit here waiting for me to fumble or prove you right about something going wrong. You don't need a guard dog at the gate when the grass is already cut."

Jean opened her mouth. Closed it.

"All you have to do is drive in a lane you're comfortable in," he said. "I'm fine in the passenger seat. I'd rather get this right than get it fast."

And like that, her shoulders dropped, a little.

They finished the night softer than they started. Less wine, more water. Less armor, more eye contact.

And when he kissed her cheek before she got in the car, she didn't flinch. She smiled.

Back home, Jean sat on her bed with the card from Khalil in one hand and a glass of whiskey in the other. She ripped it once. Then again. Then again. Then again. Until it looked like what it was— irrelevant. She dumped it in the trash. Texted Green Smoothie: "Still think about your voice when it's quiet."

He replied: "I think about your silence when it isn't."

Jean didn't respond. She didn't need to. Not yet.

She curled into her sheets, phone on her chest, and finally—finally —slept without flinching.

Danielle was standing in front of her refrigerator, holding oat milk like it was a metaphor.
The bottle was half-empty. She didn't remember drinking it. She had a therapy client in 20 minutes, a mild tension headache, and an email from a ghost sitting untouched in her inbox.
Selena's text from last night was still on her screen: "That depends on how soft your lips still are by the second one."

Danielle had stared at that line longer than she'd admit. Then muted the thread, like some intimacy safety net.

The problem wasn't the silence. It was the quiet it left behind. Twenty minutes later, Danielle sat across from a woman wearing crystals and describing her emotional landscape as "a little feral, but mostly fine."

Danielle nodded. Took notes. Tried not to dissociate. But her brain was crawling with everything she wasn't saying. The ex hadn't reached out since that one-line "Hey."

But her Instagram stories had been watched every day since. Right on time. Always around 2 a. m. The digital version of knocking on a door you no longer have a key to.

Danielle tried to ignore it. Tried to laugh it off with herself. But some part of her—the therapist, the woman, the recovering romantic—still wanted to ask: "What do you want?"

Not out loud. Not. … energetically. Because even if she never replied, it still meant something that the email came. Didn't it?

Group Chat: Velour Veterans □□

Kiki: I walked in on Ramon eating a peach and moaning like he was auditioning for OnlyFans.

Ramon: It was a good peach.

CC: If Ramon ever joins OnlyFans I expect a promo code and a preview.

Danielle: I need peace. And unmoaning fruit.

Asha: This is why I'm celibate. Men be moaning wrong.

Jean: What's the correct moan?

Asha: Like they know I got options. Not like they saw God.

CC: Amen. I want reverence. Not worship. This ain't a prayer circle.

Danielle laughed. laughed. And that helped. A little. But then the notification slid across her screen again. "Instagram: [Name Redacted] viewed your story."

She hadn't posted anything sexy. a picture of her tea. A playlist screenshot. A meme about emotional labor.
Still… seen. Always seen. She put her phone down. And stared at the ceiling.

Later that night, she and Selena FaceTimed. Casual. Low-pressure.

Selena had her bonnet on. Danielle had under-eye patches and her "I'm Not Dating You But I'm Still Hot" tank top.

"Long day?" Selena asked.

"Emotionally full."

Selena nodded. "Wanna talk about it?"

Danielle hesitated. Then: "Not yet. But thank you."

"Okay," Selena said. "You hungry or nah?"

Danielle blinked. "Wait... are you sending food to my place right now?"

"I already did "

Danielle grinned. "What did you send?"

"Something with carbs and grace."

Twenty minutes later, a delivery bag showed up: Jamaican oxtail stew, plantains, rice and peas, and a sticky note taped to the lid: "You don't always have to be the one holding space. Let somebody feed you."

Danielle sat on the floor and ate it with her fingers. Because forks felt too formal for this tenderness.

After dinner, she poured a glass of wine and reopened the email. Still no follow-up. Still no reply needed. But this time, she didn't close it immediately. She reread it. "Hey. I saw you the other day. You look good."

She typed to see it. "Thank you. I'm in a different place now." She stared at the words. Then deleted them. Typed again. "You don't get access because you miss me in hindsight."

Deleted it. Typed one last time: "Ghosts don't get VIP access." She didn't send that either.

She let it sit on the screen for a minute. Then she closed the tab. Not archived. Not saved. closed. That was the reply.

The group chat popped again.

CC: Okay. I'm drunk and lonely. But in a cute way.

Kiki: That's called "regular lonely " bitch.

CC: No. This is like… I want someone to moisturize my back and leave me alone afterward.

Danielle: You're describing married people.

Jean: Back rubs and boundaries. The dream.

Asha: I want someone who folds my towels and knows when not to talk to me.

Ramon: So y'all want emotionally intelligent ghosts with house skills.

CC: No. We want love. But only on Tuesday and only if they come pre-shrunk.

Danielle muted the thread again and went to her bathroom, removed her eye patches, and rinsed her face. She stared at herself in the mirror. "I'm doing good," she said.

Then corrected herself. "I'm doing better." That felt more honest.

Back in bed, she opened her messages and finally replied to Selena: "Thanks for the food. You're dangerous."

Selena responded almost instantly: "Dangerous how?"

Danielle smirked. "Like I might start liking you before I finish healing. And I don't wanna confuse the two."

Selena left it on read for three minutes. Then replied: "That's okay. I'm not afraid of your healing. I wanna be part of the reason it finishes."

Danielle blinked. Heart skipped once. Maybe twice. Then she put the phone down and whispered, "Okay." Not to Selena. To herself.

Velour Social was humming.

Not loud, not chaotic— full enough to feel alive without having to yell across the table. The crew had taken over their usual velvet booth, drinks in hand, and Danielle was glowing like a new relationship in soft light.

She didn't try to hide it this time. She wore white—crisp, structured, with gold hoops and a lip that said kiss me if you can keep up.

Jean clocked it the second she walked in. "Oh, we wearing happiness now?"

Danielle grinned. "Not happiness. alignment "

"Mm-hmm."

Kiki leaned in. "You look moisturized and mildly digmatized. But we support it "

Danielle laughed. "It's not even like that. It's … good. Easy. Like I'm not performing or explaining or calculating all the time."

Asha nodded. "That's how. When you don't feel like you have to be on."

Danielle sipped. "Exactly." She glanced over at Jean, who was unusually quiet. Not closed off. … unavailable. Danielle nudged her. "You good?"

Jean blinked. "I'm fine "

"You haven't said one shady thing in ten minutes."

"I'm drinking my drink."

Danielle smirked. "You still talking to—"

Jean cut her off. "Let's not do this."

Danielle nodded. Backed off. Understood.

Jean hadn't given Green Smoothie a name yet, and she wasn't planning to. Not until he earned it. Not until the attention felt like presence. Not good lines, but good follow-through.

Still… her fingers slid to her phone. Typed a quick message under the table: "You'd like the music here tonight."

He replied almost instantly. "Send me a clip. Let me hear what you're hearing."

She smiled in spite of herself. CC caught it. "Oh? We texting during Velour hours now? The rules—no love notes during the trauma circle."

"Shut up," Jean muttered, cheeks pink.

Danielle raised her glass. "To growth."

Jean clinked it. "To denial."

Kiki cackled.

That's when CC leaned forward. Quiet first. Then loud. "You bitches thought I was being extra when I said I was celibate, but I meant it." The table froze.

"What now?" Ramon asked, almost dropping his glass.

"I said," CC repeated, dramatic and dead serious, "I am celibate. For real. I'm saving this pussy for a worthy man."

Danielle blinked. "You… you definitely don't have a pussy."

CC didn't flinch. "Bitch, have you never heard of man pussy? It's like woman pussy—only better. Especially for men that are gay."

A beat. Then laughter exploded.

Kiki choked on her drink.

Jean leaned back. "I'm not doing this with you tonight."

"No, be serious," CC said, suddenly steady. "Y'all know I'm always playing, always flirting, always fucking. But I've been thinking a lot."

He sipped. Looked at his drink like it might finish the thought for him. "Yes, I'm gay. Yes, I've fucked women. Yes, I've definitely fucked men. And yes, I've been fucked—but what I can't remember?"

The table stilled. "I can't remember the last time I felt loved. Like loved "

Asha leaned in, silent now.

"A big dick and a pretty face has gotten me far " CC continued. "Real far. But I don't wanna go further. Not like that. I want love. Like, real-ass love. Not somebody who kisses me so good I forget my name, or jerks my dick with eye contact. I want someone who listens when I talk. Who sees me when I'm not in glitter or lashes or funny one-liners."

He paused. "I want someone who hears what I'm saying without waiting for a punchline. Someone who don't look at my lips, but wants to know what they've been through. Who doesn't look at my ass and wonder how it moves in the right pants, but asks how I got this thick and still carry grace."

No one spoke.

"I'm done handing out pieces of myself to people who only want the parts they can touch. I'm waiting now. For the one who wants to love me whole. Fully."

Danielle's eyes welled slightly. "That's real."

Jean nodded once. "That's grown."

CC exhaled. "So yeah. I'm celibate Not 'I'm bored' celibate. Not 'I can't find nobody' celibate. I'm intentional celibate. Until love shows up, this pussy is locked. VIP only."

A beat passed. Then Jean raised her glass. "To CC's man pussy."

Danielle laughed. "And to Jean getting some dick she doesn't ghost."

"BITCH!" Jean shouted, nearly spilling her drink.

The table roared.

Asha wiped tears. "Okay, I needed that."

Ramon raised a glass. "To the whole table wanting more than what we started with."

Kiki smiled. "To all of us wanting something real."

CC tapped his glass against theirs. "To not settling for sparkles when we deserve fucking fireworks."

Danielle whispered to herself, "And still wanting peace."

Jean looked around the table. Every single one of them had changed. Not fully. Not permanently. But something had shifted. The drinks were still flowing. The jokes still flying.
But under all of it? A deeper truth. They weren't out for fun anymore. They wanted more.
Even if they didn't know how to ask for it yet.

Chapter 7: Your Name Is What We Say It Is

Jean hadn't heard from Green Smoothie in a few days—not that she was checking. (She was.)

Danielle was quiet but glowing. A few days had passed since the date with Selena. And while she still didn't know if it would last, she had to admit it felt different. Healthier. Still sexy as hell. But slower. More deliberate.

Jean called her on FaceTime. "You look too cute today. Spill it."

Danielle smirked. "It's nothing to spell. It was a great night. I don't wanna ruin it by overanalyzing."

Jean raised a brow. "So you mean you don't want us to ruin it "

"That too."

"You gonna go to Kiki and Ramon's tonight?"

"Nah, staying in. Catching up on work. I'll see you at karaoke."

Group Chat: Velour Veterans □□

Jamal: Y'all. I got a date tonight. A real one. Black. Beautiful. Not AI-generated. Bringing her to Velour. Don't be weird.

Danielle: Did you meet her at church or Craigslist?

CC: Request denied. Bring her at your own risk.

Kiki: We'll be respectful… unless she orders a lemon drop with a straw.

Jean: I'm only judging if she wears kitten heels and says "vibes" too often.

Asha: Make sure she don't call him Jamal. That's the only trigger word I'm honoring tonight.

Velour Social was already buzzing when Jean walked in wearing highlighter and secrets. Danielle followed close behind, radiating soft but contained confidence. Her hair was up, her earrings were lethal, and her shirt read HEALING IN PROGRESS. DO NOT DISTURB—UNLESS YOU FINE.

Asha greeted them from behind the bar with a nod. "Y'all early," she said. "That means the drama hasn't started yet."

"Good," Jean replied. "I like to stretch before the chaos."

Danielle leaned on the counter. "Make mine something pretty but emotionally balanced."

"Same," Jean said. "Except mine should be broken with trust issues."

Asha rolled her eyes and went to work.

Ten minutes later, the front doors opened like a prophecy and in walked Jamal. Or as he insisted on being called tonight, David.

Everyone turned. CC clutched his chest like a church mother seeing Beyoncé walk in barefoot. Because the woman on his arm? She was fine. Natural curls. Golden brown skin. Flowy black dress. Radiated peace and almond body butter.

"Shit," Danielle whispered. "He brought a soul cycle instructor with cheekbones."

Jean sipped. "The real question is… does she know he calls himself Jamal in public?"

Kiki leaned in. "She looks normal. Like real-normal. She might be tax bracket normal."

CC (smiling bright): "Welcome! Hope you came for trauma and tapas!"

Jamal introduced her quickly—name: Jasmine, voice soft, handshake firm. She smiled like she wasn't new to this.

"Blink twice," CC whispered, "if he told you he was Afro-Asian with a streetwear line."

Jasmine smiled. "Nope. But he did say y'all were funny."

"Girl " CC replied, "funny is not what I call forgiving."

Then came Kiki and Ramon, walking in slightly apart. Kiki's face was powdered to perfection, lips glossy, heels militant. Ramon followed, slightly hunched like someone who'd been yelled at all afternoon.

Danielle said, "Y'all walking like you left couple's therapy and a court summons"

Kiki didn't smile. "Ask your boy why he called me a raggedy Black bitch while pulling on my seven-hundred-dollar ethically installed extensions."

The table went silent. Jean blinked. "Wait… What?"

Ramon looked around. "She said she wanted it rough!"

Asha clapped her hands once. "Sir. There's rough. And then there's reckless."

CC said, "And then there's choosing violence on Black hair. That's not rough. That's unholy."

Asha: "Let me be clear. Dirty talk is 'you like that, don't you'? Degradation is 'you raggedy Black bitch.' One keeps the coochie wet. The other gets your PlayStation repossessed."

Kiki nodded like a judge in a televised divorce court. "I told him I was in the mood for disrespect, not destruction."

Ramon: "She kept getting mad every time I asked permission midstroke, so I winged it!"

Jean nearly dropped her drink.

Danielle buried her face in her hands. "You winged it? With Black hair and identity politics on the line?"

Ramon threw up his hands. "I panicked!"

Asha said, dead serious, "Real or extended, you never pull a Black woman's hair without explicit and enthusiastic permission in writing. Preferably notarized."

Kiki sipped her drink like she had no plans to smile until August.

The conversation devolved into laughter—mostly at Ramon's expense—and as things were calming down... Selena walked in. She wasn't with them. She was with two friends—stylish, tall, clearly gay, and clearly hers. She wore dark green satin, confidence, and no apologies.
Danielle clocked her.

Selena saw her. They exchanged nods. Nothing more. But something inside Danielle pulled slightly. Jean noticed. Didn't say a word.

As the group settled deeper into drinks and light jabs, Asha delivered another round and whispered to CC, "That man over there at the bar? He's been watching you like he wants to get baptized."

CC turned. Tall. Asian. Beautiful. Open shirt. Gold chain. Smiling.

"Lord " CC said. "Send help. Or a towel." He walked over slowly. The man didn't move.

"Hey," he said. "You're CC, right?"

"Depends," CC replied. "You asking as a fan or a hopeful applicant?"

"Little of both."

"Mmm." CC squinted. "I don't trust men with perfect teeth and shoulder veins. That's demon dick architecture."

The man laughed. "I'm Kenji. I work in film distribution. Not the fun kind."

"What's the fun kind?"

"Porn. Or documentaries about wine "

CC smirked. "So you distribute trauma and subtitles?"

"Basically." They laughed.

Kenji leaned in. "If I kissed you right now, would it mess up your celibacy or reroute it?"

That line would've had CC in someone's car two months ago. Instead… "You'd think," CC said, "but not tonight. Not yet."

He sipped his drink, scanned Kenji again, and exhaled. "The old me would've taken you home, tried to impress you with things I don't even value anymore. But I'm trying something different "

Kenji smiled, undeterred. "That's sexy. Not many people admit that out loud."

CC shrugged. "Evolution's a bitch."

Kenji handed over his phone. "Well, in case your new version accepts callback auditions…"

They exchanged numbers. Real numbers. No burner.

CC tapped his nails on the screen. "You're the only man who made me laugh this hard without touching me."

Kenji grinned. "Yet."

They didn't kiss. But the tension was real. And when Kenji walked away, CC whispered to himself: "Look at me. Evolving."

He finished his drink and floated back to the table, lighter than when he left.

Across the room, Jasmine laughed at something Jamal—David—was saying.

Kiki was leaning into Ramon again. slightly.

Jean was watching Danielle.

And Danielle was watching Selena.

The room was full of almosts, maybes, and might-have-beens. And none of them knew what tomorrow would bring. But tonight?

Tonight was messy, loud, and unforgettable. And that, for now, was enough.

Danielle was on her third drink, watching Selena laugh with her friends like the night didn't feel different. She hadn't looked Danielle's way in a while. Which, somehow, felt worse than being stared at.

Jean was sipping something strong and silent.

CC had been quiet too, ever since his encounter with Kenji. Not in a sad way—thoughtful.

Then it happened. The mic at the front of Velour crackled to life. A host in gold boots and bad decisions grabbed it like it owed him child support.

"Alright, babies. We've tallied the votes, we've reviewed the trauma, and we've decided who gets to walk away as tonight's messiest maven of romantic mayhem."

The room erupted in cheers. The host flipped his notes dramatically. "Let's count it down."

"In third place…To the woman whose brunch date showed up with her ex sitting in the car like a parole officer… baby, we see you. That's drama with a parking pass."

Danielle blinked. The group turned. Kiki wheezed. "That was you?!"

Danielle shrugged. "It was a bad month."

"In second place…To the savage queen who thought she was dating Idris Elba but got exposed when her man broke character mid-thrust and yelled 'Deadass!' like a Brooklyn hype man. Sis. You almost made it."

Jean spit her drink.

CC hollered. "You lied to me! You said he was British!"

"He was!" Jean hissed. "Until he wasn't!"

"And in first place…To the icon, the legend, the person who tried to rebuke gayness with prayer, oil, and penetration. Sir, your ass— and your story—will live forever."

CC stood up, bowed like royalty, and whispered, "Minister of Footwork strikes again."

They were each handed a tiny gold trophy shaped like a broken heart with a bandaid across it. The crowd roared. The crew laughed so hard they were wiping tears.

Kiki: "We swept the trauma awards. We're the Beyoncé, Kelly, and Michelle of dating disasters."

CC: "Correction. I'm Beyoncé. Danielle is Michelle. Jean is definitely Kelly 'cause she keeps pretending she's not in love with someone."

Jean rolled her eyes. "I hate you."

Danielle said, "We didn't win. We dominated. Like trauma Olympics."

They all clinked glasses. Then Jean got quiet again. Not withdrawn. still. Danielle noticed. CC noticed. But neither said anything.

A few minutes later, Selena made her way over. Alone. She smiled. "Congrats on your trophy," she said.

Danielle raised an eyebrow. "You heard it?"

"Heard? Girl, the crowd almost rioted. That story had legs."

Danielle laughed once. "Apparently so did the ex."

Selena leaned on the table, casual. "Someone said I used to be the ex in those stories."

Danielle's expression shifted. Slightly. "Oh?" she said, careful.

"Yeah. Said I threw a drink on somebody at brunch and then left with her wife."

Danielle blinked. "Did you?"

Selena laughed. "Yes. But it wasn't like that."

Danielle's tone cooled. "It sounds exactly like that."

Selena tilted her head. "Is that what we're doing?"

"I'm saying. If I heard something like that, and then dated the person, I'd be curious."

Selena stayed calm. "Danielle, I've been a whole situation. I've been a trilogy. Possibly a reboot."

Danielle didn't smile. Selena softened. "But that's not who I am now. Or trying to be. Don't take any of that too seriously. Keep the outside out. While we're building, there's no room for outside contractors."

Danielle sipped slowly. "Sure."

Selena watched her. "You good?"

"I'm fine." The tone was ice.

Selena lingered for a second, then nodded. "Okay. I'll see you around."

She walked off. Danielle didn't watch her go. Jean finally spoke. "You're not fine."

Danielle shrugged. "I'm realizing some shit."

Jean nodded. "That's allowed. Just don't burn down the house over something someone else used to be."

Danielle didn't reply. She tucked the trophy in her purse and leaned back like she was done talking for the night.

CC stepped outside for air. Kenji was gone. Left a text that said,

"Let me know if your celibacy ever takes a vacation."

CC didn't respond. Just smiled to himself and whispered, "Not yet." He looked up at the stars, then down at the trophy in his hand. The broken heart. The bandaid. He laughed. "Cute. But I want the whole thing." He didn't go back inside. Instead, he walked down the block slowly, letting the air hit him clean.

Inside, Jean checked her phone. Green Smoothie had sent her a photo. A cocktail he'd tried at a new spot. Caption: "Looks like something you'd drink. Strong, cute, and likely to ruin me." Jean didn't reply. She looked up. Saw a man at the bar who looked like a walking mistake. He smiled at her. She smiled back. Didn't move. But didn't not think about it.

Then she caught herself. Closed her phone. Whispered, "Not tonight." But she still ordered one more drink. In case.

The night wound down slowly. The crew parted ways, each carrying something home besides the trophies. Something quieter. Unspoken. But real. They were all laughing.
But the laughter that comes after you realize how much healing costs. And how much joy is worth.

Chapter 8: Emotional Baggage Claim

Danielle wasn't the type to linger in bed. But this morning? She sat still, phone in hand, thumb hovering over Selena's last message. "I had fun last night. Hope your trophy doesn't talk too much shit while you sleep."

It was playful. It was easy. It should've made her smile. Instead, she reread it three times and drafted a reply she never sent. Then deleted it. Then sent something dry: "Same. Hope your friends behaved "

Dot dot dot. Selena replied almost instantly. "They always behave when they know I'm the one worth behaving for."

Danielle rolled her eyes. But a smile cracked anyway.

Across town, Jean's phone buzzed. She'd rolled out of bed, head pounding slightly, lip balm still intact.

CC's message lit her screen. "Your nephew is fine and disrespectful. Pray for me."

Attached: a full-bodied, well-lit, proudly centered dick pic.

Jean blinked.

CC's follow-up came quick: "I'm calling him nephew 'cause he younger and I might accidentally cradle him after. But damn "

Jean responded with a one-word reply: "Mercy."

Five seconds later, CC FaceTimed her. Jean answered half-eye-open, bonnet still on.
"I can't stand you," she said.

CC held the phone up to his own expression—one of exaggerated grief. "Why do men think sending a dick pic immediately puts them in the 'wanna fuck' category? Like we haven't seen prettier, bigger, and better."

Jean raised an eyebrow. "Or like their dick is a security clearance. As if I'm gonna ignore every red flag because their tip got good lighting."

CC laughed. "I hate the big ones. Not because they're big, but because they're lazy. Big dick destroyers are used to rearranging insides without trying. So they stop trying "

Jean nodded. "Yes. But this pussy got elasticity. She can handle the work."

CC began singing, "You better work… work it girl!"

He struck a half-pose with the phone. "RuPaul wasn't talking about the runway. She was talking about the dick."

They both cackled. Jean wiped a tear. "Size is fine. But I'll take above average that doesn't bend in the middle. I like my dick hard as a ex-con whose mother left him at an orphanage."

CC screamed and hung up. Jean smiled at the screen for a beat longer than she meant to.

Then closed it. Then opened it again. Then finally tossed it across the bed. She had things to do.

She also had… a missed call from Green Smoothie. And a voicemail. She stared at the bubble. Hovered. Then hit play. "No pressure, wanted to say I think about you more than I should. And it doesn't scare me. Hope that's okay "

Jean stopped it halfway through. Deleted it. Then immediately regretted it. But the regret didn't make her go back. It made her quiet.

Group Chat: Velour Veterans ☐☐

Jamal: Y'all. She tapped my shoulder.

Kiki: During sex?

Jamal: During oral. I was going in. I thought I was killing it.

Danielle: Shoulder tap during head = "you're not good at this, but I'm trying to be polite."

CC: Shoulder tap = "bless your heart." It's southern for "get the fuck up."

Jean: Ouch.

Jamal: Y'all suck. Anyway, I got on top and started giving her

ALL the dick. She was moaning, pulling her legs back further, telling me deeper…

Ramon: …then what?

Jamal: Then she flipped me. Got on top. Rode me like she was tryna punish somebody.

Danielle: So… your dick was under review and failed the audition?

Asha: Sounds like she had to take over 'cause you were giving lazy missionary with non-union pelvis energy.

CC: I like my dick black and strong. Clearly, she likes hers with a little tiny bit of cream.

Jamal: FUCK y'all. I like my women strong like my coffee.

CC: And clearly she likes hers diluted.

Jean: She drowned you, boo. You were a learning curve.

Jean laughed so hard she dropped her toothbrush. Still brushing, she sent Danielle a quick message. "You good?"

Danielle replied: "Define good."

Jean didn't push. sent a heart emoji.

Later that afternoon, Danielle and Selena were on a call. It started light. Recap of the night. Dumb things CC said. Brunch plans. Then Danielle brought it up. "I like you," she said. "But I'm not gonna ignore red flags because the kiss was good."

Selena's tone shifted. Still calm. But different."I'm all for red flags I deliver on my own," she said, "but I refuse to acknowledge or accept any red flag ownership that's curated by outside people—all of whom you don't even know."

Danielle was silent. Selena continued. "I get giving consideration to your loyal council of friends. That's friends looking to protect friends—with limited information. But your flags? They're created by noise and nonsense. And I won't acknowledge that bullshit."

Still calm. Still sharp. "I won't address it again. If it creates a shift in this beautiful, perfumed, and wet pussy space we're in, I can assure you—it won't be red flags that end us. It'll be my exit."

Danielle sat with that. Then Selena delivered the final cut. "I don't do long-haul shit when every pothole makes you pull over and inspect the tires."

There was a silence. Danielle was about to say something—But Selena beat her to it.

"I gotta go." Click. Call ended.

Danielle sat still. Looked at her phone like it had insulted her mother. Then tossed it across the couch and stared at the ceiling. No tears. No smile. Still. She had some time before the veterans showed up and her turn to play hostess.

Danielle's condo looked like what would happen if Pottery Barn got a PhD and a partner at Deloitte. Cream walls. Moody light. Coffee table books about erotic psychology. Throw rugs that whispered, "Try it, bitch."

Shoes were off at the door. Jean tossed hers into the hallway like she was rebelling against the entire aesthetic.

Kiki whispered to Ramon, "Don't you dare walk on that rug in socks." He nodded like a student in Catholic school.

Everyone had arrived. Drinks were poured. No music. No distractions. plush couches, brutal honesty, and the unofficial sacred tradition of the crew: The Airing of Grievances.

Asha stood first, arms out like a tired referee. "I got a lotta problems with you people. GO."

Jean said, "Ramon, raggedy Black bitches are your mama. And she's Spanish. And still your mama."

Ramon ducked and laughed. "I was trying to be nasty!"

Kiki rolled her eyes. "You succeeded. Nasty and racist."

Ramon threw up his hands. "I said sorry!"

Asha stood again, "CC, I saw you talking to Bruce Lee last night. If he don't do nails or offer some Asian discount, you're banned."

CC said defensively, "Bitch. He's cute!"

Asha pointed out, "You are a size queen, and he doesn't stand a chance!"

Jean said, "He got a pic. It's… standard Asian issue."

CC was grinning, "You uncultured heifers wanna see?"

He held up his phone. The group leaned in. Silence. Faces twisted like the Wi-Fi went out.

Only Ramon nodded. "It's not bad. Respectable."

They all turned to Kiki with that same face. The pity one. Kiki said, "I know. I'm carrying this man's last name and medium dick forever. Shut up."

Jamal stood up, "I got a problem with all y'all."

Jean said, "Do tell, Mixed Milk Dud."

Jamal said, "Y'all made me think she tapped my shoulder 'cause the head was bad. It wasn't! It was great! She couldn't wait to get the dick."

Danielle said, "No one taps away from greatness. We moan, we hover, we grind. Tap means, 'Thank you, next'."

Jean added, "Anytime we say 'deeper,' we know there's no more dick in there. Never in the history of sex have I said 'deeper' and been pleasantly surprised."

The room erupted. Jamal sat down with a sigh. "Y'all are evil."

CC said, grinning, "I got a problem with Jean."

Jean replied, "I'm sure you do, bitch."

CC continued, "This bitch is secret happy. She got a mystery man and ain't said nothing. SPILL IT."

Jean was smirking. "Nothing to spill yet. But I will. You messy bitch."

They high-fived and sipped like enemies who wrote love letters in secret.

Kiki was next. "I got a problem with Ramon." She smacked him in the back of the head. "If I wanna be slutted out by you, then slut me out properly."

Ramon said defensively, "I tried!"

Kiki went on, "I forgive your ignorant stroke. But next time your punishment is eating my ass after takeout Indian food."

The group SCREAMED.

Jean added, "Not curry cunnilingus."
Asha said, "Bitch, that's a hate crime."

Finally, Danielle stood. Everyone hushed. She sipped her drink. Looked at the ceiling. Then said: "I got a problem with all of you."

Pause. "Because none of y'all eat pussy."

Ramon, raising his hand, said, "I do."

They all laughed.

Danielle continued, "And none of you know what it's like to wanna lick it. To crave it. To dream about women like a goddamn walking hallucination. So sometimes, I feel alone in that."

The room quieted for a beat. Not heavy. Just real.

Jean stood slowly. "Come talk to me for a sec."

They stepped into Danielle's kitchen, past the untouched charcuterie and emotionally unavailable hummus.

Jean looked at her and said, "You okay?"

Danielle replied, "I'm trying." She leaned on the counter. "I keep thinking I'm healed. Like… functional. And then something dumb happens—like someone warning me about Selena, or her clapping back too hard—and suddenly I'm replaying every relationship in my head like a fucking courtroom montage."

Jean nodded. "Been there."

Danielle exhaled. "I know I'm bringing old files into new situations. But it's hard to know what's instinct… and what's trauma playing dress up."

Jean poured them both another drink. Then said, "We gotta learn the difference between a real red flag… and the ones we tie to a stick ourselves to justify running."

Danielle smiled. Barely. "I'm working on it."

Jean raised her glass. "Then cheers to working. Not running."

They clinked glasses.

Back in the living room, CC was already arguing with Kiki about the ethics of pegging a man who used to coach high school football.

Asha said, "I swear, if y'all mess up Danielle's rug with any of this noise—"

Danielle returned and said, "It's fine. The rug forgives us. For now."
Jean said, "But my trauma doesn't."

"That's 'cause you carry it in your BBL," Jamal said.

Danielle: "And I carry mine in my tongue. Ask somebody."

Ramon was grinning, "We know."

The crew laughed, loud and long, until the weight of their grown-up chaos dissolved into something lighter. Not gone… shared.

Later that night, after the laughter, the roasts, the curry-flavored threats and dick pic diplomacy—everyone trickled out of Danielle's condo in waves. Jean stayed back to help tidy up. Not because she wanted to. Because she didn't want to go home.

Danielle walked her to the door eventually, wine still in hand. "You good?" she asked.

Jean nodded. Too fast. Then shrugged. "I think so."

Danielle leaned against the wall. "You didn't say much about mystery man."

Jean smirked. "That's because y'all don't know how to handle anything delicate. You bitches try to roast intimacy."

"Guilty."

"But… he's fine. Kind. Doesn't overshare. Doesn't overthink."

Danielle smiled. "So you're waiting for the other shoe to drop."

Jean didn't answer. hugged her. Tighter than usual. Danielle clocked it but didn't press. She closed the door, turned off the lights, and let the silence sit.

Jean got home to a quiet that was too quiet. She dropped her keys in the dish, pulled off her lashes, and flopped on the couch like she'd been running for days.

She picked up her phone. No new messages. She opened Green Smoothie's thread anyway.
Still there. Still no pressure. Still sweet. She stared at his last message: "Tell me something you've never told anyone."

She sighed, then opened her photo gallery. She found an old screenshot—something a past lover had written to her. A man who broke her heart, but knew how to write like it meant something.

It was a long message—sweet, manipulative, poetic. The message that makes you think dysfunction is romantic. She meant to send it to Danielle, with a caption that read:
"This is why I can't trust words no matter how pretty they sound."
She hit send.

But she realized too late: It didn't go to Danielle. It went to Green Smoothie. "Shit."

She froze. Then stared.

Dot. Dot. Dot. He was typing. Her stomach dropped.

Green Smoothie: "Tell me if I'm walking into a repeat chapter. I've got my own pages too."

Jean sat on the floor. Not because she was tired. Because it felt like a safe place to fall. She didn't reply. Didn't delete, just stared.

The next day, Danielle woke up to no messages. None from Selena. None from anyone.

Which was fine. She was fine. Mostly.

She checked Instagram. Scrolled. Liked a photo. Muted three others. Stared at a reel of a girl cooking brunch half-naked with a girlfriend in the background. Felt something she didn't wanna name.

Closed the app. Checked her email. Deleted four old burner messages from people she'd already written off. Cleaned her inbox like she was scrubbing her own past.

Then she saw it. One new message. From Selena. Not a text. An email. A single line: "If you're still deciding, decide in silence. I don't wanna audition while you second-guess the script."

Danielle stared at it for five minutes. Then deleted it. Not because she didn't care. But because she cared too much to argue.

She placed her phone face down and went to make coffee barefoot on hardwood that cost too much to ignore.

Jean eventually replied to Green Smoothie: "That wasn't meant for you. But maybe it was."

Dot. Dot. Dot. No reply. She waited.

Twelve minutes. Then 30. Then an hour. Nothing.

So she did the only thing she knew how to do. She called Danielle. "Say something smart," she said when Danielle answered.

Danielle exhaled. "What did you do?"

Jean told her. Danielle didn't laugh. Didn't gasp. Instead she said, "You want him to know the truth. But not like that."

Jean groaned. "Exactly."

Danielle sipped. "Now you have to sit in it."

Jean whispered, "Fuck."

"Yup." Silence.
Danielle finally broke it. "I got an email, too."

Jean perked up. "Selena?"

"Yeah."

"Bad?"

"Not bad … boundary-setting."

"Did it work?"

Danielle didn't answer right away. Then said, "I deleted it."

Jean nodded like she could see it. "We're out here self-sabotaging in luxury housing," Jean muttered.

"Designer chaos." They laughed. For now.

Chapter 9: Trust Issues in 4K

Jean finally texted Green Smoothie back.

She'd been sitting on the couch for half an hour, phone in one hand, wine in the other, pretending to scroll through TikTok while rereading his last message like it had hidden cheat codes.

She could've ignored it again. Could've hit him with a meme, a ha-ha, a delay tactic. Instead, she typed: "Maybe I thought I was ready. But clearly I'm not "

She didn't expect a fast response. But it came fast anyway.

"I could call you on your bullshit more politely. But you don't strike me as the woman that likes that shit."

She blinked.

Then he followed with: "Drop your guard. Keep your knife in your pocket. And know what it feels like to enjoy someone freely."

"If the blade needs to come out, it's right there in your back pocket —pull it out. But to walk around with a blade in your hand, your guard up, and a snub nose. 38 tucked in your boot to go out on a date? That would exhaust me too."

Jean's chest got tight, a little.

Then came the final line: "Let yourself off the hook a little bit. And once you realize that even with the most sophisticated systems and alarms ringing, they can't stop the devastation of a tsunami… maybe the brilliant ones don't prepare for the storm, but damn if they don't know how to recover."

She read it twice. Then locked her phone and stared at the ceiling like it owed her an apology. She didn't reply. Not yet. But this time… she smiled, a little.

Meanwhile, CC was in the middle of a pre-fuck playlist and a pre-fuck cleaning ritual—candles lit, playlist on, ass moisturized with expensive intention—when the mood died mid-text.

The Asian guy—Kenji—was cute. Charming. And had finally broken through CC's no-fuck-fast wall. Until he didn't.

The message came through as CC was fluffing throw pillows. "You'll be the first Black man I've ever had. Or… had me. Guess I'm finally checking the last box 😈"

CC read it. Paused. Took a deep breath. Then replied with surgical precision: "Go fuck some others. I'm nobody's experiment."

Kenji backpedaled immediately. "Wait. I was kidding. I have been with Black men. I thought it'd make you feel special…"

That did it. CC put down his drink. Stared at the phone like it called him out his name.
Then typed: "I don't mind joking. Bullshitting. Flirting. But where I draw the line is lying—to get some dick, to get your below-average meat wet, or to make yourself feel better. Don't lie to me.

Not to me. Especially not for me."

"If you haven't fucked a Black man by now in 2025, something's already wrong with you. And if you feel like you gotta lie to get some ass, there's shit wrong with you I won't even begin to unpack. Blocked."

He didn't even wait for a reply. He sent the message, turned off the playlist, blew out the candles, and walked away.

Group Chat: Velour Veterans □□

CC: Bitch. I blocked Bruce Lee with the weak meat. That's a wrap.

Jean: What happened? I thought he was your new blend.

Danielle: Y'all exchanged real numbers. That's like gay marriage.

Asha: You gave up burners for him.

CC: Girl, he said I'd be his first Black man. Like I'm some history class elective.

Kiki: Oop.

Ramon: That's bad, huh?

Jean: Bad? That's fetish-level foolishness.

CC: And THEN—wait for it—he says he lied, to make me feel special.

Danielle: ... oh no.

CC: I told him: go find your first somewhere else. This ain't Black dick trial day on Hulu.

Jean: This the type of shit that make me delete my whole dating app folder and go straight to sleep.

CC: And let's be clear—if you lie to me to slide in my sheets? You're not my type. You're a case study.

Asha: He tried to unlock the rainbow with a lie. Denied.

CC: Exactly. I don't do lies. I do luxury.

Danielle screenshot the whole exchange and sent it to Jean directly: This bitch said 'not Black dick trial day on Hulu.' I'm SCREAMING.

Jean responded with a row of laughing emojis. Then paused. Then messaged:
Also... I finally replied to Smoothie."

Danielle: AND?

Jean: He called me on my bullshit. But in a poetic, deeply unbothered way.

Danielle: You like it?

Jean: I don't hate it.

Danielle: That's your version of love. I support it.

No rooftop chaos. No random hookups. No emotional breakdowns. Just a few hard truths, one blocked liar, and Jean realizing that maybe, maybe, she's not as broken as she thought. Just bruised. And bruises heal. Even the pretty ones.

Asha had her glass in hand like it was court-ordered and started pacing like a preacher about to drop scripture. "I swear to God, if one more man takes off his socks and reveals a toe situation that looks like his foot survived Vietnam, I'm gonna throw a sandal at somebody."
The group was already giggling.

"Had a man last week tell me he doesn't believe in monogamy or foot care. Like polyamory comes with a fungus."

Jean choked on her drink.

"Then there was this other one. Beautiful teeth. Perfect fade. Took me out to dinner, was respectful, funny, smart…. and then we get back to his place, and he says, 'I'm not into head.' I was like whose?"

CC clutched his chest.

"Girl," Asha said, holding up a finger, "when I asked for clarification, he says, 'I don't think women giving oral is respectful to the divine feminine'."

Danielle blinked. "What the fuck?"

"I said—so your dick is too holy for head?"

Kiki said, "That's not divine. That's denial."

Asha continued. "THEN I had the nerve to go out with a fine ass gym rat. the type. Smooth skin. Gold chain. Protein shake in the car. We get home, we fuck, and mid stroke, he calls me—wait for it—'a strong 7 with potential'."

"Bitch what? !" CC yelled.

"I stopped mid-thrust and said, 'Sir, I'm gonna need you to nut and leave'."

They were all dying. Then Asha looked at Danielle. "Real question though. And don't judge me."

Danielle said, "I'm listening."

"I had this girl friend—lowercase G, not caps—and she used a strap on me so good I saw the Lord. Like big dick energy with no balls attached."

Danielle coughed into her wine.

Jean said, "Go on, bitch. I'm fake considering lesbianism."

Danielle raised an eyebrow.

Asha added quickly, "But I can't eat pussy. I … I can't. I won't. I don't even like peaches unless they're in a cobbler."

CC burst out laughing.

Asha said, dead serious: "So like… is it frowned upon to receive strap but not return the favor?"

Danielle sipped her drink slowly. "You trying to be a headless lesbian?"

Asha nodded. "A pillow princess. A strap-only queen."

Jean: "That's not gay. That's theft."

Ramon: "That's a debit card with no PIN."

Kiki: "That's community fraud."

They were wheezing.

Asha shrugged. "Fine. Guess I'm still stuck with men and their post-nut podcast opinions."

CC wiped tears from his eyes. "If you become a lesbian, let me be your sponsor. You're not ready."

They all clinked glasses.

Danielle's phone buzzed again. It was from Selena. She hesitated, then read it out loud.
"You're different. Not in a predictable way. In a 'maybe I'll stay up late to talk to you' way."

Everyone gave the same slow eyebrow raise. Danielle smiled but looked uncertain. "I'm gonna share it. One second."

She started typing—her usual setup when sharing a screenshot with the crew group thread.
She captioned it: "See? This is what. She's either perfect or completely unreadable. I can't win."

CC reached for her phone. "Where is it, bitch? I didn't get it."

Jean checked hers. "Nothing came through."

A beat passed. Danielle's face dropped. "Oh my God."

Kiki leaned in. "Wait…. what?"

Danielle held up her phone like it was evidence at a murder trial. "I sent it… to her."

Silence. Then—gasps.

Asha covered her mouth. "No the fuck you didn't."

Jean's jaw dropped. "Bitch."

Ramon winced like he'd been slapped. "That's a death blow."

CC leaned across the table. "Tell me you unsent it."

Danielle whispered, "She saw it already."

They all recoiled in unison. Jean grabbed Danielle's hand. "Okay. Deep breath. Did she say anything?"

"No."

"Did she block you?"

"Not yet."

"Then there's still hope."

CC sipped his drink like it had healing properties. "Bitch, you hit send like it was a bomb and threw it into her lap."

Asha shook her head. "You out here doing recon and forgot what side you're on."

Danielle leaned back, defeated. "Fuck."

No one said anything for a second. Then CC, trying to lighten the mood, raised a finger.
"So... we not gonna circle back to Asha's cobbler comment?"

Asha: "Still stands."

The laughter crept back in. But under the table, Jean gave Danielle's hand a soft squeeze.
No more jokes. a quiet anchor. And for now... that was enough.

Danielle stared at her phone like it had pulled a gun on her. The message thread—the one that used to be blue, light, and playful—was now green.

Her last text had been a full apology. Not a weak-ass half-apology.

A real one. Thoughtful. Honest. Owning the mistake. "I didn't mean for you to see that. I was venting to friends, which I know doesn't make it better. But I like you. A lot. And I'm sorry I let my fear get loud."

No response. Only a green bubble where connection used to be.

Jean walked into the living room and froze when she saw Danielle's face.

"Shit," Jean whispered.

Danielle shook her head. "It's not even the message. It's… the silence."

Jean sat next to her, quiet for a beat. Then offered, "Maybe her phone died."

Danielle stared. Jean smirked. "What? It could've. Or maybe she's in a tunnel."

Danielle gave her the driest look known to woman. Jean tried again. "Maybe she's building a greenhouse in her backyard and that's why your texts turned green."

"Bitch."

Jean raised both hands. "Okay. Okay. Too soon."

Danielle laughed— once. But it cracked her composure. The tears came quietly, embarrassingly fast. She wiped one before it fell, but Jean saw it. Jean didn't make it weird. She slid closer. "Well, bitch," she said, "let's shut up and hold hands in silence."

Danielle nodded, and they did. For a while.

Later that night, Jean finally opened the thread with Green Smoothie. She typed:
"You got room for one more storm?"

His reply came ten minutes later. "Yes. But on one condition."

Jean exhaled. "I don't do conditions. If you want the business Jean, I promise you—you will not survive negotiations."

He sent back a laughing emoji. Then: "Fair."

"Will you let me cook for you?" Jean nearly threw her phone across the room. Fuck no. No fucking way.

"Cooking is intimate. You'd be better off asking to bend me over a balcony somewhere."

His reply came instantly: "Duly noted. But not ruling out the balcony either."

Jean smiled in spite of herself. "So now what?"

"You pick where we go next. I'm interested to see how you date a man you like but not that much."

Jean responded with a thinking emoji.

He added: "You can even bring your knife. Keep it in your back pocket."

Jean read it twice. Then typed: "Fine. But if you say one wrong thing, I'm stabbing you in the ankle."

"I'd expect nothing less."

Group Chat: Velour Veterans □□

CC: ATTENTION BITCHES !! Karaoke night is in TWO WEEKS. Learn your songs. Rehearse your bridges. Get your life. Everybody's getting served. @Jamal—no songs with the N-word in them. I will not be able to save you. You will get stomped out by the bar staff, the DJ, and two old ladies playing spades in the corner. Also yes, I will be joining you ungrateful hoes. Prepare accordingly. □□□□□

Danielle: You're yelling.

Jean: But he's right.

Asha: Don't test me. I've been rehearsing Toni Braxton in the car.

Ramon: I got Boyz II Men locked and loaded.

Kiki: Your deep voice can't save you from being off-key.

CC: Bitch we ready. Get your snacks. Get your notes. And get your lungs.

And like that, the air lightened.

Danielle still wasn't okay. Jean wasn't either. But they were back in motion. And sometimes… that's enough.

Chapter 10: Sound Check & Sore Spots

One week later, still no word from Selena.

Danielle had done the whole routine—apologized twice, left it alone, gave space. But now the blue iMessage bubbles were still green, and the silence was too loud to ignore. She was tired of jumping to check her phone. Tired of pretending it didn't matter.

She opened her dating app folder, stared at the icons… and hovered. That weird, comforting familiarity tugged at her like an old pair of sweatpants. Maybe it was time to go back to what she knew: short-lived flings, half-interesting profiles, and burner emails tied to bad decisions. The world of dating women wasn't safer—it was newer. But even the new had started to feel disappointing.

Across town, Jean was doing what she did best when emotionally unsettled—working her ass off but not giving a damn. She was technically at work. Laptop open. Coffee half-drunk. Calendar full. But her head was floating.

So was Danielle's. They both floated through the week. Float-ghosted.

Meanwhile, the crew group chat had turned into a full-blown karaoke war room.

Ramon: "I'm not singing. Last time I did, I got analyzed like I wrote the damn song."

Kiki: "Because you picked a song about loving big asses. Knowing damn well I don't have one."

Ramon: "You got big, pretty, full tits and a big-lipped fat pussy. You don't need an ass."

Kiki: "Don't do that. Ass is a trigger. Compliment the rest, but don't invoke the cheeks."

Asha: "Let's put that on a shirt: 'Don't invoke the cheeks'."

CC: "Singing Anaconda in solidarity with Kiki now."

Jean: "Y'all are dumb."

Danielle: "Ramon got dragged and still thinks he was the victim. Impressive."

Jean had been silent for a while. Then: "Okay, so what are we thinking—Whitney ballad or something petty?"

CC: "You do petty like it's your birthright. Live in it."

Green Smoothie had been texting regularly. Sweet, short, never clingy. Jean hadn't seen him in person again yet. Part of her didn't want to ruin the vibe. Part of her didn't trust the vibe.
But she was tired too.

So that night, she did the unthinkable.

J: Hey. There's a karaoke night next week. At my spot. It's wild.

Loud. A little messy. Come.

GS: Is that a real invite or a setup?

J: Both.

GS: Will I survive?

J: Don't be fake. Don't lie. Don't try too hard. And you'll be fine.

GS: So it's a group interview.

J: Correct.

GS: What's the dress code?

J: Confidence and something that won't get you roasted by a gay man in leopard print.

GS sent back a laughing emoji, then a thumbs up.

And like that—Jean had made her move. But the rest? Still unwritten.

It had been eight days. Still nothing. Danielle wasn't checking her phone anymore. She had stopped hoping. Stopped waiting. Started preparing for the silence to be the end of it. Selena was gone. And if she wasn't, she was damn good at pretending to be. Until the text came. after 2:00 p.m.

Selena: I wasn't trying to hurt you. I needed space. That text hit harder than I expected. I didn't know what to say.

Danielle stared at it, unsure what to write back. She sat in it. Let the weight of it press down.
Then the phone rang. Selena.

Danielle answered, slowly. Hey.

Selena exhaled. Maybe a phone conversation is better than a text.

Danielle didn't disagree.

Selena started: I wasn't trying to hurt you. I … needed space. That text hit harder than I expected. I didn't know what to say.

Danielle took a breath: If you needed space, that's fair. But I thought we were at least above the point of ghosting. Even if communication meant 'fuck off, I'm done with you'—that would've been better than silence.

Selena went quiet.

Then: Fair… I missed you. Terribly. I'm sorry for that. When can I see you again?

Danielle's heart skipped—but her brain kept pace: If she could ghost me over a mistake… what happens when something serious happens? What if someone lies on me? Would she believe it without even asking me? Would she leave again?

She almost didn't say it. But she did.

Danielle: I'm gonna be real with you. Retreating at the first thing you don't like is some bullshit I can't get with. I'm not perfect. Neither are you. You told me your past was in the past. I left it there. But mine lives with me. Every day. I survive it with the people I trust. My crew.

Selena was quiet again.

Danielle kept going: So yeah, we talk. Yeah, we roast. We do it to each other too. It's how we breathe through our mess. They pick me up when people run. They stay. Even when I fall apart.

Selena said: That's childish. You're all grown. It's giving modern day Mean Girls.

Danielle didn't flinch: It's only mean if it's malicious. It's only petty if it's public. We talk in our circle. Our safe one. There's no malice in that. biased love and truth.

Selena snapped: Until you send the wrong text.

Danielle sighed: Touché. But I apologized. And I meant it. That's all I owe you. I won't keep bleeding for a paper cut. You have a good night.

She hung up. Then whispered to herself: Fuck that. I choose me… over you choosing you… for me.

She sat back. Didn't cry. Didn't scream. She sat in it. And somehow… that made her feel stronger than she had all week. She went from wanting to war with Selena to warring for herself.

Because the Velour Veterans weren't a group chat—they were a goddamn mighty morphin' battle unit. Stronger than any Transformer, fiercer than the Thundercats, more loyal than a Power Ranger.

And when shit hit the fan, they didn't flinch—They formed up. Like always.

Danielle didn't miss Selena anymore. She thought she would. Thought it would sting. Thought maybe she'd cry again. But real heartbreak lingers longer than a week. What she felt now wasn't sadness—it was breath. Room to finally inhale. Selena had done her a favor. Her timing was perfect. Because now Danielle could walk away, not with bitterness—but with clarity.

And tonight wasn't about ghosts. It was karaoke night. And the Velour Veterans did not come to play. Everybody showed up in their best, most ridiculous fits.

Asha had on gold thigh-high boots and a denim corset that made no sense with the weather but all the sense with her attitude.

Ramon came in with a leather vest over no shirt and a bandana like he was cosplaying an extra from a 90s R&B video.

Kiki had on a long ponytail and a bodycon dress that shimmered like a fresh text thread.

And then there was Church Candy. Leopard bodysuit—at least half a size too small. Dick print? Present. Unapologetically so. He wore not one, but three hats—stacked on his head like gay Russian nesting dolls. He had a chain around his neck attached to nothing —except for the imaginary teacup Yorkie he swore was named "Bitch Please."

The crowd was buzzing.

Kiki: So where is Green Smoothie?

Asha: He better not be fine. I'm petty and I'd hate to not like him.

CC: I'm not calling nobody Green Smoothie all night. What's his real name again?

Jean:… Shit.

Then—he walked in. Jean damn near forgot how to blink.

Perfectly fitted jeans. Shirt hugging his arms like it knew what it was doing. Beard tight. Fade sharp enough to slice cheese. Dick print respectful but undeniable.

Jean stepped forward to introduce him—then blanked. She had been calling him "Green Smoothie" for so long she genuinely forgot his damn name.

Before the awkward pause hit, he extended a hand. "It's a pleasure to meet y'all. My name's Dothan."

CC: Dothan? That's not a name. That's a GPS destination.

Asha: That sound like a town with one gas station and a jail full of your cousins.

Dothan: Two gas stations. And the jail's under renovation.

Kiki: Okay! You got jokes.

Jean: Be careful. They smell fear.

Dothan: Good thing I used to work animal control.

They all paused. Looked at CC.

CC gave a slow, dramatic blink: Okay, Green Smoothie… you might fit in.

Dothan: Are you still gonna call me Green Smoothie?

CC: Your name is what we say it is. Be thankful. (Snap)

And with that, the show began.

First up was Asha. She kicked off with her own hybrid version of "Girls Wanna Have Fun" blended with SZA's "Kill Bill." By the time she got to "I might kill my ex," the room was screaming and somebody's drink had already spilled.

Then came Jean. She strutted up, mic in hand, and channeled Beyoncé with "Irreplaceable."

"You must not know 'bout me…" The crowd went wild.

When it was CC's turn, he grabbed the mic like he was born for it and launched into CeeLo Green's "F**k You," changing the names mid-song depending on who pissed him off that month. Every "fuck you" was louder than the last, and when he pointed at Jamal mid-verse, Jamal ducked behind Jasmine like it was a drive-by.

Danielle took the mic next. She didn't warn anyone. She grabbed it and went straight into Adele. "Nevermind, I'll find someone like you…"

She was off-key. Loud. And dead serious. Everyone started to laugh—until they saw her face. She was singing her truth.

Kiki and Ramon went up together and tried to duet Bruno Mars and Sexyy Red. They forgot every word except "booty" and "girl." It was a disaster. It was iconic.

And then… Jamal stood. Jasmine on his arm. He raised both hands. "My turn."

CC put his hands over his face in preemptive shame.

Jamal stepped up. Grabbed the mic. And started to sing "Ebony Eyes" by Rick James and Smokey Robinson. And he wasn't bad. Like… decent.

When he hit the Smokey part with real emotion, the crowd blinked. Then CC walked up behind him—grabbing the second mic and jumped into the Rick James verse with everything in his flamboyant soul.

Together, they serenaded Jasmine like two drama kids who found each other at last. Enemies became friends. And the Velour Veterans? They howled, hollered, hugged, and harmonized.

Because if there was one thing they knew how to do—it was show up, sing loud, and survive whatever came next. Together. Like always.

Chapter 11: You Up? (Don't Answer.)

It had been four days since karaoke night, and the emotional glitter still hadn't fully settled.

Velour was quiet now, like a confession booth that had seen too much.

The couches still smelled faintly of spilled martinis and judgment, and someone's boa had been left hanging from the flower wall like a gay sacrifice. Danielle wasn't sure if it belonged to CC or the woman in leather pants who sang "If I Ain't Got You" like she was auditioning for revenge.

Jean had been in silent mode most of the week—emails only, minimal emojis. Danielle didn't ask questions. She knew better. When Jean went quiet, it wasn't depression. It was data collection.

Danielle, on the other hand, had been fielding too many messages from too many women who didn't remember how to flirt without trauma bonding. She was tired. Not sad. … post-emotional. Like someone who'd done the cleanse and now couldn't stomach sugar.

The group chat pinged.

Velour Veterans (Muted □)

Kiki: So… Jasmine still here?

Asha: WAIT. You mean with Jamal?

CC: Are we being punk'd? Is this a long play? Did she lose a bet?

Jamal: Lmaoooo. Y'all so pressed. Yes. She's still here. Unlike some of y'all, she wants to teach me her body. And I'm learning.

Jamal (again): Also... I had no idea squirting was real. I thought that shit was edited.

CC:☹

CC: Bitch boy, that's piss. Don't drink it.

Kiki: DEADDDDDD 😫😫😫😫

Danielle: Jamal out here getting baptized in brunch pee and thinking he found God.

Jean: I hate it here.

Ramon: I'm impressed somebody lasted longer than a week.

Asha: Congrats Jamal. You made it past the trial version.

CC: Proud of you, little vanilla dick king. Go forth and ruin less lives.

Danielle laughed out loud—genuine, tired, almost grateful. Then her screen lit up with a new message. Not from the group chat. From... someone named Monet.

The preview said: Hey beautiful. I've been thinking about our convo all week. You free tonight?

Danielle blinked. Who the hell is Monet?

She opened the thread and scrolled up. Barely anything there. Two lines from Saturday night. A compliment. A flame emoji. A location tag from a wine bar they were all at briefly.
She didn't hesitate.

Danielle typed: Look, I don't have time for any games. I don't remember who you are.

Then she paused. Looked at the profile picture. The woman was beautiful—like, FaceTime-without-a-filter beautiful. Skin like buttered tea, eyes like something you should say grace before staring into.

The memory snapped back faintly: Monet had leaned over at the bar and whispered something flirty about Danielle's ring. She wore velvet. Laughed like her pussy had a playlist.

Still... something about her was off. Not a red flag. a missing receipt.

Danielle took a breath. She wasn't going to force it. Let the red flags show up organically. She hit send.

Across town, Jean was curled up on her sectional, hair wrapped, a face mask on, and a glass of wine she swore was her last for the night in hand.

The chat pinged again.

CC: Now that we've addressed Jamal's newfound talent for slip-and-slides, can I say something?

CC (again): Jean. I see you, bitch. You been quiet, but that energy still glowing. You and Green Smoothie got a lil … rhythm now.

Jean rolled her eyes so hard she almost strained a muscle: Stop calling him that.

CC: Excuse me?

Jean: I said stop calling him that. We're not naming my people. That's the rule. You name your own. I name mine.

CC: May I REMIND YOU of our sacred code?

CC: Your name is what we say it is, Article 3, Section: Petty.

Jean: And I'm updating the bylaws. Effective today, his name is NOT Green Fucking Smoothie.

CC: Fiiiiiine bitch □

Kiki: She put her foot down. That means she like him.

Danielle: She ain't been this snappy since the Turtleneck Sausage incident.

CC shivered in trauma. Jean smirked a little. She didn't want too like this man. He was too calm, too clean, too…. real. But the way he looked at her? Like he was trying to memorize her laugh? That shit was spiritual warfare.

Then Danielle's phone buzzed with a new notification. Selena. Of course.

Subject: "I Want You To Know…"

She opened it without flinching:
Hey D. I've been sitting with what happened, and I wanted to be honest. I still believe what I said was valid, even if it hurt you. I felt what I felt, and I don't apologize for being in my truth. But I miss you. I miss us. And if there's still a window… I'd love to talk. I still care. Terribly.—Selena

Danielle stared at the screen for a second. Then another. And then… nothing.

No tears. No ache. No mental gymnastics. She simply whispered, "That's a you problem."

She didn't reply. Didn't even save it. She slid the thread into archive and whispered, "Alexa, play 'Closure' by Summer Walker."

Velour Social was quieter than usual—at least for now. It was that midweek lull between paychecks and poor decisions. The playlist was slow, the lights were soft, and Asha was already behind the bar with her sleeves rolled up and a look on her face that said she wasn't here for the bullshit but welcomed it if it came correct.

Jean was already seated, sipping something dark and neat. She wore all black like she was mourning patience. Danielle slid into the booth across from her, freshly perfumed, emotionally unbothered, and about two "Hey stranger" texts away from snapping someone's neck.

They didn't greet each other right away. Jean finally said, "You look light."

Danielle smirked. "I'm trying. Letting shit go is cheaper than therapy. Even if I am the therapy."

Jean nodded. "So. Update me."

Danielle pulled her phone out and slid it across the table. A picture of Monet glowed from the screen—gorgeous, effortless, unnervingly curated.

Jean raised a brow. "She's fine. Too fine. Like… AI-generated with a skincare deal."

Danielle laughed. "Exactly. She sent me a photo from a hammock with a smoothie in one hand and a book in the other. Captioned it 'My soft life is sacred'."

Jean blinked. "Was it at least a real book?"

" 'The Alchemist.'"

Jean groaned. "The red flag starter pack."

"I know," Danielle said, sighing. "But I can't tell if I'm being cautious or cynical. I don't wanna fall for a personality someone made up on Canva."

Jean leaned in. "Then don't. Let her show you who she is in silence, not in stories. The real ones trip over their own truths eventually. Watch."

Danielle nodded, holding that advice a little longer than she expected to.

Then Jean exhaled and sipped again. "So… Dothan texted me."

Danielle perked up. "Did he call himself Green Smoothie?"

Jean side-eyed her. "Don't start."

Danielle smirked. "What did he say?"

Jean pulled her phone out. "'If your week's as heavy as mine, maybe we lighten it together'."

Danielle blinked. "Okay, poet. I see you."

"I haven't responded," Jean admitted. "I like him. But I'm waiting for the ghost in him to show up."

"You're not afraid to feel," Danielle said. "You're afraid to be wrong again."

Jean sat with that. Didn't argue. Didn't blink. That's when the front door opened, and Velour's temperature dropped five degrees.

Selena. She walked in wearing jeans that clung to all her like old promises and a blazer like she came to serve a summons. Her hair was slicked back. Her lips were red. Her energy was not invited.

Danielle caught her immediately and turned to Jean.

"Give me a sec." Jean watched without asking questions. adjusted her glass and turned slightly toward the bar—close enough to intervene, far enough to let it unfold.

Danielle met Selena near the back hallway, out of earshot of the bar but within full view of Asha, who subtly turned the music down and stood taller.

Danielle folded her arms. "What are you doing here?"

Selena crossed hers. "I don't like being ignored."

Danielle's brow arched. "That's funny coming from someone who ignored me for eight days."

Selena rolled her eyes. "I needed space."

Danielle's voice was flat. "And during your little clarity retreat, I didn't seek you out, didn't show up uninvited, didn't beg for closure I didn't owe. What makes you think this is welcome now?"

Selena stepped closer. "Because I know you. I know you still feel something."

Danielle's face didn't move. "… a version of me that tolerated your chaos. That version has been updated. You're talking to the premium subscription now. No ads, no returns, no fucks left."

Selena's voice rose. "You're acting like none of it mattered."

"You're acting like you didn't disappear and then pop back up like I'm a fucking errand you forgot to run," Danielle shot back.

Selena's voice got sharper. Louder. "Because you make everything so cold. You act like emotions are threats."

Danielle didn't flinch. "Let's not confuse my classy and dignified demeanor with my ability to shed that skin when necessary. And let's not mistake your raised voice for anything but an invitation to violence."

She took a step closer. "I am not only not the one—but I will be sure you never fucking forget it."

Selena blinked, jaw clenched. And as she opened her mouth again, Asha, with zero hesitation, hit the Bluetooth and pressed play.

Big Sean's voice poured through the speakers: ☐ "I don't fuck with youuuu. You little stupid ass bitch I ain't fuckin' with you…"
☐

Danielle looked up at the ceiling, then smiled. "Oh. They're playing our song." She walked off.

Selena stood there, trying to hold her posture together, rage brewing in her mascara. She barked, "You're a fucking robot of a person!"

Jean didn't look up. Danielle didn't flinch. And Asha? She stepped out from behind the bar, struck a robotic pose, and said, "Take me to your leader."

Jean and Danielle joined her in perfect sync—arms stiff, heads tilted, voices monotone:
"Take me to your leader."

Selena stormed out like a TikTok tantrum with nowhere to go. And like that, the bar snapped back to normal.
A beat passed. Then the front door opened again, and the rest of the crew walked in, mid-laugh, mid-gossip, mid-life.

Kiki stopped cold. "What the hell happened?"

Danielle slid back into the booth like nothing occurred. "A reboot."

Ramon glanced at Asha. "We missed something, didn't we?"

Asha didn't answer. She poured a round.

CC took off his sunglasses dramatically. "Well, damn. Somebody give Danielle her flowers and a flamethrower."

Jean looked at them all, still sipping, still calculating something in her head. Then she said it—clear, sharp, and absolute. "I'm done hesitating."

Everyone turned. "I'm ready to move forward. With Dothan."

Danielle smiled slowly. Jean nodded. "No sense in falling for someone and I can't stay because the dick and tongue game is trash. I'm too young to say 'Well, he's nice to me' or 'This is as good as it gets'."

She leaned forward, eyes lit now. "Fuck that. It's on."

Chapter 12: And That's Why We Don't Get Excited Too Early

"Okay but can we talk about the limp elephant in the room?" CC asked, swirling his mimosa like it had secrets in it.

Jean didn't look up from her coffee. Danielle coughed into her napkin. Kiki blinked. Ramon just sipped slowly, like a man who'd learned never to speak first when emotions were loading.

It was Sunday brunch, and the table was still warm from last night's drama. Asha was running late. Jamal was supposedly deep in "domestic vibes" with Jasmine and sent a group text that just read: "Y'all pray for me. She's talking baby names and I just learned where the G-spot is."

Jean hadn't said a word since she sat down. Danielle tried. "We don't have to—"

"No," Jean cut in. "Let's go ahead and unpack it."

She set her fork down like she was about to operate on herself without anesthesia. "I invited him over."

CC's eyes lit up. "Green Smoothie?!"

Jean didn't blink. "Dothan. I invited Dothan over."

She took a sip of her drink like it was communion, then exhaled. "Look... I set the scene. Candles. Music. I wore the silk. He showed up smelling like he moisturized with ambition. We kissed. We laughed. Grown energy. Right "

The table leaned in.

"We get to the bedroom. I'm thinking, okay, let's see if the smoothie is thick enough to drink."

Danielle snorted.

"And then…" Jean raised her eyebrows. "Nothing. Flatline. Not even a wiggle."

"Girl," CC whispered.

"I thought okay, maybe nerves. So I offer a little assistance—nothing. Try again—nothing. So I try to keep it light, you know? I joke—said, 'So this is what they meant by green smoothie. Thick but no stamina'."

Danielle winced. Kiki covered her mouth. J

ean kept going. "He pulls back and says, 'What?' Like I insulted his ancestors. I say, 'It's a joke.' He tells me maybe don't joke right now. I say, 'I'm just keeping it light. It's not the first limp dick I've seen. Won't be the last'."

Ramon blinked. "Oh shit."

Jean looked at him. "Oh, it gets better." She straightened in her seat, like bracing herself for the next layer. "He stands up and says, 'You always gotta lead with your mouth. Just once, I wish you'd shut the fuck up and let someone just… be'."

Everyone went still.

"Yup," Jean said flatly. "Told me to shut the fuck up in my house with his limp dick."

CC: "Oh hell no."

Danielle: "What did you say?"

Jean's smile was tight. "I said, 'I didn't realize silence was the cure for your erectile dysfunction'."

The table exploded—then fell quiet again.

Jean nodded. "Yeah. That's when it went from soft to savage."

"Jean," Kiki said gently, but Jean waved her hand.

"I know. But I was trying to keep some dignity while watching the Titanic sink in my bed. Anyway, he says, 'This isn't about my dick.' I say, 'Oh it's not? Because your dick was the one that RSVP'd to this party and didn't show up'."

Even Ramon winced.

"Then," Jean said, quieter now, "he looked at me and said… 'You ever think maybe your mouth isn't what makes people run'?"

She paused.

" 'That it's not your beauty or your confidence or your mouth—but the fact that you're unreachable'?"

CC's lips parted, but no sound came out.

Danielle's hand gently touched Jean's arm, but Jean didn't stop. "Then he said… 'You claim you're alone by choice. But the choice is everybody else's—not yours'."

Silence. And for once, Jean didn't try to fill it. "I told him, 'Well, that's one way to lose your erection and your chance.' He didn't laugh. Just left."

She exhaled. "I crumpled on the floor like a clearance dress from Zara."

The silence at the table was soft, thick, real.

Then CC, always the breaker of emotional tension, said, "You roasted him. But damn."

Jean gave a single, tired nod. "I felt every word. I told him off, but… I heard him. And what makes it worse is—he wasn't all wrong."

Danielle squeezed her hand. "You okay?"

Jean shook her head. "No. But I will be."

CC reached over and tapped her glass. "To soft dicks and hard truths."

Jean tapped back. "To being alone on purpose. Even if it started by accident."

Kiki, softly: "You weren't wrong for trying."

Ramon added, "And you're not weak for feeling it."

Jean didn't cry. Didn't flinch. But her next sip felt heavier.

Danielle leaned in. "What he said? About being unreachable."

Jean nodded.

"It wasn't a lie," she said. "But it wasn't the truth either. Danielle whispered, "That's the part that hurts the most. When someone says something that's not fully false."

Jean smiled bitterly. "It's like an insult and a diagnosis in one."

The table chuckled softly. Then CC, trying to cut the tension, asked, "So are we calling him Flaccid Fury now or…?"

Jean snorted. "No. We're not giving him anything else. Not names. Not energy. Not emails."

Danielle raised a toast. "To chapters closed." Everyone echoed back, glass to glass:
"To chapters closed."

They sat in the quiet for a moment longer—no music, no jokes, no distractions.

Jean didn't say anything else, but the space around her shifted. She wasn't glass about to shatter. She was iron that just remembered it could rust.

Danielle clocked it, then looked down at her own phone like it buzzed—even though it hadn't. She didn't want to be the next one up, but her silence had started to hum. And this crew was too good at hearing things no one said.

So when Ramon asked, "Anyone else got something to get off their chest?" and CC fake-gasped with a hand to his imaginary pearls, Danielle knew it was time.

She looked up. "Okay. Fine."

Jean smirked but didn't turn her head.

Danielle exhaled. "Monet texted me again."

CC lit up. "Ooooh! Did she send a pic? Was it titty or tame?"

Danielle rolled her eyes. "Calm down, Safari. It was a selfie in her car. Seatbelt across the chest. Captioned: 'Hope your day's as beautiful as you'."

"Awww." Kiki cooed.

Danielle didn't smile.

CC leaned in. "You're not impressed?"

"It's not that I'm not impressed. It's that… I'm not moved."

Jean, still not looking up, muttered, "Say more."

Danielle turned her phone toward the table. "This is her vibe. Always perfect lighting. Always a curated caption. Always saying the right thing. She's warm. She's attentive. But I can't feel her."

"Is the chemistry off?" Ramon asked.

"It's not chemistry," Danielle said. "It's access."

She paused, then found the words. "Monet gives me everything but herself. It's all airbrushed care and poetic checkins. But she never talks about anything real. Her ex, her fears, her shit. It's like I'm dating a really well-edited hologram."

CC blinked. "Not a hologram."

Danielle continued. "I've tried to open doors. Asked her if she's been in love before—she said, 'Yes, but I think I confuse love with loyalty.' Which sounds deep… but she never followed up. Just changed the subject."

Kiki nodded slowly. "That's a performance answer. Like when someone says they're an empath but never notice your moods."

Danielle laughed—short and sharp. "Exactly "

Jean finally turned her head. "So what are you gonna do?"

Danielle looked out the window, like the answer might be floating in traffic. "I don't know yet. But I do know this—if I wanted surface-level affection from a beautiful stranger, I'd go back to men."

Everyone oooooohed. Ramon crossed himself like a guilty Catholic. CC grabbed his drink and whispered, "May her chakra rest in peace."

Danielle took a sip of water, then said it out loud. "I want more. I want ugly honesty. I want someone to take their mask off before I have to rip it off."

"You want love, not a highlight reel," Jean said.

Danielle met her eyes. "Exactly."

And there it was—shared disappointment between two people who hadn't even lost anyone yet. Just the feeling that what was being offered might never match what was needed.

"Text just came in," Danielle added. "She said, 'Hope your week's off to a soft start'."

CC blinked. "Is she dating you or writing you lullabies?"

Danielle showed them her reply. "Appreciate it. We should talk soon. Like, actually talk."

Ramon asked, "Did she respond?" Danielle shook her head.

Jean leaned back. "Maybe that's your answer."

Asha finally arrived, slightly out of breath but still fine as hell. She tossed her bag behind the bar and pointed at the group.

"I know I'm late, but somebody better catch me up before I start reading lips."

CC snapped: "Jean almost caught a charge. Danielle might be dating a screensaver. Ramon still fine. Kiki judging us in silence. And I haven't caused chaos yet, but I'm working on it."

Asha raised a brow. "Sounds like Sunday." The group chuckled, tension easing.

Danielle pulled her phone out again. Nothing new. Jean, watching her, spoke softly. "You okay?"

Danielle didn't answer right away. "I'm not crying. I'm not spiraling. But I feel like I'm carrying a balloon that's been leaking slowly for a week."

CC nodded. "That's grief before it arrives."

Danielle nodded back. "And I'm mad at myself for being disappointed before anything bad actually happens."

"You're not mad,"Kiki said. "You're preparing."

Danielle smiled. "Same thing."

Jean said, "You want her to prove you wrong."

Danielle replied: "I want her to know me. Not just pursue me like I'm a slot machine that might pay out with enough good behavior."

The table grew quiet again. Then CC, unable to sit in sincerity too long, raised his glass. "To being known. Fully. Loudly. Before somebody tries to love us in lowercase."

Danielle clinked glasses. "To soft landings and hard truths."

Kiki raised hers. "To the courage to admit when something looks good but feels empty."

Jean said nothing. She just tapped her glass last. And that said everything.

Asha wiped her hands on a bar towel and leaned across the table. "You know what we haven't done in a minute?" she asked, deadpan.

Everyone looked up.

"Email reconciliation," she said. "And don't act brand new."

CC gasped like he'd just remembered like an appointment he was late for.

"Oh bitch—yes. We've been so busy processing heartbreak and soft penises, I almost forgot what matters."

Danielle smirked. "What matters is accountability and archiving."

Jean nodded. "Closure with flair."

Kiki sipped her mimosa. "Are we doing this by ghost story, sexual trauma, or emotional damage tier list?"

"Surprise us," Ramon said. "The bar's already low."

Danielle exhaled. "Fine. I'll start. Because if I don't tell this story, I'm gonna take it to my grave and still be mad."

The group leaned in. "I dated this woman for about three months. Thought she was grounded, sensual, emotionally smart. We go out one night, I start my period—not a big deal. I go to the bathroom to change my pad, and this bitch follows me in there like she's my OB-GYN."

CC choked on air. Danielle held up a finger. "No no, it gets better. I'm standing there, pants down, pad off—and she picks up the fucking trash can, holds it under me, and says, 'I just want you to know I'm here for you. I understand'."

Jean covered her face.

"She said it with tears in her eyes," Danielle added. "Like it was some kind of sacred ritual."

CC gasped, "NOT THE PERIOD ALTAR."

Danielle said, "And when I told her to get the fuck out, she looked insulted. Like I'd just rejected her love language."

Kiki wheezed. "Was she wearing white linen?!"

"She was wearing a poncho," Danielle replied. "I never recovered."

Asha clinked her glass against Danielle's. "Okay. I have one. It's not emotional—it's visual trauma."

CC whispered, "Yes. Please."

"I met this man online. Grown, confident, definitely had a script—but whatever. He says he left something at his house, we gotta swing by real quick. Fine. I'm thinking maybe it's a lie and it's his mama's house. Nope. This motherfucker had a house like Scarface. It was real. Big. Clean. He lived there."

Jean raised an eyebrow. "So what's the problem?"

Asha said, "As soon as we walk in, I notice two things: gold teeth and spray paint."

CC froze. "Excuse me?"

"Not grills," Asha said. "Gold crowns. From like… the '70s. The kind that say 'I chew with history'."

Danielle was already crying.

"And he had a bald spot," Asha continued. "But instead of just being bald, he spray-painted it black. Like literally—sprayed it. But dinner was hot, and I was starving. By the time the waiter brought the wine, that spray started to melt. It slid down the back of his neck like a Banksy mural."

CC screamed. Ramon wiped tears. "That's not hair. That's runoff."

Kiki asked, "Did he ever come back around?"

"Oh he did " Asha nodded. "A few months later. This time? Hair plugs. Looked like someone tried to staple Astroturf to his scalp."

The whole table lost it. Asha sipped, satisfied. Jean said, "Alright. I got one."

Everyone leaned in like she was about to read them bedtime trauma.

"I was seeing this guy who wrote me poetry. Like deep, heavy shit. Thoughtful. Soft. Sexy. Then he ghosted me after we slept together. No warning, just poof. Nine months later, he emails me a voice memo of him playing guitar and singing lyrics he wrote for me."

Danielle raised a brow. "Was it good "

"Sounded like acoustic diarrhea," Jean said. "And the chorus was 'You were never really mine, but you still haunt my hands'."

Asha gagged. "Haunt your hands? Sir, was I a ghost or a glove?"

Jean added, "He attached a photo of my foot from our first date."

Everyone stopped. CC blinked. "A photo of your foot?"

Jean nodded. "Captioned: 'Wherever you walk, I'll still ache'."

Kiki stood up and walked away. CC clutched his chest. "Oh this is biblical."

Jean smirked. "I replied with a picture of my middle finger and the word 'Boo'."

The table howled. "Okay, wait," CC said. "I got one."

Danielle leaned back. "Let's go."

CC exhaled. "I fell for a church man. Handsome. Deep voice. Said all the right things. Made me feel safe. We dated for four months. He prayed over my food and my backshots."

Asha whispered, "Sacred."

"Then he disappeared. Cold vanish. I sent two messages—nothing. Third week, I stop trying. He resurfaces two months later saying, 'God was testing my restraint. I wasn't ready to let temptation win'"

Ramon: "You were temptation?"

CC nodded. "I said, 'God may not be finished with you, but I am.' Then blocked him while playing Kirk Franklin."

Kiki clapped. "With praise hands?"

"Bitch, with cymbals," CC said. They all laughed. Then the tone softened.

Danielle checked her phone again. Still no new reply. Jean noticed. "Nothing?"

Danielle shook her head. "She sent me a 'hope you feel held' text yesterday. Still no follow-up. Just soft sentences and no substance."

CC reached over. "You deserve more than being a poem someone writes to make themselves feel deep."

Danielle smiled weakly. "I'm starting to believe that."

Jean looked down at her phone, took a breath, and opened her draft folder. "Alright," she said. "I'm sending this."

Danielle read over her shoulder. "You didn't break me. But you did show me a mirror I didn't want to look in. I'll heal with grace—and from a distance "

Jean hit send. The table watched her closely. She didn't cry. She didn't flinch. But she didn't smile either. Her face settled like someone who finally closed a window after months of cold air leaking in.

CC raised his glass. "To the ones who left. To the ones who lingered. And to the inboxes we finally deleted."

Everyone echoed: "To email reconciliation."

They toasted. And this time? No one needed to say another word.

Chapter 13: Do You Smell That? That's Your Soul Leaving.

Two weeks later, the group had fallen back into their rituals—drinks, deep sighs, wild stories, and the occasional group text that said, simply: "Meet at Velour. We need to cuss."

It was Thursday night now. Low crowd, low lighting, high potential for chaos.

Jean leaned on the bar, glass in hand, looking fully moisturized—without us saying it—and deceptively peaceful.

Danielle raised her glass. "To new chapters and no returns."

Kiki clinked. "To hot people with good hygiene."

"Relevant," Jean muttered.

CC turned dramatically. "You have a story. I feel it in my taint."

Ramon covered his face. "God help us."

Jean exhaled. "Okay. Y'all wanna hear about the worst date I've had since I accidentally matched with my cousin's ex-husband?"

"Yes," Danielle whispered, already smiling.

"So… my aunt decided to hook me up. Said he was respectful, educated, had a great job. I check his Instagram—cool enough. Real teeth. Good skin. I figured, fuck it. I'll try"

CC leaned in. "That's always the beginning of the end."

Jean nodded. "First five minutes? All good. He opened the door, paid for parking, complimented my outfit without sounding like he wanted to wear it."

Ramon: "Sounds decent."

Jean held up a finger. "Until he opened his mouth."

A pause. "No, like—really opened his mouth. His breath? Baby, it was biblical. Like the third plague of Egypt—but hotter."

The table howled.

"Y'all, I have never smelled anything like it. It was like if regret had a mouth. Like burnt rubber mixed with betrayal. I swear one nostril went completely numb."

Danielle coughed. "Did you say anything?"

"At first I thought maybe it was a fluke," Jean said. "Like maybe he had a bad shrimp or smoked something ancient. So I did the polite lean-back."

CC whispered, "The social matrix backslide."

Jean continued. "I considered digging in my bag for some Bath & Body Works room spray. I really did. But I knew if I sprayed that shit in public, I'd catch an assault charge."

Kiki wheezed. "What did you do?"

Jean said, "I reached in my bag and faked a sinus problem. Found one of those car vent air fresheners I'd forgotten to throw out. Rubbed it between my fingers like it was Vicks and held them near my nose."

Danielle replied, "You're lying."

Jean said, "Girl, I was fighting for my life." The laughter was uncontrollable.

"Then he leans in for a kiss," Jean said. Everyone went still.

"I didn't mean to—but my reflexes kicked in and I flinched like he was throwing a punch. I even balled my fist like I was about to swing."

Ramon: "You almost clocked him?"

Jean nodded. "He looked shocked. I looked traumatized."

"What did he say?" Asha asked.

"He backed up and said, 'Damn, you didn't seem this prudish over text.' And I said, 'Sir, your breath smells like you flossed with Satan's pubes. I have toilet paper in my purse—you want some to wipe your teeth'?"

Danielle spit her drink.

"I told him, 'Nothing coming out of your mouth should smell that ungodly unless your soul is leaving your body'."

The table was howling.

"I left before the entrees arrived," Jean finished. "Texted my aunt that I'd never forgive her and ordered Jamaican takeout to disinfect my spirit."

Kiki wiped a tear. "God, I love it here."

Asha pointed. "So wait—are you off dating for now?"

Jean shrugged. "Actually… no."

Danielle raised an eyebrow.

"There's this guy I see at the gym," Jean said, sipping. "I don't work out. I go in, get a protein shake, and pretend I'm scouting machines."

"Accurate," CC muttered.

"Anyway " Jean continued, "I kept noticing him. Clean cut, chill energy, gave me the gym nod like he knew I wasn't doing shit but respected my outfit. And last week? He walked over and spoke."

Danielle grinned. "Oh "

"Simple convo," Jean said. "Cool voice. No weird jokes. Didn't ask if I squat. Didn't try to train me."

"Yet," CC whispered.

Jean smirked. "We exchanged info. Texted a bit. He hasn't said anything dumb yet."

"Name?" Ramon asked.

Jean sipped. "Derrick. But we're calling him 'Gym Smoothie' until further notice."

"Better than Green Smoothie," Danielle said, and they all nodded.

"Do we like him?" Asha asked.

"I don't know yet," Jean admitted. "But so far, I don't hate him. And he smells like cedar and ambition."

"Amen," CC whispered.

Then Danielle tapped her phone and smiled.

"Ohhhh," CC said. "That's a face."

Danielle held up a message thread. "So… remember that woman I matched with months ago but never met? Things got busy, we both fell off. She reached out again. Been texting. Real conversation. No random selfies or poems. Just vibes."

Jean raised her glass. "We love a second shot."

"Too early to tell," Danielle said. "But I could really see it. She's got these lips…"

CC interrupted: "Oh here we go."

Danielle grinned. "The kind of lips that could really go to town on my clit. Like Cinnamon Toast Crunch is angry and needs some milk."

The whole table screamed. CC nearly fell off his seat. "Bitch, you know you need some dick to get some milk, right?"

Danielle shot back: "That's why you're dry now. No dairy in hell, ho."

Ramon had to walk away. Even Jean clapped. Then CC, trying to recover, casually said, "Anyway. I might have something new too."

Silence.

Danielle leaned forward. "What you mean?"

CC sipped slowly. "I'm just saying… there's a certain someone who been texting me with grown energy and better grammar than I'm used to."

Kiki smirked. "Who is he?"

"I didn't say it was a he " CC replied.

Asha blinked. "Is it not?"

CC's smile was slow, soft, and telling. "I didn't say that either."

Jean narrowed her eyes. "You like this one?"

CC shrugged. "I'm… curious."

Danielle raised her glass. "To curiosity."

CC clinked. "And controlled chaos."

As the table burst into laughter again, Jean's phone buzzed. She glanced at it, then pocketed it fast.

"Gym Smoothie?" Danielle teased.

Jean didn't answer. She just smiled. And for the first time in a while? It didn't feel sarcastic. It felt like a maybe. And maybe… was finally enough.

The drinks had just hit the table when CC stiffened. "I smell narcissism," he whispered. "And sandalwood."

Jean followed his eyes and hissed, "Oh no. Not this bitch."

Kiki squinted. "Is that—?"

"Yep," Asha said flatly. "She's back."

Selena. Looking flawless, of course. Hair slicked into a high bun, matte lip, and a camel trench coat draped over her shoulders like she was auditioning for Lesbian Scandal. And as if her entrance wasn't dramatic enough, she brought two friends—both instantly hateable.

One was chewing gum like she was trying to kill it. The other was glued to her phone, taking selfies at odd angles like it was a sponsored event.

"Not her bringing backup dancers," Danielle muttered.

Asha folded her arms. "They look like they met in a pyramid scheme."

"She's walking over," CC announced, sliding his glass away like he was about to throw it.

Selena approached the table slowly, eyes locked on Danielle.

"Hey," she said softly, ignoring the daggers being thrown from every other direction.

Danielle blinked, surprised but calm. "Hey."

"Can I talk to you for a second?" Selena asked. "Outside?"

Kiki said nothing but uncrossed her legs like she was ready.

Danielle held up a hand and nodded. "It's fine. I've got it."

The table tensed, but no one moved.

Danielle followed Selena toward the front of Velour, her boots clicking steady across the tile. As they stepped out into the night air, the door thudded shut behind them.

Selena turned, hands in her coat pockets, eyes soft.

"I just… wanted to say I'm sorry," she said. "I shouldn't have said what I did, and I definitely shouldn't have shown up the way I did."

Danielle stood still. "Okay "

Selena's voice cracked slightly. "I was hurt. Not just by you, but by myself. You didn't deserve that."

Danielle nodded once. "No hard feelings."

Selena looked surprised. "Really?"

"I don't hold grudges," Danielle said. "But I don't hold space either."

Selena laughed lightly, nervously. "Damn. That's poetic."

Danielle just stared.

After a beat, Selena stepped closer. "Can I…?"

Danielle stepped back—just half a foot. "Let's not."

Selena nodded. "Okay."

Danielle turned to walk back inside. And that's when it happened.

A sudden pull. Fingertips curling around her wrist. The next second, Selena's mouth was on hers—soft, hot, devastating. It wasn't just a kiss—it was a claim. Like she was trying to remind

Danielle of something she'd forgotten, or worse—feel something she swore she was done with.

Danielle inhaled sharply against it. But her body didn't move.

Just for a second, she remembered when Selena said, "I don't want to own you. I want to recognize you. Fully. In every room, every dark, every day."

And for a second, Danielle had believed her. Until she didn't.

Selena's hands moved slowly, deliberately—almost up the hem of Danielle's skirt.

Danielle broke the kiss like she'd come up for air after drowning. She grabbed Selena's wrist—not hard, but enough.

"See?" she whispered. "That's exactly why I can't do this."

Selena's lips parted to speak, but Danielle shook her head.

"Goodbye," she said. Then turned and walked—fast—back inside. When she stepped through the door, the crew was already standing like they were about to stage an intervention.

Jean narrowed her eyes. "She kiss you?"

Danielle blinked, still breathless. "She kissed me like she owned my mouth. Touched me like she forgot we were outside."

CC stepped back, fanned his face, and said, "Bitch, did you start scissoring on the sidewalk? I saw her hand—don't play."

Danielle sat down, smoothed her skirt, and downed half her drink.

Kiki leaned in. "You good?"

"I'm fine," Danielle said, cheeks flushed. "It was just a kiss."

CC sipped. "Kisses don't make you tremble like you just saw Jesus."

Asha, ever the sniper, asked: "Was it good?"

Danielle paused. "It was ruin-your-day good."

Jean grimaced. "Damn. Those are the worst kind."

"They linger," CC added. "Like trauma with tongue."

Ramon blinked. "Y'all got bars tonight."

They all laughed. The tension finally broke. Jean tilted her head. "She brought two friends. Who the hell were they?"

"Does it matter?" Danielle asked. "They were giving MLM conference energy."

"I kept waiting for them to offer us skincare or ask if we were open to new opportunities," Kiki added.

CC leaned in, serious now. "But for real… that kiss shook you."

Danielle didn't answer at first. Just looked down at her hand—like it had betrayed her. "I'm not going back," she said. "Just needed the reminder."

Jean nodded. "We all fall for that one person who kisses like clarity and fucks like confusion." The table hummed with agreement.

Danielle smiled again—smaller this time. "You ever wonder if some people come back just to make sure they still have a hold on you?"

"Every damn day," CC whispered.

Danielle straightened up. "Well, that leash just got cut."

"Period," Asha said, raising her glass. The toast was quiet but heavy.

Then Jean broke it. "Alright. Somebody tell a dumb sex story or flash a nipple. We're too emotional again."

CC reached for his shirt button. "Say less." And just like that, the world tilted back into place. Almost.

Across the bar, near the back where the lights were lowest, Selena stood with her two silent friends. She wasn't talking. Wasn't smiling. Just watching. Locked in. Eyes on Danielle like she was studying something she still wanted to own.

The table was still buzzing from the aftershock of Selena's kiss. Danielle stirred her drink like she was mixing up her self-control. Jean checked her phone. Asha just muttered, "That bitch really brought friends."

And CC? He cleared his throat, stood up dramatically, and said, "If y'all see me smiling next week, it's because I got my back blown out by a man who doesn't abbreviate his texts and eats butt with intention."

Everyone burst out laughing.

Jean fanned her face. "As long as he doesn't abbreviate his shower."

Danielle smirked. "Or the aftercare."

"Okay, yes," CC said, pointing. "Let the church say rinse and repeat."

Kiki held up her glass. "To all the men who wash between the cheeks."

Ramon added, "And the women who make 'em."

The toast clinked. Spirits rising.

Danielle leaned back. "Okay… I need to confess something."

CC leaned forward. "Yes, tell us about the titty pic she sent you that made you lose your religion."

Danielle laughed. "Not that. But close."

The group waited.

"I like her," she said, simple and steady. "The new one. The one I just reconnected with. She's not flashy. She's not trying too hard. She just… feels easy. Comfortable."

Jean nodded. "That's dangerous."

"Exactly," Danielle said. "It makes me want to run. Which is how I know I need to stop."

Kiki said, "Growth looks good on you."

"I'm trying," Danielle said. "But if this woman holds my hand too long or texts back too fast, I'm gonna block her just out of trauma."

CC patted her shoulder. "We'll be here to delete the draft if you do."

Asha sipped. "Or send a titty in apology."

"Speaking of drafts " Jean said, pulling out her phone. "I think it's time."

Danielle raised an eyebrow. "For what?"

Jean scrolled. "I've been texting Gym Smoothie."

The table snapped to attention. CC shrieked, "You didn't tell us that!"

Jean smirked. "I needed to see if he was real before I let y'all get involved."

Asha clapped. "So is he?"

Jean nodded. "He's chill. Smart. Hot enough to make me regret every ex. And he asked if I wanted to meet up after this."

"Oooooh," the whole crew said in unison.

"I told him I might be free," Jean said. "But I wasn't sure."

Danielle tilted her head. "Are you sure now?"

Jean looked around the table. At her friends. Her peace. Her earned joy. She tapped out a message under the table. Then she looked up and said, "I'm sure."

Right then, the front door opened—and in walked Jamal, holding hands with Jasmine.

The group had seen her at karaoke night, sure—but tonight? She looked like she just got promoted to Executive Director of Fine. Sleek black pantsuit, red lips, natural curls framing her cheekbones like art. She walked like her credit score had a personal assistant.

CC whispered, "Okay, Michelle Obama—but make it 'don't text my man after 8pm'."

Jamal beamed. "What's up, fam?"

Jean said, "Y'all are officially the most confusing couple I know."

Danielle gave him a slow clap.

Kiki whispered to Ramon, "She's still out of his league."

Ramon replied, "And he still knows."

Jamal pulled out a chair for Jasmine, who sat like she ran the spot.

CC blinked. "Okay. Explain."

Jamal grinned. "She got me doing yoga, therapy, and skincare. I own a silk pillowcase now."

Danielle raised an eyebrow. "Who are you?"

"Someone who uses coasters without being asked," Jasmine said, sipping her drink.

Jean whispered, "A respectful hostage."

Jamal laughed. "Listen, I'm just trying to keep up. She got her own everything. I've never dated someone who didn't ask me if I had roommates."

Kiki smiled. "We love a grown woman."

CC leaned in. "Does she suck dick with her soul or just her throat?"

Jamal turned red. "I'm not answering that."

Jasmine didn't flinch. "I do it with intention. Like it's my purpose."

CC blinked. "Well damn. I just fell in love too."

Jamal buried his face in his hands. The group erupted. Then things settled again. Jean's phone buzzed. She looked, read it, and smiled.

Danielle raised an eyebrow. "What he say?"

Jean held up her screen:

Gym Smoothie: Be ready in 30. No gym. Just cardio.

The table screamed. CC knocked over a chair. Kiki jumped up. Jean stood like a queen.

"I'm going home," she said. "I have a dick appointment with a man who uses full sentences."

"Do you need us to walk you out?" Danielle asked.

"I got this," Jean said. "But if I don't text by midnight, assume I died happily and scatter my ashes at Sephora."

Jamal stood and bowed. "We salute you."

Jean kissed two cheeks and grabbed her purse Then paused.

"Oh, and I've already decided—if it's over seven inches and hard on its own before I do anything, I'm letting him hit raw dog."

CC screamed. Jasmine spit her drink. Jean kept going. "I don't care. Green Smoothie never technically made it inside, and I have one raw dog per 'I like you, really like you, and your dick is hard' quota."

Danielle nearly fell out of her chair.

Jean shrugged. "Y'all know I'm a woman of principle." Then she was gone.

The group sat in silence for a second. Then Danielle said, "So… CC. You meeting your mystery man tomorrow?"

CC smirked. "Yup. Dinner and drinks. If he brings flowers, I'm letting him spit in my mouth."

Jasmine blinked. "Damn."

Danielle nodded. "That's fair."

Asha held up her glass. "To new chapters."

"To intentional orgasms," CC added.

Danielle raised hers too. "To only responding to emails that don't send us backward."

They clinked again.

Jamal whispered, "Y'all are wild."

Kiki looked at Jasmine. "Girl, welcome to the group."

Jasmine smiled. "I'm already terrified." And just like that, they all laughed again.

Wild. Happy. And for once, ready for whatever came next.

Chapter 14: Cardio, Confusion, and a Cold Splash of Clarity

Two days after her cardio-based resurrection, Jean slid into the booth at Silk & Sand like a woman who'd earned every muscle ache and memory.

This wasn't Velour Social. It was giving resort lobby meets influencer brunch. The music leaned Taylor Swift. The lights were soft gold. The cocktail list had items like "Soft Launch Sangria" and "Post-Orgasmic Paloma." But the drinks hit, and the crew? They made any place theirs.

Asha looked around, whispering, "If anyone from Velour sees me in here, I was never here."

Jean raised an eyebrow. "You cheating on your bar job?"

"I'm scoping the competition," Asha said. "If I ever need to jump ship, I wanna know what I'm walking into." Everyone froze.

CC narrowed his eyes. "You ever say that out loud again, you're dead to us."

Danielle nodded. "You'll be banned from group chats and every future happy hour."

Ramon added, "We'll treat you like someone who orders bottom-shelf tequila on purpose."

Asha held up her drink. "Y'all loyal to Velour like it paid your student loans."

Kiki lifted hers. "Because it's homebase. And you don't disrespect homebase."

Jean smirked. "But this booth is cute."

"Okay, slut," CC said. "You're glowing. Spill the tea. Start with the cardio."

Danielle laughed. "Yeah, you came in here like you just got stretched out and baptized."

Jean leaned back, legs crossed, posture perfect. "Y'all ready?"

"Don't play," Kiki said. "We canceled plans for this."

Jean took a sip of her drink. "His name is Elliot."

Everyone blinked.

"Wait," Danielle said. "Gym Smoothie has a name?"

"Elliot?" Ramon repeated. "With a full spelling?"

Jean nodded. "One T. Like he was born with nuance."

CC gasped. "So it took two orgasms and a protein shake for him to earn a name?"

"We don't normally allow that without a formal Email Reconciliation," Danielle added.

CC raised a finger. "May I remind the circle: We do not speak the names of the dead and the damned unless it's a sanctioned ceremony—or your name is what we say it is."

Jean shrugged. "Well, the dick was divine. So he earned it."

Danielle crossed her arms. "Okay. Give us the scene."

Jean leaned in. "I get to his place. Shirtless. Slight sheen. Smelled like body wash and unspoken promises. I'm already halfway wet from the scent alone."

Kiki whispered, "Amen."

"He makes me a bourbon ginger with a fancy-ass cube. I'm suspicious, but impressed. We sit. We talk. Not fake deep. Real. Adult. And then he says, 'You nervous? Want me to help you relax'?"

CC clasped his chest. "Bitch, what'd you say?"

Jean smirked. "'I thought that's what the bourbon was for'."

Ramon clapped once. "Strong opener."

Jean continued. "We kiss. He's soft but assertive. His tongue moved like it read instructions first."

CC gasped. "A man who reads?!"

Jean kept going. "He took off my clothes like they were rental couture. Careful, steady, but with intention. When he got between my legs? I made a sound I didn't know I could make."

Danielle leaned in. "What kind of sound?"

Jean said, "It was like a whisper moan. A spiritual exhale. I felt like he was speaking to my grandmother in tongues."

Kiki threw a napkin.

Jean nodded. "He licked like he was meeting my ancestors. I came twice before his dick even made a guest appearance."

"And the dick?" CC prompted.

She grinned. "Thick. Curved. Strong. Came with rhythm and restraint. He put in work. Hit every wall with purpose. I forgot my name and remembered my middle one."

Danielle fanned herself. "Stop. I'm sore from listening."

Jean paused. "And then… midstroke… this man leans in and says —"

Everyone froze.

"'I know this is the best dick that you've ever had in that delicious wet pussy of yours'."

The table groaned Kiki buried her face. "Why do they always ruin it with some extra shit?"

Danielle shook her head. "Delicious wet pussy? That's not sexy. That's a food review."

Jean held up a hand. "I paused. In my spirit. Because it was good. But now you want credit before the semester ends?"

Ramon said, "Give the grade when the work is done."

Jean nodded. "I still let him finish. But the sentence lingered."

Danielle leaned in. "Okay, so be real—was it the best?"

Jean tilted her head. "Look. I don't normally resurrect the dead, but I could name at least five better."

CC gasped. "I want names."

"Fake ones " Jean clarified. "But memorable."

She held up fingers. "Patchy Beard. Small Arm. Soldier Boy. Fifth Quarter. And Parole Bae."

Ramon blinked. "These sound like failed SoundCloud rappers."

Jean laughed. "Patchy Beard had inconsistent facial hair but full-body consistency. Small Arm had one short arm but exceptional grip. Soldier Boy gave tactical strokes. Fifth Quarter used to play college ball—I still flinch when I hear whistles. Parole Bae? Fresh out. Fucked like he needed to reclaim his time."

Danielle wiped tears. "You need a museum exhibit."

Jean grinned. "Moral of the story? You gotta hit this pussy like it's the cannibal's last meal and Survivor just merged the tribes."

"YES!" Danielle yelled. "Naked and Afraid: Survivor Edition!"

And with that, CC raised his glass. "To the throat goats."

They all clinked glasses and shouted in sync: "Baaaaaaaaaaa!"
Even the bartender looked over.

Jean finished her drink and smiled. "Elliot thought he was getting
off easy. But before he left, I sucked his soul out of him. Now that
big dick is just out here wandering the streets—empty."

Danielle clutched her nonexistent pearls. "That's haunting."

Kiki whispered, "I'm ovulating now."

Asha shook her head. "I need to reschedule my whole rotation."

CC leaned in. "You seeing him again?"

Jean shrugged. "If he texts. I'm not chasing. I got what I needed.
Closure in multiple positions."

Ramon lifted his glass. "To cardio."

Danielle added, "To coming first—and last."

Asha said, "To not needing to explain why you left your wig on
the floor."

Kiki said, "To real grown woman behavior."

The group toasted again. Glasses clinked. Goat sounds faded.

And then CC's phone lit up. He smiled. Just slightly. Danielle saw
it. Jean did too.

No questions. No pressure. Just the kind of quiet grin that meant:
This one might be different. The kind of moment that earns its own
chapter.

As the laughter finally faded from Jean's post-orgasmic
monologue, Danielle took a long sip of her drink and tried not to

let her face betray the tiny, almost dangerous thing growing in her chest: Hope.

Jean smoothed her hair like a woman who had both made peace with and taken dominion over her edges. She looked satisfied, smug, and completely unbothered by the chaos she'd just triggered.

"And just like that," CC said, dramatically fanning himself, "Gym Smoothie has a name."

Asha leaned toward Danielle and whispered, "Elliot again? Damn. James E. running out of names or what?"

Danielle snorted into her glass. "You're a mess."

Asha sat back like nothing happened. "Anyway."

Jean pulled out her phone and sighed. "I'm still not texting him first. He knows what this is."

Danielle raised an eyebrow. "Are you sure he does?"

CC clutched his nonexistent pearls. "Are you accusing her of leading with mystery and vagueness like the rest of us don't?"

Jean cut her eyes. "Don't project, bitch."

Ramon tapped his glass. "Okay, since Jean broke the ceiling with that cardio confessional, I feel like it's only right we move on. Danielle? You've been too quiet lately."

The table turned. Danielle smirked. "Well, things are… moving. Surprisingly well, actually."

Jean tilted her head. "So what's the verdict?"

Danielle shrugged, but the smile she tried to hide gave her away. "Let's just say she got lips like she's been training for the Clit Olympics. I don't know if I wanna date her or franchise her."

CC wheezed. "You trying to put her on payroll?"

"Honestly?" Danielle said. "I'm okay waking up broke if she's there. The conversation, the vibe—real smooth. No pressure. No awkward tension. It's just… easy. Which is terrifying."

"Why terrifying?" Kiki asked.

"Because I'm used to needing a therapist and a lockpick to figure out if someone's worth texting back," Danielle said. "Now I'm like, wait—is this peace? Or prelude to heartbreak?"

Asha nodded. "You describing emotional sobriety."

"Maybe," Danielle said. "I'm suspicious of how good it feels."

Jean looked over. "So are we talking potential relationship here, or just someone who knows how to season tofu and read body language?"

"I don't know yet," Danielle admitted. "But I haven't been this tempted to overshare in a long time. And that alone is dangerous."

"Damn," CC said. "We need to keep this one in the vault."

"She's saved in my phone as 'Corporate Conference'," Danielle added. "I still don't know her real name."

Ramon blinked. "That's either romantic or reckless."

"Can't it be both?" Danielle said.

Jean raised her glass. "To both." They all clinked glasses.

"Okay," Kiki said. "But CC—you been suspiciously happy over there. What's your update?"

CC looked like someone just asked him to perform at a church he left on bad terms. He blinked slowly. "Okay… okay. Fine. There's someone."

Danielle gasped. "Spill."

"His name is Pastor Stroke."

Asha choked. "Pastor Stroke?!"

"I didn't name him that to his face," CC said. "But it fits. We met at a gospel hip-hop brunch. Don't judge me—I was lured in by free mimosas and a cousin with questionable taste in men and music."

Ramon laughed. "What kind of brunch plays gospel and trap?"

"Exactly," CC said. "But there he was. DJing. Dressed like an usher from a church that just found out about Spotify. He smelled like sage and unspoken accountability."

Jean whispered, "Lord."

"We didn't even kiss," CC said. "But the way he looked at me? Like he knew what I was thinking before I did. It was annoying. And hot. And unsettling."

"So what's the vibe now?" Kiki asked.

"He texted me later that night," CC said. "Said: 'I hope this doesn't offend you, but I felt a calm in your presence today'."

Danielle put her hand over her heart. "Okay, that's a soft launch into emotional intimacy."

"He's been consistent," CC said. "No weird texts. No overcompensating. Just… solid. And I don't trust it."

Jean squinted. "You like him."

CC nodded once. "I don't wanna. But yeah."

"Damn," Asha said. "That's big."

"He got that energy that make you delete hoes without feelin' like you lost anything," CC added.

"Whew," Jean exhaled. "That's not even dick. That's divine intervention."

"I'm not calling it anything yet," CC said. "But when he texts me just to make sure I ate lunch, I reconsider all my trauma."

"You know what this sounds like?" Ramon said. "Actual emotional availability."

CC blinked. "Is that what that is?"

"Mm-hmm," Kiki said. "You allergic to it, but you'll be okay."

A beat passed. Asha raised her glass. "To no longer dating out of boredom or codependency."

Jean clinked hers. "To people who don't treat peace like punishment."

Ramon said, "To deleting numbers and not even feeling it."

Danielle added, "To whatever this healthy shit is… we're trying it anyway."

They clinked glasses again. No goat sounds this time—just honest ones.

"Okay, now hold on," Kiki said. "Can we pause for a second and acknowledge something?" They all turned to her.

"Look at us," she said. "Getting real stories about real people. Not just being the comedic relief because of our fuckups."

Danielle laughed. "Damn. Dare I say… we're growing up?"

Jean placed a dramatic hand over her chest. "Is this our First Wives Club moment?"

"Right," Danielle said. "Like… are we evolving from Love & Hip Hop: Atlanta and Miami to actual grown-ass women with a plan?"

Asha said, "Bitch, I can't choose. So we blended both."

Danielle nodded. "Exactly. We're out here raising the bar—but still ready to throw a drink if needed."

"Speaking of grown," CC said, leaning back, "Can we talk about how the fuck Trick Daddy is now the voice of wisdom?"

"THANK you," Danielle said. "Like—how the fuck is Trick Daddy… Florida Evans if she was a man and a hitmaker in the '90s… suddenly the elder trying to guide this generation through its dating chaos?"

Jean choked on her drink.

"Like, seriously," Danielle continued. "He out here offering insights like he's the Yoda of Miami. When this is the same man who, in Naan N**a*, said—and I quote—'You don't know naan who do more freaky stuff… eat coochie with legs up… then I blow all in your butt'."

Kiki covered her mouth. "Oh my God."

"Now that's the voice of reason?" Danielle said. "Trick Daddy? Bad teeth, worse skin, and an internal monologue that's clearly still in 2001?"

Asha wiped tears. "Florida Evans if she was a man has me crying."

Ramon added, "That quote made my soul leave the chat."

Jean shook her head. "It's like the world flipped and now we're all looking for guidance from people who once gave us STDs and bad mixtapes."

Danielle leaned back. "Anyway, I'm done. That's all I got."

They all paused again. And just for a second, the whole table sat in it—growth, chaos, and all. But not for long. A phone buzzed. Then another. The group looked around.

Jean raised an eyebrow. "Alright. Who opened the gates of hell?"

And just like that… the storm was coming. It started with a buzz. Then another. Phones lit up around the table like someone had pulled the emergency lever on everyone's past.

CC looked down first. "Who the fuck…"

He opened his phone, squinted, and burst out laughing. "Oh, now this is rich. Bitch-boy Bible verse just sent me a selfie like we didn't end with him saying I was a walking temptation sent by Satan."

Jean leaned in. "Is that the one who said your moans disturbed his spirit?"

"The very one," CC said, still scrolling. "Caption just says: 'Thinking about you lately. Hope you're well.' Like hellfire don't have Wi-Fi."

Danielle's phone buzzed next. She saw the contact preview and went cold. Selena. She didn't open the message. She didn't need to. The name alone was its own kind of nausea. Eight days of silence, one explosion, and now… this?

Jean glanced over. "You good?"

Danielle gave the smallest nod, then flipped her phone upside down. "Next."

Asha laughed without mirth. "Is it a full moon? Or did someone leak our blocked lists to the public?"

Ramon raised a hand. "It's like emotional spam season. You get a message, you get a message…"

Kiki's phone stayed silent. She grinned and held it up. "Married privilege, bitches."

"Must be nice," Jean muttered, swiping hers open. A message from Itchy Dick Energy.

She hadn't saved his number under that name, but the group had. The man had come to Velour once in a grey suit that screamed credit repair scam and a dick that had left Jean with a yeast infection so memorable it almost got its own holiday.

The message just read: "You still think about me?"

Jean rolled her eyes. "Only when my pH is off, sir."

CC snorted. "Not sir…"

Kiki folded her arms. "I don't know what's worse—the message or the fact that they think it's gonna work."

Asha added, "That's the real red flag. The audacity."

Danielle finally spoke. "It's not just audacity—it's math. They circle back hoping the odds are different. Hoping the damage they did has faded enough for us to forget it even hurt."

Jean exhaled. "Alright. Since we're clearly under cosmic attack, can we do a little circle-back story time?" They nodded.

"Let's get it out of our systems," she said. "Who spun the block on you recently?"

CC started. "So… y'all remember Jerome from my thicc boy summer phase?" They nodded.

"Well. This man once told me—TO MY FACE—that being with me was like being trapped in a beautiful but sinful temptation. Like I was the devil's reward for men who strayed too far from the light."

Danielle blinked. "Is this Lucifer fan fiction or real life?"

"Real life, bitch," CC said. "Last week, he hits me with: 'I miss our connection. You brought light into my life'."

Ramon gasped. "Not the same bitch who said you were darkness?"

CC held up his phone. "I said, 'Yeah, hellfire got energy too. Burn in it'."

Jean took a sip.

"I had a man once fly me out to Miami for a long weekend, then ghost me the moment we landed back in JFK. Like, I swear to God, he vanished like TSA pulled his soul." They groaned.

"This man DMs me last night talking about, 'Made a playlist that reminded me of you'."

"What was on it?" Asha asked.

"Probably Beyoncé's Irreplaceable and Future's Mask Off," Jean said. "I didn't even open the link. I replied: 'Did you also pack your balls this time or just the same excuses'?"

Danielle went next. "This girl I dated during peak pandemic who told me I was too emotionally unavailable to date seriously… she disappeared, resurfaced, blocked me again, then slid in my DMs this morning."

"Oh lord," CC groaned.

"She sent a picture. No caption. Just her, nude, bent over in a very… specific way."

"Ass to camera?" Asha guessed.

"Direct shot," Danielle said. "I replied: 'Still cold to the touch?' and she wrote back: 'Only when you're not in it'."

Kiki wheezed. "Bitch, what does that even mean?"

Jean whispered, "It means she's still delusional."

They all sat back for a second, the air suddenly heavier than before.

"Funny how they all reappear like we're waiting," Jean said. "Like we're just sitting here hoping they return better."

Kiki nodded. "They don't want you healed. They want access to the part of you that tolerated them."

Danielle's voice was quiet. "That's why we email. So we can delete them and say…"

In unison: "No. Not that email."

Jean pulled out her phone and stared at an old thread. No message had come in this time—but she'd kept the email. A relic of a man who almost had her convinced she was hard to love.

She opened the message. Read the first line. Then hit backspace. And back again. Until all the letters disappeared. She didn't send a thing.

She just whispered, "I'm not entertaining the past. I want something that sees me now—not who I was when I was lonely."

CC raised his glass. "To present tense dick. And future tense commitment."

Jean smirked. "To people who can eat, stroke, and shut the fuck up about it after."

They laughed—but it wasn't loud. It was low. Real. The kind of laugh that says you've seen some shit and survived it. The kind of laugh you earn.

A few minutes passed in calm. But calm never lasts. Jean's phone buzzed again—this time, the name made her eyebrows lift. She didn't say a word. Just stared.

Danielle caught the look. "What?"

Jean locked her screen. "Nothing," she said.

But her hand was trembling under the table. And the storm? It was officially back in session.

Chapter 15: The Person, The Pattern, or the Possession

Every time they walked into CC's place, it felt like he'd robbed a boutique hotel and staged it like a runway shoot for Architectural Digest. Tonight was no different.

The entryway had been transformed into an homage to high-glam safari meets queer fantasy: palm-leaf wallpaper, zebra-striped stairs, and gold-accented furniture that somehow didn't look tacky in the slightest. The crown jewel was the rooftop. Private, breezy, with sweeping views of the city—and a lit bar cart stationed next to a glowing neon sign that read: Stay Petty. Stay Paid. Stay Home.

"You got a jungle in your hallway now?" Asha asked, spinning slowly. "I swear you had velvet wallpaper last time."

"Seasonal aesthetic," CC said, shrugging as he floated by in a lime green satin robe and metallic sandals. "I reinvent. You bitches just get dressed."

Jean walked in with Danielle behind her and tilted her head at a new painting on the wall. "Is that… you? Naked? On a horse?"

"Yes, bitch. And the horse was into it."

They gathered on the rooftop, drinks in hand, night air brushing over their bare arms like a promise of something about to unfold.

It was just the core crew tonight. No Jamal. No Ramon or Kiki. Just the ones who'd been through too many nights together to pretend their lives weren't shifting.

Jean was already seated—legs crossed, one heel dangling, glow steady. Her drink matched her mood: classy but low-key pissed off.

"You good?" Asha asked.

Jean nodded. "Just thinking."

"About Elliot?"

Jean took a long sip. "He wanted to see me tonight."

Danielle raised an eyebrow. "And you said no?"

"I said I wasn't in the mood to eat clean and correct his overconfidence all night. I already sucked the soul out of him once. I'm not giving it back just because he missed the sound of applause." They cackled.

CC fanned himself with a sequined coaster. "You better ration your miracles, bitch."

Asha said, "He really said he was the best you ever had, didn't he?"

Jean nodded. "That dumbass line almost ruined it. You could've ruined a perfect dick with a sentence."

Danielle raised her glass. "To dick that doesn't need a Yelp review." They clinked glasses.

CC tapped the rim of his. "And may we never again sleep with a man whose confidence is louder than his stroke game." They howled.

But once the noise faded, Jean went quiet again. Asha noticed. "You sure you're good?"

Jean gave a half-smile. "Yeah. Just thinking about how something can feel so good and still so… familiar. Like, not in a bad way. But in a way that makes you nervous."

Danielle nodded. "Familiar isn't always safety. Sometimes it's just a warning in better clothes."

"Exactly," Jean said. "He hasn't done anything wrong. He's just confident. But something about the way he moves, it reminds me of shit I've already survived."

CC tilted his head. "Bitch, you not in love—you in déjà dick." Danielle wheezed.

"Blink twice," CC continued, "and you're back in a pattern with new cologne and a different Spotify playlist." Jean laughed, but there was a truth in her face that didn't leave with the sound.

They drifted into separate pockets of silence. The music was soft. The skyline twinkled. A rare, real peace sat on top of them like a weighted blanket they hadn't realized they needed.

Danielle hadn't spoken much yet. But her mind was too loud to let her enjoy the quiet. She hadn't seen Corporate Conference since the last kiss. But the texts? Every day. Affirming. Kind. Hot.

She hadn't given in yet. Not out of disinterest—but fear. Something she wasn't proud of. Not anymore. Jean looked over. "You okay over there?"

Danielle sipped her drink. "She's been patient."

"Too patient?" Asha asked.

Danielle smiled slightly. "No. Just… not used to it. No pressure. No expectation. Just space."

"And that bothers you?" Jean asked.

Danielle shrugged. "It bothers my trauma."

Everyone paused.

"I've given people less of me, and they've stayed longer. And now here's someone who seems capable, consistent—and all I can think about is what happens if she leaves after I finally let go."

Asha nodded. "So you're protecting yourself."

"I'm delaying a freefall," Danielle said. "But I know it's coming."

"You want to sleep with her?" CC asked.

Danielle didn't hesitate. "Absolutely."

The room held it.

Jean blinked. "So…?"

"I will," Danielle said. "But I'm not gonna tell y'all when. Not this time."

CC sat up. "Wait—what?"

"I mean it," Danielle said. "If it goes wrong, I don't want the usual rituals. I don't want the same comfort cycle. The group therapy. The pep talks. The jokes that hide the pain."

Jean tilted her head. "You don't trust us?"

Danielle shook her head. "I do. But I'm starting to think I trust you more than I trust myself. And that's backwards. If it breaks me, I need to learn how to do the repair. Solo."

Asha sat with that. "Damn."

CC poured more champagne into Danielle's glass.

"To pussy decisions made in silence."

"To growth," Jean added.

Danielle raised her glass. "And to Cinnamon Toast Crunch. Because lord knows, that mouth still haunts me."

They all laughed. But the laughter was quieter now. Like they knew the storm wasn't gone—it was just further out.

The drinks got stronger as the night stretched longer. CC had candles now—lit without a single match, probably by divine gay magic—and they flickered along the glass wall leading to his rooftop. The playlist had slowed into something soft but rich, and for once, nobody was rushing to interrupt it with a twerk song or trap anthem.

It was that rare pause. The kind they didn't name out loud for fear of jinxing it.

Danielle sat with her feet tucked under her, a second drink in her hand, but her mind elsewhere. Corporate Conference hadn't texted in the last two hours. That wasn't unusual. But tonight, Danielle noticed her noticing.

It was subtle, but still. She remembered the last few days.

"You didn't text me back for a bit. Was everything okay?"

"Where are you headed now? I know you had plans earlier…"

"Text me when you get home, please. I just want to know you're good."

None of it had come with venom. None of it screamed possessive. But it wasn't volume that raised alarms in Danielle's mind—it was patterns.

The last time she let herself fall, she ended up justifying red flags until they looked like home decor. This time, she wanted better sight.

And yet… her body still wanted what it wanted. It wasn't scared. But her mind? Her mind had notes. She took another sip. Didn't speak.

"You ever date someone who just… kept tabs like they were the IRS?" CC asked suddenly.

Danielle looked up. Asha grinned. "This about Pastor Stroke or someone else?"

"Someone else," CC said. "Back in my early twenties. This man used to send 'Good morning' texts with GPS coordinates. Like, 'Hope you slept well—also, you still at the gym on 14th'?"

"Wait, what?" Jean blinked.

"I thought it was love," CC said. "I thought he was just invested. Checking in. Being present."

"And he wasn't?" Asha asked.

"No, bitch. He was tracking me like I was a stolen Amazon package. The man once asked why my phone had been on 'Do Not Disturb' for three hours. I said I was watching a movie. He said, 'What movie blocks me from your thoughts'?" Everyone groaned.

"Hell," CC said. "It was hell. He wasn't protecting me. He just liked knowing where I was at all times because it made him feel bigger."

Danielle didn't speak. But she heard it. All of it.

Asha refilled her glass, then sat forward. "I had one like that too. Soft-voice guy. Always wore white. Spoke in affirmations."

Jean smirked. "The spiritual narcissist?"

"The one and only," Asha said. "He used to say, 'I don't ask where you are because I doubt you—I ask because I want to share in your freedom'."

"That sounds like a cult brochure," CC whispered.

"It was," Asha said. "A one-man cult. He wanted me to feel watched, not seen. Every 'checkin' was really a boundary test."

Danielle exhaled. Quietly. Like her body needed to confess but her mouth had no intention of joining the conversation.

The stories continued, one or two more rounds, each with a shared theme: people who used intimacy as a leash, affection as a cage.

Jean finally said, "It's so easy to confuse love with visibility. But being seen isn't always the same as being safe."

Danielle's mind locked onto that one. She hadn't told anyone what Corporate Conference said last night.

"I really like knowing you're mine. Not in a weird way—just in a 'you're my person' kind of way." It hadn't raised an alarm then. But it whispered to her now.

The problem wasn't her. The problem was what her body still held. The trauma hadn't vanished just because things were going well. The body didn't only remember war—it remembered the walls it built to survive it.

And right now, her instincts weren't telling her to run. They were telling her to pay attention. Danielle leaned back and stared at the flickering candles.

The group was still talking. Still sharing stories, jokes, lessons from past entanglements. But she wasn't in the middle of it.

She was beside it. Listening. Processing. Separating what was hers from what wasn't.

Later—after the laughter softened, after CC changed outfits (again), after Jean turned her glass upside down and said she was done drinking for the night—Danielle made her choice.

Not out loud. Not with announcement. Just inside. She was going to sleep with Corporate Conference. Not because she was reckless. But because she was ready. And if the aftermath brought pain? She'd handle it. Alone.

Not out of pride. Not out of shame. But because the comfort rituals —the "girl, he ain't shit" chorus, the popcorn and groupchat hugs, the long convos where everyone passed around blame like snacks —weren't where the real healing happened.

She wanted to heal on purpose this time. Not just with support, but with discipline.

If it broke her? She'd rebuild.

If it elevated her? She'd accept it.

But either way, the moment would belong to her.

Not the group. Not the analysis. Just her.

The night wound down slowly.

Asha yawned. Jean leaned into the back of the couch. CC put his feet up and groaned dramatically, like he'd carried the emotional labor of the entire evening on his fabulous shoulders.

And Danielle? She didn't say much more. But her silence wasn't fear. It was decision.

The candles hadn't gone out. If anything, they burned lower, but brighter—like the room knew it was the kind of night that needed soft edges and steady light.

A few hours had passed since the jokes, since the reflections about possessiveness, déjà dick, and choosing pain on purpose. Now, the drinks were gone, replaced by mismatched mugs of espresso, cappuccinos, and whatever CC called "warm milk with grown-up trauma foam."

Jean sat closest to the windows, one bare leg crossed over the other, her phone facedown on the table. Danielle leaned against the countertop, coffee in hand, quiet but present. Asha lounged with a fuzzy throw blanket over her knees like it was a fireside chat.

CC emerged with a tray stacked with more tiny cups, sugar cubes, and a single almond cookie no one remembered buying. His robe had changed—again. This one was dark plum with embroidery that spelled out "Glory Be, But Don't Test Me."

"Alright, who wants bougie foam or bitter truth?" he asked, setting the tray down.

"I'll take both," Jean said. "But only if the truth comes with oat milk."

It was calm. Grown calm.

Nobody was rushing to rehash a date or break down a breakup. The room wasn't wound tight like it used to be, where every silence meant someone was about to cry or yell.

Tonight, the quiet felt earned. Jean sipped her drink. Her phone buzzed once.

She didn't look at it. She knew it was Elliot. She knew because he was consistent. And part of her loved that. But another part—the part that had ignored red flags in the past, the part that clung to men who smiled while they drained her—was watching.

She didn't open the message. She didn't delete it either. "I'm not spiraling. I'm studying." That's what she told herself. And this time, she meant it.

Danielle hadn't spoken since the coffee came out. She didn't need to. Everyone knew. Not the specifics—but the energy.

There was a calm around her that hadn't been there in a while. Not peace, exactly. More like readiness. She was going to sleep with Corporate Conference. She just hadn't said it. And no one asked. Because she'd already decided.

CC took the last mug and settled next to the espresso machine, watching the steam drift up like thoughts he didn't want to say out loud. Then he did. "She scares me."

Everyone turned. Danielle raised an eyebrow. "You "

He nodded. "Pastor Stroke. That man scares the fuck outta me."

Jean leaned forward, elbows on knees. "Why?"

"Because he sees me," CC said. "Like, actually sees me. Not just the outfits and the quick tongue. The other parts. The stuff I don't bring out for everybody."

"Isn't that what you want?" Asha asked.

"Yes. And no," he said. "I prayed for a man who was soft with me. Who didn't need to be chased or decoded. Who showed up. But now that I got it…"

He trailed off. Jean filled in the blank. "You want to ruin it before it ruins you."

CC nodded once.

Danielle sipped slowly. "So don't."

They didn't pile on him. Didn't joke. Didn't make it a thing. Jean just said, "Sounds like love might like you back this time."

Danielle added: "Let it " CC sat with that.

It was almost midnight. No one was in a rush, but the wind had picked up. The rooftop felt cooler. Softer. Time to start thinking about leaving.

Jean got up first. Stretched. Checked her phone but didn't open the text.

Danielle followed, grabbing her bag and hugging Asha on the way out. No one said too much. Just the usual: "Text me when you're home." "Let me know you made it safe." "Love you."

But this time, it wasn't performative. It was simple. Adult. Quiet love.

CC stayed behind. He cleared the mugs, turned off the neon sign, and walked through his apartment barefoot, letting the silence wrap around him like a robe.

He sat down with his own drink—warm milk and a splash of bourbon, because healing needed help sometimes—and stared at his phone. There was a message from Pastor Stroke. "Can I see you tomorrow? I want to hold you."

He smiled. Typed: "I want that too." Then deleted it.

Typed again: "Maybe." Deleted that too.

He left it on read. Sipped his drink. Watched the candles flicker. And whispered to himself:

"Maybe it's not the person. Maybe it's the pattern. And that's what really needs to go."

Chapter 16: Trauma, Tongue, and Temptation

The first red flag wasn't loud. It was the kind that waved softly, almost beautifully.

Gym Smoothie—Elliot—was confident. Sure of himself in a way that was hot at first, but then started to lean a little sharp. The way he made her feel wanted, the way his hands pulled her hips in like home—it all hit. But there was something he didn't say.

And then something else. And then something else.

It started with the locked Instagram. Not private—locked. No tags. No stories. Only three posts. All of them were generic thirst traps: beach, gym, locker room selfie. Every man was allowed boundaries, of course. But Jean's instincts didn't ignore patterns just because they were packaged in abs and almond-shaped eyes.

Then came the dodged question about family. A short comment about his schedule being "complicated." The way he never once invited her to his place. The silence when she mentioned birthdays or holidays.

"He's hiding something," Jean told herself, fingers already moving.

She'd promised herself she wasn't gonna be "that bitch" again. But when a woman's gut twitches, and her resources are only one click removed from the DMV, what exactly is she supposed to do? Wait for peace to disappoint her later?

She opened her laptop. Jean didn't go straight to his real name. That would be too obvious. She used one of her burner IG accounts—one that had just enough photos to look real. She'd used it before on a cousin's cheating fiancé, and once to catch a man in her own building lying about being divorced.

Her fake profile sent the follow request. Within an hour, she was in. Elliot had another account. A full one. And he didn't hide a damn thing in there.

Graduation pictures. Family cookouts. Him in a suit, looking proud and too fucking happy. Next to a seventeen-year-old boy with caramel skin and Elliot's nose.

Jean zoomed in. Over and over. "No way this is his cousin."

More photos. More tags. The teen was listed in one caption as "My boy. My reason."

And then came the one that silenced the whole room inside her head. A birthday post from six months ago.

The caption: "Another one without her. I hope she's proud of us, J. I miss her every day. We're doing okay. I promise."

The woman in the photo? Stunning. Stunning enough to make Jean's fingers freeze mid-scroll. Asian. Elegant. Radiant in a way that didn't try—it just was.

The kind of beauty Jean rarely compared herself to because she didn't know how to compete. Not like this. She stared. Then slammed her laptop shut.

Elliot texted a few minutes later: You around tomorrow? Would love to see you.

Jean replied: Sure. Let's go somewhere new. I'll meet you there.

They met at a new bistro near his gym. Not the Social. She wasn't gonna let this blow up at home. Jean arrived first. Sat in the corner, facing the door, drink already ordered, posture like she was about to fire someone.

Elliot showed up in black joggers, fresh cut, and a face that looked too at ease for what was coming. "Hey, gorgeous."

She didn't smile. "Sit down."

He tilted his head. "Everything okay?"

Jean blinked slowly. "It's funny. We've slept together, kissed like we meant it, and talked about childhoods. But I've never seen your house. Never met a friend. And I didn't know you had a fucking mixed teenage son."

Elliot froze mid-motion. Didn't sit. Jean pressed on. "You gonna lie or sit down?" He sat.

She leaned in. "It's always the pretty motherfuckers. You get a little body, start going to the gym, and now you're too cute to disclose shit like you got a whole ass family." He didn't interrupt.

"I mean, is that your baby mama? The one you conveniently forgot to mention while you were buried in my pussy talking about how this was the best you ever had? You forget to mention the mixed Tiger Woods tribute act you're raising?" Still—nothing.

Jean scoffed. "You men get a couple compliments and suddenly think you're allowed to treat people like puzzles. Newsflash: I'm not the bitch you breadcrumb." Silence.

Then Elliot blinked once. "You done?"

Jean leaned back. "Go off"

He took a deep breath. And then, "You ever been insulted so thoroughly, so often, that it becomes the only language you believe in?" Jean didn't respond.

"I used to be 85 pounds heavier," he said. "I was the joke. I was the one who got ghosted before the first date even happened. I worked. Every single day. Changed my body. Changed how I moved. But the way you came in here?" He shook his head.

"That's not about me. That's about what you're scared of. And instead of asking a single question, you dug through my life like it was a clearance bin." Jean looked down, then up. But not at him.

"You want to know who the boy is?" he asked. "He's not my son. Not by blood. His mom was my girlfriend. She was abused—by the person before me. And when she died, I did the only thing I could. I raised him. I filed papers. I gave him a home." Jean's face cracked—but didn't break.

"I didn't tell you because I don't owe everyone my story. Especially not someone who might not be around next week. That's not secrecy. That's survival." Then he stood slowly.

And delivered the part that would burn long after he walked away. "Fucking women like you," he said, "do well for themselves, put up such a barrier that you feel like anybody should climb a mountain to fucking talk to you. First—don't flatter yourself."

He looked her dead in the eye. "I can peep you're from around the way just like me. And I don't know how to get where you are in life, but I always believed the way there was through integrity and being exactly who you are—or at least who you can be." Jean swallowed. Hard.

"You believe you're entitled to someone's life story and haven't even earned the right to the opening chapter. You don't take the time to build anything—you just inspect. You probe. And then you try to guess what the truth is because you don't like not knowing."

He pulled a folded hundred-dollar bill from his wallet and set it gently on the table which was at least twice as much as the tab.

"Try being a normal fucking person next time. Ask. You might get an answer. Or you might get a boundary. Either way, at least it'll be honest." Then he looked at her one last time.

"Please don't ever call me again. And if you wouldn't mind discarding my personal details that you conveniently looked up, that would be great too. This round's on me."

And then—he was gone. Didn't look back. Didn't slam the door. Didn't ghost her. Just walked the fuck out.

Jean didn't move for a full five minutes. Her face was still. But her soul? Her soul had just been rearranged.

Danielle didn't pack for a sleepover. She packed like a woman who accessorizes her readiness.

Her Louis Vuitton Neverfull bag was lined with exactly what she needed: small toiletries, two pairs of panties, her softest maxi dress, and a charger with a lightning port—not USB-C, not Android-compatible. A charger that said, I planned for tonight, but I'll never say that out loud.

Corporate Conference had invited her to dinner. Nothing wild. No promises. No guarantees. But Danielle knew what was building between them. It had been humming at the edges for weeks.

They started with wine and tapas at her place. Neat. Minimal. The kitchen was clean and modern, with matte-black finishes and a candle that smelled like something upscale and slightly dangerous. A smoky vanilla maybe. Something leather-adjacent.

They sat on the couch, laughing at a work story Danielle told about a couple who came in for couples counseling but spent the entire session trying to out-therapist one another using phrases they clearly pulled from TikTok.

"She said he was love-bombing her. He said she was emotionally unavailable and stuck in a hyper-independent survival loop."

Corporate laughed. "Not hyper-independent survival loop—that's a fancy way of saying 'I don't need you but I want you to want me anyway'."

"Exactly," Danielle said. "And then he said she had main character syndrome, but with poor supporting cast energy." Corporate nearly spit her wine.

It was easy. Fun. But Danielle didn't wait for the perfect moment.

She cleared her throat. "Look—I like you. And I don't want to mess this up by letting something small grow legs. I don't like being questioned. About my whereabouts, time gaps, whatever. Please don't take that the wrong way—it's not personal. The woman I work for has given me a serious chunk of her practice, and it keeps me busy as hell "

Corporate set her wine glass down gently. "Thank you for saying that. I can respect it. Truly."

She exhaled. "You have to forgive my slight insecurities. They're less about control and more about… safety. Well-being. I'll say what most people don't say out loud—fucking ID and true crime have absolutely ruined my life. I can't go a week without thinking that somebody I care about is gonna get snatched by a crazy person—or worse, is the crazy person."

Danielle nodded slowly. "I get it. I really do. I limit myself to one episode. That's it. One at the most. More than that is just too much darkness to let into your soul. And the wild part? We've normalized it. Not because of the darkness—because we enjoy the crazy."

"Exactly. We pretend we're just being cautious, but really we're just feeding the paranoia." They locked eyes.

Corporate smiled. "Do you want an espresso for the ride home?" Danielle tilted her head. "I didn't know I had a ride home."

Corporate stood up. "Oh." She turned toward the hallway, unbuttoning her shirt as she walked. Danielle didn't move at first. Just watched. Cinnamon Toast Crunch growled. Then she followed.

The bedroom was simple but lush. Dark green walls. Gold-trimmed lamps. The sheets were cream and crisp, and the bed looked like the kind of place where intentions went to live out their purpose.

Danielle barely got her shoes off before Corporate was in her face, kissing her deeply. Her mouth was soft but assertive, and her hands were already on Danielle's waist, pulling her in.

They collapsed onto the bed like they'd done it before in a dream. Corporate moved fast—but not rushed. She knew exactly what she was doing.

Danielle gasped the first time she felt her tongue. It was exact. Precise. Rhythmic. Danielle came fast—too fast—and covered her mouth with the back of her hand. "Oh my God."

Corporate laughed and slid up beside her. "So I see that you like a little fingering with your cunnilingus."

Danielle grinned through her breath. "I mean, you could've at least warned me."

"You looked like the type who doesn't like surprises."

"Apparently I was wrong."

Danielle flipped her over without warning and returned the favor. She kissed every part of her thighs, worked her way up with teasing strokes, then dove in like she was building a case for sainthood.

Corporate moaned loud enough to make the flickering candle on the nightstand tremble. After several minutes, they collapsed next to each other again. Breathing hard. Sweaty. Laughing. It felt good. It felt real.

Then Corporate reached into the drawer. Danielle expected a vibrator. But she came back with a strap-on. Danielle blinked. "Okay."

Corporate smiled. "There's always room for dessert." She guided Danielle to the edge of the bed. Lifted her legs back with confidence. And entered her with a motion so smooth it was almost spiritual.

Danielle gripped the sheets. She wasn't ready. But somehow—she was.

Corporate moved with intention. Controlled. Powerfully slow. Then fast. Then slow again. She didn't just fuck—she read. She listened. And every stroke answered Danielle's need without her ever having to say a word.

Danielle moaned. Loud. Honest. And when she came, she pulled Corporate's body all the way against hers, held her there, and felt the kind of peace that only came after choosing to stay in the moment.

They collapsed. Again. Still breathing hard. Still laughing.

Danielle let her hand rest gently on Corporate's stomach.

She wasn't performing. She wasn't self-censoring. She wasn't even processing. She was just… present. And proud.

Not because she'd finally let someone in. But because she did it with both eyes open and no illusions about the risk. No fantasy. No escape hatch. Just honesty. And a neatly packed overnight bag that said: You don't have to announce your readiness. You just have to be it.

The sun hit differently when your heart was confused. It wasn't just rising—it was judging.

And it had the nerve to be bright as hell, sneaking through the edges of Church Candy's blackout curtains like a nosy aunt with a gossip addiction.

He sat upright in bed. Perfect posture. Legs crossed. A silk robe with tigers on it. One slipper on, one mysteriously missing. He wasn't sure if he slept or just blinked for six hours. But his soul was definitely up.

His bedroom looked like Prince had redecorated during a coke high in Versailles. Velvet headboard, purple candles, gold-framed mirror with a fur stole tossed over the edge like it had just fainted dramatically. And yet, in all that beauty, CC looked like a boy.

A grown-ass boy, but a boy nonetheless. His phone buzzed. It was from him.

Pastor Stroke: "Just thinking about your laugh this morning. Hope you're having a good day, starshine." CC didn't respond.

He wanted to. God, did he want to. But his fingers didn't move. Instead, he got out of bed, robe flowing like a cape, and walked to the kitchen with the silent energy of someone debating if their feelings were just indigestion from a bad charcuterie board.

The espresso machine purred like a satisfied cat. Steam rose. He poured his milk first—because he was raised with class—and stood there, swirling his cup, side-eyeing his own emotions.

He hated this. Not because the man wasn't wonderful. But because he was.

"I like him too much," CC whispered to nobody, like the lead in a daytime soap monologue. "That's the problem. That's the fuckin' problem." He took a sip.

"That man got me sittin' in a $300 robe, lips dry, questioning the meaning of sunlight."

He walked to the window, flung the curtain open like a pastor about to make a point. The city didn't care. It never did.

Last night had been normal. Which made it dangerous.

They watched a dumb movie. Ate Thai food. Talked about their dreams and childhoods. Pastor Stroke told a story about getting in trouble in the sixth grade for drawing a naked body in science class and labeling it with correct anatomical terms.

"And my mama didn't even yell," he'd said. "She just said, 'If you're gonna be nasty, at least be correct'." CC had laughed so hard he almost spilled pad see ew on the throw pillows.

And then, out of nowhere, the man kissed him. Gently. No tongue. No groping. Just… meaning.

It rattled him. They didn't have sex. And somehow that made it worse.

Because CC had never—not once—been left hard and hugged. Not in his adult life. It was intimacy without performance. And it scared the glitter out of him.

The group chat was quiet this morning.

Jean hadn't said a word. Danielle was radio silent. Nobody was planning a brunch or uploading memes about karmic vengeance via yeast infections.

And CC? He was standing in the middle of his luxury condo like the second act of a gay gospel musical called Lord, Is That My Husband or Just Another Lesson?

He walked to the couch. Sat down in his leopard print armchair. Took another sip of coffee. Looked at his phone. Still no reply. He could say something. Good morning. You too, sunshine. You ever seen a grown man cry while moisturized and stunning? Nope.

He couldn't do it. Not because he didn't want to. Because he did. Too much.

He scrolled to their earlier conversations.

"When are you free next?"

"What do you think about going to that art exhibit you mentioned?"

"You looked amazing tonight. But more than that, you felt like peace."

That last one made CC audibly groan. "Ugh. Bitch, what the fuck is this?"

He wasn't built for this much softness. His heart wore heels and talked shit. It didn't know how to do peace.

He tossed his phone onto the couch, missed, and watched it bounce off a cushion and land facedown on the floor like it was emotionally exhausted too.

"Fine," he said. "Don't nobody say nothin', then."

He turned on some quiet music. No lyrics. Just sounds. Jazz or something jazz-adjacent. The candles from last night were still flickering. The scent of vanilla and oud lingered like memories that refused to leave.

And then he sat back. Held the coffee in both hands. Sipped. Didn't post. Didn't text. Didn't call.

It was peaceful. And terrifying. And not a single person knew what the fuck he was going through. Which, for once… was exactly how he wanted it.

Chapter 17: Split Screens & Solo Scenes

It had been two weeks since karaoke night. No one said it out loud, but the group had drifted. Not in a bad way—just in a grown one.

Nobody ghosted. Nobody flaked. The thread was still active every couple of days. But it lacked heat. No rants. No drunk selfies. No emergency brunches scheduled at 1 a. m.

They were in that weird in-between. Still friends. Still tethered. But for the first time, everyone had their own mess, and nobody felt like narrating it in real time.

Kiki was the first to test the thread again: We were funnier when we were toxic.

The message hung there. No likes, no reply bubbles. Just an audience too tired to clap.

Three hours later, CC came in like a drag queen late to brunch— fashionably, but without the sparkle: That wasn't funny. That was a collective psychotic break on a drink minimum.

Danielle responded with a photo. Her hand curled around a whiskey glass, a therapy workbook in the background. No caption. None needed.

Jean followed: I don't do chapters anymore. In books or in life.

Ramon: You do drafts tho.

Asha, always lurking but rarely loud, added: Y'all remember when our biggest stress was whose ex might show up at Velour?

CC: My biggest stress now is deciding if I'm gonna cry or exfoliate.

The crew laughed—quietly, to themselves, in their respective apartments or homes. Not the raucous belly-deep kind of laughter that spilled out during happy hour or after too much mezcal. This was different. Like hearing your own echo and realizing the cave's gotten bigger.

Jean was mid-pour when the thread finally broke her trance. She glanced at the messages and let herself smirk. Just for a second. Then the bourbon hit her lips and washed it away.

She wasn't lonely. Not really. She'd been on a few dates in the last couple of weeks. Nothing dramatic. Nobody awful. Nobody unforgettable, either.

Tonight's contender was handsome, emotionally literate, had great teeth, and knew how to say "let's split the check" without making her want to punch him. She had even let herself enjoy it for a few moments. Until he reached for her hand across the table, and all she could think about was how much energy it would take to fake softness again.

He texted her as she left the car: "Tonight was lovely. Hope to see you again soon."

Jean typed: "Same. Let's do it again." Then deleted it. She tossed her phone on the bed, poured one more drink, and let the silence coat the walls.

Danielle, curled up in bed with one leg sticking out from under a linen throw, stared at her screen. Corporate Conference had just sent a selfie—messy bun, no makeup, sprawled on the couch with a book.

Caption: "Still like me?"

Danielle stared at it a second longer than she expected. Replied: "Especially when I forget to question it."

The rest of the conversation trailed off. Corporate Conference fell asleep mid-text.

Danielle placed the phone screen-down on her nightstand and turned off the light.

No overthinking. No fireworks. Just peace.

She hadn't told the group much about Corporate. Not because she was hiding her—but because, for once, she wasn't performing her healing. There was no arc to pitch, no mess to confess. Just two women sharing time and oxygen.

Across the city, CC was wrapped in his leopard print throw, one hand massaging coconut oil into his cuticles, the other scrolling through his old thread with Pastor Stroke.

The last message still sat there, unread: "I had a good time too. You're dangerous, Candy."

He'd typed a dozen replies. Deleted all of them. They were either too thirsty, too dramatic, or too him.

Finally, he put the thread away and opened the group chat.

CC: Raise your hand if you've rewatched old stroke videos and regretted growing as a person.

Jean: Multiple tabs. One regret.

Danielle: If I had a dick it would've been tired.

Kiki: Get out my search history.

Ramon: Y'all need Jesus.

Asha chimed in next: Mine has him sitting on the edge of the bed, slow stroke, full eye contact, talking real soft about how I always run from good dick. I've never made it to the part where he finishes. That clip is undefeated.

CC: Bitch.

Jean: Send the audio. For research.

Danielle: Why are all of ours emotionally damaging and sexually elite? That's the formula now?

Asha: If it didn't come with post-nut therapy needs, was it even worth it?

CC: Screaming.

Ramon: You're all insane. But I get it.

The thread flared for a moment—sharp, chaotic, oddly soothing. Then, quiet again.

Kiki tilted her phone toward Ramon. "They still funny," she said.

Ramon didn't look up from the TV. "Yeah?"

"But it ain't the same."

"It's been two weeks. Let people breathe."

Kiki leaned against the headboard. "I know. But I don't like it."

"Why?" he asked.

"Because it used to be messy, but it was our messy. Now everybody's out here healing in private, and I feel like I'm watching a bunch of grown-ass folks try to become… adults."

Ramon muted the TV. "And that's a bad thing?"

Kiki gave him a long, annoyed glance. "You ever miss Velour on a Friday when the music's too loud, CC show up in a cape, Jean got her third drink and starts monologuing about men being mediocre, and Danielle pretends to hate us but always stays until the end?"

Ramon chuckled. "Every damn week."

She shook her head. "We used to live vicariously through the chaos. Now look at us. You got me eating grilled salmon and watching people get catfished by inmates."

"It's a good show."

"It's a depressing show."

Kiki unlocked her phone and started typing—slowly, deliberately.

Kiki: I miss y'all. Come to our place. Dinner. Booze. Not optional.

CC: Who cooking tho?

Kiki: Me. Don't be cute.

Danielle: I'll bring wine.
Jean: [heart reacts]

Ramon: Y'all better show up. We got the good mezcal.

CC: I'm there. But I'm not helping clean.

Asha: I'll DJ. But I'm only playing slow jams.

Kiki: Do what you want. Just show up. The thread slowed again. But this time, it didn't feel like silence. It felt like the moment before the toast. Before the hug. Before someone says, "I needed this."

They weren't back yet. But they were circling home.

The dinner was set. Kiki had picked the date. Ramon had cleaned the grill. Everyone said yes, no maybe, no need to check back in. The RSVP was groupwide and sacred.

But in the days leading up to it, the thread started acting like its old self—just a little. It wasn't as loud or reckless, but it wasn't silent anymore either. They were in that sweet space between healing and joking again. Not quite healed. But not afraid of the light, either.

It was Danielle who dropped the gem: I won't be able to stay late. Corporate and I are flying to Vegas Saturday to see Wizard of Oz at the Sphere.

The reactions rolled in instantly.

CC: Damn bitch, you are just about as gay as I am now.

Ramon: Lmao.

Asha: You don't have to be gay to love Wizard of Oz. I absolutely love Wizard of Oz and dick.

Jean: Same. Huge fan of both.

Kiki: Same. Rainbow skirts and raw dog. It's about balance.

Danielle: Y'all are so stupid.

CC: I am DELIGHTED. This is gay excellence.

Danielle: It's a Sphere show, not a U-Haul lease signing. Relax.

CC: No. You're officially one of us. Gay brunch mandatory next month.

Jean: I wanna come. For the food. And the trauma.

It wasn't just banter. It was something more. Everyone felt it. They were finally getting back into the rhythm of being themselves around each other—without pretending the last few weeks hadn't happened.

Jean wasn't avoiding her feelings. She'd just quarantined them. She took them out on walks, fed them old text threads and playlists that hadn't aged well, and let them sit quietly in a corner. They didn't scream anymore. They just breathed. That was enough.

She was walking near the river when she saw Asha on the same path. They waved, then walked side by side, no plan, no small talk needed.

"You ever feel like you can only be soft with one person at a time?" Jean asked, staring ahead. Asha didn't respond right away. She just nodded and waited.

"I let that man drag me," Jean said. "And he wasn't wrong. That's the part that fucked me up. He wasn't lying. Just… honest. Brutally honest. And calm. Like he knew I wouldn't be able to handle it."

"You handled it," Asha said.

Jean smirked. "Barely. But yeah. I didn't spiral. I just—paused." She glanced at Asha and slowed her pace.

"I've done this thing for years. Performed 'open.' Like I'm this deeply available, emotionally fluent, fully unpacked woman. But really? I'm polished pain. That's the truth. Clean on the outside, chaos inside."

Asha looked over. "You've done that for all of us. In different ways. Especially the serial dater. You gave us polished perspective when we were just messy feelings."

Jean nodded slowly. "What really stuck with me is what he said before he left. Word for word: 'You believe you're entitled to someone's life story and haven't even earned the right to the opening chapter;. "

Asha whistled low. "Damn. That's…. harsh. But surgical."

"It cut because it was real," Jean said. "And I keep replaying it."

Asha gave her a sideways glance. "You gonna ever reach back out to him?"

Jean barked a dry laugh. "Bitch, I said I'm evolving. I didn't say that Jesus performed a miracle."

Asha laughed too, then bumped her shoulder gently. "Just checking."

Jean sighed. "I've reopened a few old email threads. Not the blocked ones. Just the ones I didn't delete. It's not desperation. I just… want to see who people are when I'm not doing all the screening and overthinking."

"Anyone surprise you "

Jean hesitated. "One. Maybe. I don't wanna jinx it by saying too much. But it feels different. I think I used to build guards so strong nobody could get through without fighting. And I confused the ones who gave up with the ones who weren't worthy "

"And now?"

"Now I'm realizing… maybe I was the locked door. And all they ever did was knock."

Asha didn't offer a fix. She didn't say "you deserve love," or "time heals." She just let Jean walk beside her in silence. That was enough.

Danielle was finishing her last bite of dinner when her phone lit up with a message from Corporate Conference.

Corporate: You're still coming over after dinner with your friends, right? I'm still pouting that I wasn't invited.

Danielle chuckled and leaned back against the kitchen counter.

Danielle: Of course I'm coming over. Trust me—we're in a reconstruction phase. I'm not sure how safe it would be for any stranger to walk into that right now.

Corporate: Mmm. So it's hostile territory?

Danielle: No. It's a demolition zone. But I've got the blueprints.

Corporate: If you're really sorry for excluding me, I'll allow one apology in the form of strap.

Danielle: If you're truly upset, you can punish me with that strap again.

Corporate: Let me find out you still out here like a dick.

Danielle: A pretty woman that knows my body and I can get fucked at the end of it. Reason 1, 265 that I'm gay.

They both laughed—separately, in their respective spaces—but it was the kind of laugh that echoed in text. The kind that made you read it twice and smile again anyway.

Danielle hadn't felt this settled in years. Not perfect. Not euphoric. Just… good. Grounded. And not a single part of her wanted to break that moment into pieces for the group chat.

She packed her overnight bag with her standard items—a maxi dress, extra panties, two toothbrushes, and a full-size bottle of lube. But this time, she packed them openly. No oversized purse disguise. No backup exit strategy.

She wasn't in love. But she was exactly where she wanted to be—and that was more than enough for now.

The day before dinner was unusually still. Nobody had much to say. It was like they were all waiting for something—but nobody knew what.

Kiki: (Dropped a picture in the group chat around 3 p. m. A table half set. Wine glasses in a perfect triangle. A bottle of tequila waiting like a guest who showed up too early.) Y'all better not flake. I bought expensive-ass napkins.

Jean: [heart emoji]

Asha: Don't worry, I'm just coming to judge everyone.
CC: You always do.

Ramon: I'm smoking wings and ribs. Act accordingly.

Danielle: Bringing real wine. No Trader Joe's rosé this time.

CC: You've changed.

Danielle: Correct.

Across the city, Jean was home early. She had a glass of red wine, a blanket across her lap, and an old documentary playing in the background. Her phone was facedown. No tabs open. No texts waiting.

She didn't feel broken. She didn't feel fixed. Just… real. She was still thinking about what Elliot said, and it still made her flinch—in a good way. Like stitches pulling skin closed.

Danielle was packing. This time, she didn't hide anything in an oversized purse. She laid everything on the bed—folded maxi dress, fresh panties, two toothbrushes, and a full-size bottle of lube. It wasn't a big deal. It was just her standard overnight bag, and she was finally packing it like she meant it.

She took a picture of it, bag still open.

Danielle: You know they say what happens in Vegas stays in Vegas.

Corporate: Unless it's an STD or pregnancy.

Danielle: Exactly.

Corporate: That's true, but what I was thinking is maybe while we're out there, we get a little risqué and go to one of those sex clubs. Not to do anything—just watch other people fuck, get turned on, and fuck each other.

Danielle didn't even blink.

Danielle: Bitch, you must've never read Heavy is the Crown. I'm in the middle of reading it right now, and if you ever mention going to a swingers club or any kind of sex club again, I'll have to block you on principle alone.

Corporate: Noted. Never again.

Danielle: Good girl.

Kiki was setting the final touches on the table when Ramon walked in with the bags of ice and flowers.

"You put me on flower duty?" he asked.

"You're the husband. That's your tax."

He handed them over without argument. "You good?" he asked.

Kiki paused. "Yeah. Actually, yeah."

"No chaotic brunches. No karaoke brawls. What's happening to us?"

Kiki smiled. "Maybe we're not falling apart. Maybe we're just getting real."

And then there was CC. Silk robe. Bonnet snug. Candles flickering. One hand wrapped around a small mug of half espresso, half almond milk. The nightcap of a diva in recovery.

He opened the thread with Pastor Stroke again. The same last message. The same unread space. He didn't overthink it this time.

He flipped the camera, gave his best raised-eyebrow smirk, and snapped a quick selfie—silk and all. Sent it with one line: "Still thinking about your peace. Don't let that go to your head."

He exhaled as soon as it delivered. The reply came less than thirty seconds later. "Too late. Already there."

CC smiled. Closed the thread. Took the last sip from his mug, and sank deeper into the pillows.He didn't need more than that tonight.

Everyone had a version of the same quiet win that evening.

Jean staring at nothing and liking how it felt. Danielle, bag packed in plain sight. Kiki watching the light hit the plates just right. CC not pressing send with a novel—but with a picture. Ramon humming while he chopped herbs. Asha organizing a playlist of slow jams and ignoring every ex that had texted "just checking in."

They were still the Velour Veterans. Just a little quieter now. A little more whole. And for the first time in a long time, nobody was trying to make the silence louder than it needed to be.

Chapter 18: And Then There Were Names

"Are you excited about your trip with Corporate Conference to Vegas tomorrow?"

The question came from Asha, casual, as she passed around a fresh bottle of wine. Danielle didn't even flinch. "Her name is Christina."

The group paused—but not in shock. Just enough for the correction to land.

CC blinked. "Wait… she got a name?"

"She earned one," Danielle said simply.

Kiki grinned. "We naming hoes now?"

"We're naming women I'm dating," Danielle said, tilting her glass. "That's growth."

"Well damn," Ramon said. "Y'all so grown now."

"She didn't like Corporate Conference?" Asha asked.

"She didn't hate it," Danielle replied. "But that name wasn't built for staying power."

CC smirked. "Christina. Mmm. Sounds like she schedules her orgasms and has tax folders by color." Then he looked at her and said "Do you?"

Danielle was laughing at something CC said when Christina's tone shifted.

"So… you looked real comfortable talking to her."

Danielle blinked. "You mean the woman selling raffle tickets for the shelter?"

Christina crossed her arms but her mouth twitched like she knew she was being ridiculous.
"I'm just saying. You don't usually lean in that close for strangers."

Danielle stepped closer, voice low. "You think I'm leaning in? Try living in my head for a day. You're the only person I've leaned into in a long time."

CC leaned in between them like a referee. "And on that note, I'm giving you both a yellow card for acting like teenagers."

"She does both," Danielle said. "And they're both excellent."

Nobody clapped. Nobody overreacted. But something shifted.

It wasn't just the end of the nickname.
It was the quiet agreement that this—this thing with Christina—was real.

They were halfway through dinner when Kiki refilled CC's drink and said, "So you calling him Pastor Stroke still, or are you on real-name terms too?"

CC sipped slowly, then tilted his head. "I whispered it into a pillow once." The table chuckled.

He rolled his eyes. "Fine. His name is DeMarcus." Another moment of silence—but not from shock. Just acknowledgment.

Jean nodded. "DeMarcus. I like it. Sounds like he works out with resistance bands and says 'affirmed' instead of 'amen'."

"He does," CC said, "and he says it in tongues."

Asha raised a glass. "To DeMarcus and Christina."

"To first names and first-class dick," CC added. They clinked. Maturity had arrived—but not alone.

"So," Ramon said, leaning back with his plate clean. "You ever notice we never invite Jordan to shit?" Heads turned.

"The bartender?" Kiki asked.

"Yeah," he said. "We hang out at the Social every damn week, and not once has anyone thought, 'Let's bring Jordan'."

Asha didn't look up. "You mean John Holmes?" The whole table froze.

Jean squinted. "What?"

CC spun in his chair. "Wait a minute, bitch—how did he get a name?!"

"I thought his name was Jordan," Kiki said.

Ramon raised his brow. "Hold up. You named him John Holmes? The white porn star?"

"Legendary big dick energy," Asha said flatly. "And accurate."

Jean stared at her. "Did you sleep with him?"

Asha didn't blink. "I'm not proud of it—but yes. I took advantage of his broken heart and his big dick. So he is now John Holmes. And we are secretly seeing each other because they don't play that fraternization shit at the bar."

Kiki screamed. CC slapped the table. Ramon howled. Jean covered her face like she was in church.

"You WHAT?!" Jean gasped.

"I knew it!" CC yelled. "I BEEN knew that man had something unspoken swinging!"

"I hugged him goodbye," Asha said. "Damn near blacked out."

Ramon, tears in his eyes: "So the rumors… are true."

Jean rolled her eyes. "Dumbass. Big white dicks have never not been a real thing. Rare, but not *not* a real thing."

Asha shrugged. "Now y'all know."

Kiki cackled. "So we naming Jordan, Christina, and DeMarcus all in one night?"

"Only if they deserve it," Danielle said.

CC pointed at Asha. "I just wanna say—when I grow up, I want to be as ruthless and discreet as you."

Asha sipped calmly. "You can't be discreet in leopard print."

"Leopard is a lifestyle. Don't do me."

Jean smirked. "I've never seen you with a white guy."

Asha shrugged. "You haven't seen me with the Latin one, the Indian one, or the Chinese one either. But yes—I fucked them all." She took a bite of cornbread like it was a mic drop.

"Rainbow Coalition in this pussy." The table erupted.

"I'm selective," she added, "by experience. Not just being naïve and stubborn."

CC wiped a tear. "This is why I stay coming to these things. Every time I think we're healed and boring—BOOM. Roster shakeup and dick revelation."

Ramon lifted his glass. "To Jordan-slash-John Holmes."

"To Christina and DeMarcus," Jean added.

"To Rainbow Pussy and her coalition," Kiki said.

They drank. And for the first time in a long time, there wasn't a single fake smile at the table. No performative wounds. No hiding behind nicknames or half-truths.

Just friends, real names, and new rules: If you've made it this far, you just might earn a name.

The plates were mostly empty now. Kiki had switched to house slippers. Ramon was stacking foil containers. Asha and Jean were drying wine glasses with dishrags older than some of their relationships.

A quiet had settled over the apartment—but it wasn't awkward. It was grown.

"I haven't seen y'all this mellow since CC got that root canal and had to text all his insults for two days," Asha said.

Jean chuckled. "I saved every one of those texts."

"'I hope your food tastes like ash, bitch'," Asha recited. "Poetry."

Kiki walked in with a glass of water and no bra. The party was officially in the comfort zone.

"I love this version of us," she said, sitting down with a sigh. "Still petty. Just not… spiraling."

"I miss spiraling a little," Ramon said from the kitchen. "Spiraling had better snacks." Everyone laughed.

Jean was the last one lingering in the kitchen with Asha. The lighting was soft, the counters clean, the air thick with the smell of leftover barbecue and eucalyptus hand soap.

"You know you're glowing, right?" Asha said casually.

Jean rolled her eyes. "Don't start."

"I'm not starting anything. Just saying."

Jean leaned against the counter. "I'm not ready to chase anybody. But for the first time… I don't feel like love would be a sacrifice."

Asha tilted her head. "I always thought I had to choose between love and dignity. Like I'd have to shrink or beg or pretend not to notice shit just to keep someone."

"And now?"

"Now I think I might be willing to negotiate. Not beg. Not settle. Just… find a balance that's not all on my side of the scale."

Asha smirked. "So now you're open to dating men that are five-foot-two?"

Jean didn't miss a beat. "No. And anything that close to being identified as a little person." The room cracked up.

"FYI, anybody 4'10" or below is legally deemed a little person— and while I'm not opposed to handicaps—"

"Damn!" Ramon yelled from the other room. "That's not a handicap. That's just vertically challenged."

Jean powered through. "You must be at least 5'6" to ride this ride. And allow me to wear kitten heels—or a proper five-inch heel—if I want to. I'm not looking down at his bald spot or the potential for one." Silence. Then applause.

"You're disgusting," Asha said.

"I'm practical."

Danielle was back home, adding last-minute items to her duffel bag for tomorrow's trip.

She'd already packed the essentials earlier in the day—maxi dress, extra panties, toiletries, full-size lube. But now she was slipping in backup charger cords, lip balm, and the face mist she always forgets.

She was zipping up the side pouch when her phone lit up

Danielle smiled and FaceTimed her. Christina answered from bed —hair loosely wrapped in a silk scarf, lips glossy, white tee.

Danielle tilted the phone. "Are your little dreams done plotting my downfall?"

"I've given them instructions in case I don't survive the Vegas trip."

"Oh, we're not just surviving," Danielle said. "We're thriving. You know I packed the full-size bottle this time."

Christina blinked. "Of?"

"Lube. Obviously."

Christina cackled. "Blessed be the gay."

They were quiet for a second. Just smiling.

Christina said, "You still coming over before we leave?"

Danielle nodded. "Of course. I already told you—I don't flake."

"I know," Christina said, a little softer now. "That's kind of the problem. You're reliable. Consistent. I wasn't prepared for that "

"You'll live."

"I better."

They exchanged a look that didn't need words.

"Get some sleep," Danielle said.

"You too, soft stud."

Danielle hung up, then stared at the black screen a second longer than necessary. Not because she had doubts—but because she didn't.

Asha's phone buzzed while she was folding napkins. It was a message from Jordan.

John Holmes: Let me know when you get home safe.

She didn't reply. Not yet. But she smiled. And for her—that was the start of something.

CC was the last one to grab his things. He kissed Kiki on the cheek, gave Ramon the world's most dramatic side hug, and waved his empty thermos like a goodbye flag.

He made it to the elevator, hit the button, then paused. His phone lit up.

DeMarcus: You still thinking about my peace?

He read it. Then let the screen go dark. Not because he didn't want to answer. But because he did—and that's what scared him.

Later that night, everyone was back in their own space.

Kiki was rubbing coconut oil on her thighs. Ramon was already half asleep. Jean was watching an old indie film with subtitles and no plot. Danielle was double-checking her passport, her charger, her confidence. Asha was in her oversized tee, still smiling at nothing.

CC stood in his mirror in a silk robe, brushing his teeth like he wasn't thinking about anyone—but he was.

And for the first time in a long time, they were all exactly where they needed to be: Still complicated. Still chaotic. But grounded.

It was almost midnight when the group chat lit up again. Ramon dropped in a photo first: Kiki knocked out on the couch, head tilted back, half a brownie still in her hand. The caption read: "She swore she could rally."

Danielle replied with a screenshot of her duffel bag zipped, passport and mini lotion on top: "Rally this."

Jean followed with a photo of a single candle burning next to her half-full wine glass and a book titled The Art of Letting It Go. "Bitch, I'm trying."

Asha dropped a mirror selfie in a clay face mask. "Washed my face. Tell my exes I won."

CC didn't post a photo. He just liked everyone else's and kept the chat open like he might say something, then didn't.

Ramon turned his phone screen-down and stretched.

Kiki, still semi-conscious, murmured, "I used to think hanging out with all them single folks would make me hate being married."

Ramon smirked. "And now?"

"I realize we live through them… but also thank God we don't live with them."

He chuckled. "I don't miss dating. I just miss titties I don't have to explain things to."

She opened one eye. "You really know how to make a woman feel special."

"You married me."

She nodded, eyes closing again. "That's the dumbest smart thing I've ever done."

At her place, Jean opened a thread she hadn't deleted but also hadn't answered.

No name saved. Just an old photo icon and three back-and-forth messages from someone she once claimed was boring—but now seemed calm, consistent, available.

She reread them. Still didn't reply. But for the first time, she smiled.

"I'm not all the way healed," she whispered to no one. "But at least I'm not performing hurt anymore."

Asha's phone buzzed again.

John Holmes: "Sleep tight. I liked tonight. Even from a distance."

She didn't send a kiss emoji. Didn't even type a reply. But she stared at it for a minute before locking her phone gently, like it deserved a soft goodbye for now.

Danielle pulled her carry-on to the door and looped her coat over it. She sat on the edge of the couch, FaceTimed Christina one last time.

Christina answered from bed, sleep scarf tied tight, still wearing that lip gloss Danielle had developed a Pavlovian response to. Danielle lifted the camera. "Packed. Passport ready. Lube secured."

Christina smirked. "You keep leading with lube like it's not the person you're flying out to see."

"I lead with honesty. You've met me."

"You're right."

Danielle hesitated a second, then added, "Let's make Vegas count."

Christina tilted her head. "It already does. You're showing up."

Danielle hung up after a short exchange of slow smiles. This time, no need for a long goodnight.

CC was the last one awake. He poured a splash of milk into his espresso shot, swirled it until it formed a cloud he liked, and sat back on the corner of his couch like it was a throne.

The city outside his window blinked and pulsed. He opened his group chat again. Hovered.

Instead, he clicked to DeMarcus's thread. It lit up with a new message. One. Singular. Complete.

"I know what it means to be broken. That's why I granted you grace. I know what it means not to trust. That's why I gave you understanding. And I know you see my messages and don't reply —not to look thirsty or excited—but because either I don't excite you, or you're still playing distance games.

So here it is plain: I need you to be as excited for me as I am for you. If you're not, I will respectfully bow out. I respect your unwillingness to chase. But now you're going to have to respect my unwillingness to keep running toward you.

If you want this—say so. If you need space to heal, I'll honor that too.

But this waiting a day or two—or several hours—for a reply when you're not busy, just avoiding…. that's not timing. That's avoidance. That's a power game.

And I'm not playing.

You won't get another message from me until you're ready.

Not an ultimatum. Not an or else. Just me, out of grace for turning myself into someone I'm not.

I don't chase either."

CC sat back. The message pulsed quietly on the screen. It hurt. But it also impressed the hell out of him. Because the one thing he was afraid of—overpowering DeMarcus—wasn't real.

This man had just shown him, line by line, he'd met his match. Before he could overthink it, CC grabbed his phone and typed: "I haven't had a man call me on my shit in a long time. No more need to run. I appreciate grace—and I'm sorry. I'll do better."

He hit send. Then sat there in the stillness. Not afraid of what came next.

Chapter 19: The Ones Who Came Back

The reservation was for eight, but nine showed up. Jamal arrived late, hoodie on, head bowed like he'd just emerged from witness protection.

Velour Social hadn't changed much, but the energy around the table had. There was less performance. Less posturing. Just laughter that didn't require a setup.

"Look who decided to return to the land of the living," CC said, swirling his drink.

Jamal smiled sheepishly. "I've been around."

"No, no," CC said, waving him off. "You've been in love. There's a difference."

Danielle leaned back in her chair, one arm draped over the back like a lesbian villain who just closed a business deal. "We haven't seen you in what? A month?"

Jean added, "He popped in once on FaceTime, and Jasmine was in the background holding a spatula like a hostage negotiator." They all laughed.

"Look," Jamal started, "I'm head over heels. And terrified "

Asha raised an eyebrow. "Terrified of what?"

"Of how much I'm willing to do. Anything she wants, I just do it. No hesitation."

"That's not love, sweetie," Kiki said, sipping her wine. "That's servitude."

"Facts," Ramon said. "You gotta be the man who would do anything. But not the one who does everything."

Jean nodded. "Say yes too much, and she stops trusting your no. That's how you end up confused, broke, and full of resentment."

Jamal let it sink in. "I hear y'all. I'll… recalibrate."

CC leaned across the table and tapped the wood. "If you're gonna be a Velour Veteran, no matter if you're in a relationship, in love, out of love, or hurt—you don't get to abandon and come back when shit goes wrong. You have to be here for the good shit too."

Jamal looked him dead in the eye and nodded. "You're right. I'll do better."

Jordan brought another round to the table without being asked.

"Is it me," Danielle said, adjusting the strap on her blouse, "or is he getting finer?"

"He's stress-skinny," Jean replied. "You can always tell when a man's heartbroken and healing in the gym."

Asha didn't say a word. CC glanced her way, then mouthed, 'You better not lie to us later'.

Danielle changed the subject. "So, in case anyone was wondering —we just got back from seeing The Wizard of Oz at the Sphere."

"Oooh, gay " CC whispered like a compliment.

"Very," Danielle said, unfazed. "And incredible."

"How was it?" Kiki asked. "Like… worth the trip?"

"It's like walking inside the movie while Beyoncé personally adjusts the sound system. It's insane. Full immersion. You don't watch it—you experience it."

Jean tilted her head. "That good?"

Danielle smiled. "It was more than good. The show was amazing, yes, but the energy with Christina…"

She trailed off, but everyone heard the softness. "No pressure. No weird power dynamics. No arguing over what to do or not to do. We just… flowed. We laughed, we drank, we held hands without thinking about it. It felt natural."

Asha gave her a look. "So what you're saying is—she passed the get on a plane with me and not make me regret it test?"

"Exactly," Danielle said. "She passed it with extra credit."

CC held up his glass. "To the soft era." They all clinked.

"Speaking of," Jean said, twirling her stirrer, "I've been seeing someone."

The table froze—dramatic silence for dramatic effect.

"And no," she added, "I'm not giving y'all a nickname this time "

"Is this someone new?" Asha asked.

Jean smiled. "Not exactly. Someone I've circled with before. Timing was never right. I was always trying to interview for red flags instead of just… being a person."

Ramon said, "So, what changed?"

Jean shrugged. "I did. Or maybe he always made sense, and I was just speaking a different language."

CC narrowed his eyes. "So now you're bilingual in red flags?"

"I'm fluent in reformed fuckboy now," Jean said, raising her glass. Nobody pressed for details. Nobody needed to.

They stayed for another hour. They didn't scream or toast or do dramatic group hugs. But everyone took turns being silent just long enough to feel it: They had missed this. Not the noise. Not the therapy session energy. Just the feeling of being seen, roasted, and still loved anyway.

And they were all still here. Changed, maybe. But still standing.

The last round of drinks had been poured, and everyone was just drunk enough to be sentimental but not sloppy. The perfect cocktail for trouble.

Ramon leaned back, arm stretched behind Kiki's seat. "Alright. One round. Truth only. No dare. No qualifiers. Just say it."

Asha blinked. "We doing therapy again?"

"Nope," he said. "Just honesty hour."

Jean sipped slowly. "I love how the straight man at the table always wants to get the women to overshare."

"He's married. Doesn't count," Danielle said.

"Exactly," Kiki replied. "His secrets are mine. I legally get to know everything, even his porn habits."

"Do you actually know them?" Asha asked.

Kiki didn't blink. "Ebony POV with oil and no talking. You're welcome." The table groaned.

"Jesus," CC muttered. "Okay, who's going first?"

Jamal exhaled hard. "Fine. I'll take the first hit."

CC squinted. "We don't want a work story. Make it nasty or emotional. Preferably both."

Jamal rolled his eyes. "What's something I lost that I never admitted hurt me?"

Jean held up a finger. "Wait—your real answer isn't the time your ex asked you to eat ass and you cried in the shower after?"

"That was emotional too!" Jamal yelled, laughing along with everyone.

He composed himself. "Nah, real talk—it was my relationship with my brother. We stopped speaking over some dumb shit, and I always played it cool. But that shit crushed me. He was my best friend. And I think I stopped trusting dudes after that."

The table got quiet for a second. Then Asha whispered, "Damn."

Jean went next. "What's the worst part about dating me?"

CC immediately raised both hands. "Ooh, ooh, can I—"

"No," Jean snapped. "This one's mine."

She sat straighter, the glow from her wine catching the soft gold on her neck. "I make people feel like they have to earn my softness instead of just receiving it. I called it standards, but it was really just fear dressed in couture." Everyone stared.

Then CC said, "Why does even your trauma sound like a luxury brand?"

Jean smirked. "Because I process in Chanel."

Danielle's turn. "What's something I was wrong about in love?" She didn't wait.

"I thought I needed someone bold. I thought if she didn't challenge me, it wouldn't last. I didn't realize how rare it is to find consistency that doesn't demand a return."

Jean nodded slowly. CC raised a brow. "So you saying Corporate Conference got you out here believing in peace?"

Danielle shrugged. "We went on a whole trip and didn't argue about anything. Not what to do, what to eat, or who was wrong. I'd never had flow like that before."

"Flow?" Kiki repeated.

Danielle grinned. "Yeah. The kind where you pack lube because you know you're gonna need it—not because you're trying to make something work that don't."

CC clapped once. "Gay joy, bitch. We love to see it."

CC tapped the table. "Fine. I'll go." He cleared his throat.

"What's something I'm afraid to admit?" Everyone leaned in.

"I'm tired of being the funny one. Of always being the safe place for other people to land." The table went quiet.

"I don't know who holds me when I fall. Maybe I set it up that way. Maybe I liked being everybody's comfort blanket. But I hate it now. I hate being the stronghold and the joke and the glue and the show."

He took a long sip. "And I wanted to say 'I'm scared of getting locked jaw from all the dick I've emotionally supported but never got to taste,' but I figured I'd go with the heart truth today."

Danielle nodded. "You could've gone with both."

Kiki sighed. "Okay. What's something I had to unlearn in marriage?" She didn't look at Ramon. She didn't need to.

"That love has to feel like a fight. That if you weren't yelling, crying, or threatening to leave, it wasn't passionate." Ramon blinked.

Kiki kept going. "Ramon's peace used to piss me off. I wanted chaos. He gave me calm. And calm made me nervous."

CC whispered, "So what changed?"

Kiki grinned. "Turns out peace is patient. Peace knows how to fuck. Peace has a dick that curves slightly left and knows where the clit lives."

Ramon looked proud. "She said slightly. Too much and you're getting stabbed sideways."

Everyone laughed, but it wasn't the loud, deflecting laugh of old times. It was warmth. Reprieve. They'd all taken a hit, and no one ducked.

They didn't even realize Jordan was listening until he refilled their water and said, "Y'all sound more like adults than usual."

Jean raised her glass. "Don't get used to it." He smiled and disappeared again.

A few more drinks. A few shared desserts. No more games.

Then someone said it—maybe Asha, maybe Jean: "We really are evolving, huh?"

And CC muttered, deadpan: "Don't say that out loud. I still got two breakups and a petty season left in me." But his smile said otherwise.

The drinks had slowed. No one was racing to leave, but no one was desperate to stay either. That was how you knew the vibe was right. Not forced. Not performative. Just… honest.

Jean leaned her elbow on the table and stirred her straw around an ice cube, staring at it like it was an ex who'd almost ruined her credit.

"I went back through some old emails," she said. The table paused.

"I'm talking about the almosts. The maybes. Not the ones I blocked—those don't count. But the ones I never fully deleted."

Kiki leaned in. "What did you find?"

Jean didn't blink. "That some people never had a chance from the very beginning. Not because they weren't good—but because I already decided I wasn't gonna let them be."

Danielle nodded, eyes soft. Jean wasn't done. "This man I'm seeing now? I ghosted him when we first talked. Not because he did anything wrong, but because I was annoyed that he liked me too soon. That was enough for me to categorize him as corny."

Asha blinked. "But now?"

"I circled back. Not with games. Not with an emoji and a 'hey stranger.' I actually apologized. I told him I was brash and dismissive and that it wasn't his fault." Silence. A different kind.

"And saying it didn't make me feel weak. It made me feel honest. Like, actually honest. Not the version of honest we use when we're being savage and calling it transparency."

No one clapped. But no one broke eye contact either. Jean sat back, her point made, no need to drive it home.

Danielle picked it up like a jazz soloist sliding in with the next phrase. "I had a moment like that too. Before things really got going with Christina." Everyone listened.

"I told her the truth. That I've been in situations where I disappeared or shut down, and that it wasn't because I didn't care —it was because I thought that showing up meant giving up control."

"Damn," CC whispered.

"I didn't tell her like I was making a confession," Danielle said. "I told her like I wanted her to know me, fully. And she didn't flinch."

Jean smirked. "She doesn't strike me as a flincher."

"She's not," Danielle said. "But it wasn't about her reaction. It was about me saying it, before anything went wrong. Before any misunderstanding could happen. I even preemptively let her know when I'm about to be slammed at work. Like, 'Hey, it's one of those weeks. I'm not ghosting you. I just need space. I'm fine. I'm safe. I have a concealed carry permit. Stop worrying'." That got a laugh.

Danielle shrugged. "Since then, I haven't gotten a single 'Where are you?' text. But I've also done something I never used to—I check in. First. Without being asked "

CC tilted his head. "Look at you out here writing lesbian Psalms."

There was a beat. Then CC tapped the table with two fingers. "Okay, bitches. Since we're being vulnerable."

Everyone turned to him. "DeMarcus called me out." No gasp. Just slow blinks. Let him talk.

"You know how we do. Get a text. Let it sit. Sometimes a few hours. Sometimes a whole day. Then we finally reply with some basic-ass bullshit like 'My bad, I was sleep' or 'Just saw this'."

He paused. "DeMarcus said he's not mad I don't chase. But he's not gonna keep running toward me either."

Danielle whispered, "Whew."

"I apologized," CC said. "No sass. No delay. Just a real-ass 'I'm sorry. I'll do better.' "

Asha leaned back like she'd seen a ghost. "Wait—you apologized?"

"Openly," CC confirmed.

"Like, not with sarcasm?" Kiki asked.

"Not even a wink emoji," CC said. "Just a clean apology. And guess what? He didn't turn it into a power play. He just kept it moving. Gave me grace."

Jean nodded slowly. "That's what it looks like when someone's grown. They don't use your honesty as leverage." CC picked up his drink but didn't sip it.

"We've all sat here talking shit about everybody else's mess," he said. "And when someone talks about us, we roast them so bad they forget they might've been right." Silence.

"We're not always the main character," he added. "Sometimes we're the villain. And the lesson."

The check came, unprompted. Nobody rushed to split it. Ramon picked it up and slid his card into the folder.

"You sure?" Asha asked.

"I've watched y'all grow up," he said. "It's my pleasure."

Kiki smirked. "Damn. Was that love or indigestion?"

Ramon smiled. "Let's call it both."

They started filtering out slowly, hugs soft and unforced. A couple fist bumps, a few head nods, and just enough eye contact to say: I see you. I got you. I'm proud of you.

Outside, the night was cool and still. Jean walked ahead, coat flowing, phone untouched. No texting under the table tonight.

Danielle waited for her car, unlocking it as Christina's name popped up with a simple: "Home safe?"

She smiled and replied: "Almost. But I will be."

Behind her, CC stood by himself for a moment, letting the silence hold. Then, with a quiet sigh, he said under his breath: "Mirror season." And walked off into the dark.

Chapter 20: This Ain't New, But It's Not the Same

Jean didn't usually check her DMs on a Thursday morning, especially not the ones in the "General" tab she kept muted. But something had pulled her thumb across the screen that day—a flicker of curiosity, or boredom, or something she wasn't ready to name.

And there he was.

Message unread, weeks old, still sitting there like it hadn't been waiting: Hope you're well. No pressure. But if your schedule ever aligns with mine again, I'd love to try that drink we never got to.

She read it twice. Then typed. No emojis. Just words: I beg your pardon for my late reply.

He hadn't expected her to reply, and she could tell. His return message came quickly but cautiously: Didn't think I'd hear from you.

She answered: I didn't reach out. I just finally responded.

Then, after a beat: Is that a drink offer still on the table or did the invitation expire with the calendar year?

He sent the address of a spot she didn't know but pretended to, followed by: Tonight at 8. I'm not confirming—I'm assuming.

She smiled and whispered to herself, I like this timeline.

Now it was 7:58. She was parked around the corner, watching the front door of the place. She wasn't stalling. Just... calibrating.

"Déjà Vu". That's what she called him in her head and to the group, though he didn't know it. Not because he reminded her of someone else—but because he was someone else. Someone already familiar. They had circled each other before. It never landed. He didn't press. She didn't bend. Their lives didn't agree.

But he was smooth, always. Clean-lined beard. Well-fitting clothes. Easy voice. The kind of man you noticed without him needing to remind you. The kind you remembered without bitterness.

She didn't ghost him. She just never gave it room. Now she had space.

He stood when she walked in. Just that. No arms out. No performative smile. Just rose, tall and centered, and pulled her chair out like he did this kind of thing with women like her all the time.

"Hi " she said, sliding into the seat.

"You came," he replied.

"I said I would "

"No, you responded. That's different."

She gave him a mock-stern look. "You're starting early."

"You're late."

"Not by the clock."

He leaned forward. "Not by the calendar either?"

Jean narrowed her eyes with a smile. "I beg your pardon for me taking so long."

He grinned. "You're here now."

"Exactly."

They didn't order a full meal. Just cocktails and the crispy chicken bites he claimed were a spiritual experience. She took one, nodded, and gave him the approving silence that said you might've been right. He didn't gloat. He just handed her another.

She watched him as he talked. He didn't shift in his seat. Didn't overshare. Didn't try to play humble. She realized quickly: he didn't care about impressing her—he cared about being understood. That was rarer.

"So what've you been up to all this time?" he asked.

She gave him the polished version—travel, work, the usual. Then added, "Mostly, I've been trying not to date idiots."

He laughed. "How's that going?"

Jean tilted her head. "You tell me."

He didn't blink. "So far, I think you're succeeding."

There was no tension between them. Just awareness. The kind of awareness that doesn't need fireworks or background music. Just two people who remembered each other—clearly.

He asked about her favorite cities. She asked if he ever regretted not pushing harder the first time.

He said, "No. You didn't seem like the type who wanted to be chased."

"I wasn't."

"But now you're here."

She nodded. "Now I'm different."

"Good different or dangerous different?"

"I guess we'll find out."

They walked out together, coats over shoulders, the kind of ending that didn't beg for more.

He looked down at her shoes. "You do realize if we ever go somewhere that requires more than five steps, I'm asking for a sneaker clause in advance."

Jean smirked. "That sounds like a commitment."

He shrugged. "It's logistics. I like walking with people I don't mind listening to."

She stared at him for half a beat, then gave a quiet: "Hmm."

He didn't go in for a kiss. She didn't offer one. At her car, he just said: "Thanks for replying. It's good to see you again."

She replied, "I didn't reach out." He raised an eyebrow.

"I just responded," she repeated, smirking. Then she got in her car and drove off.

Back home, she kicked her heels off and scrolled her messages.

Déjà Vu: You ghosting again or you just like making me wait?

She typed back: Neither. I just don't rush replies anymore. I read slow. I answer slower.

A pause. Then: But I'm here. She hit send. And then she smiled.

Christina cooked with her shoes off. That was the first thing Danielle noticed when she walked in. The heels were by the front door, neatly arranged under the entryway bench like they'd never been worn.

Danielle paused at the threshold of the kitchen, eyes softening. "Look at you " she said, smiling.

Christina looked up from the stove, one eyebrow raised. "What?"

"You're barefoot in your own home. And not in a 'my feet hurt' way. Like a 'this is my place' kind of way."

Christina stirred the sauce and shrugged. "It is my place "

Danielle tilted her head. "I know. I just like when people live like it."

Dinner was light—pasta tossed in a lemon herb sauce, a salad with arugula and those little crisp fried chickpeas Christina liked. They ate on the couch with linen napkins and full glasses of wine. No TV. No music. Just the soft clink of forks and the way the night settled around them without ceremony.

Danielle picked at the chickpeas. "You ever feel like things are so peaceful you start looking for danger?"

Christina didn't flinch. "All the time."

Danielle glanced at her. "Really?"

Christina nodded. "But I stopped trusting that instinct. My peace isn't a setup. It's a reprieve."

Danielle blinked, then looked down at her plate. "That's a hard belief to hold."

"I know. But it's true."

They talked about minor things after that. Whether cilantro was worth fighting for. Why so many Black women liked British murder shows. Christina admitted she rewatched The Bodyguard every time she got seasonal depression and cried at the exact same timestamp each time.

Danielle said she never cried at movies unless someone was abandoned at a bus stop or a dog got put down.

"So, emotional detachment and a soft spot for strays?" Christina teased.

"Exactly."

After dinner, they curled into opposite corners of the couch like a soft parenthesis. Christina pulled the throw blanket over them, her hand settling against Danielle's knee. Not possessive—just present.

Danielle exhaled. "You know I don't sleep well."

"I figured."

"I used to blame the mattress."

"Of course you did."

Danielle cracked a smile. "I'm serious. I told myself it was about alignment. Neck support. Turns out, it was the silence."

Christina ran her thumb in slow circles against Danielle's knee. "What about the silence?"

"It's loud. When it's just me, it fills up the room like gas. I start thinking about everything. About nothing. About people who aren't thinking about me."

Christina paused. "And now?"

Danielle took a moment before answering. "Now it's different. But I still wait for it to turn."

"You think I'm gonna ghost you." Danielle didn't answer. She didn't have to.

Christina adjusted slightly, shifting so they faced each other more. "I'm not Selena."

"I know."

"You say that. But you still brace like I am."

Danielle closed her eyes for a second. "I don't mean to. I've just… I've never done soft."

Christina studied her. "That's not true. You do soft all the time. You just don't receive it."

Danielle's lips parted, ready to deflect, then closed again. She sat with it.

"I'm not trying to fix you," Christina said. "But I need you to recognize what you've survived without building a bunker in every room."

Danielle exhaled again. "Damn. You want a sermonette or a kiss?"

Christina smirked. "Surprise me."

They didn't have sex that night. Not because there wasn't tension. Not because the desire wasn't there. But because neither of them needed to prove anything. And that was new.

They lay in bed, tangled but not fused. Danielle let Christina wrap an arm around her waist, let the warmth settle in without asking what it cost. She didn't scroll through her phone. Didn't draft emails in her head. She just let herself exist in a space that didn't ask for defense.

It was uncomfortable. And healing. And terrifying. And beautiful. She whispered, "Thank you."

Christina, already drifting, murmured, "For what?"

Danielle didn't answer right away. "For letting me be quiet without thinking I'm shutting down."

At 2:43 a. m., Danielle woke up briefly. The room was dark, the kind of dark that didn't feel dangerous. She reached over and found Christina still there, breathing slow, arm still around her. She didn't get up. Didn't panic. Didn't go to the bathroom and check her face in the mirror like she used to—to make sure she still looked worth staying for.

She just turned slightly and rested her head against Christina's collarbone.

Back in the group chat, unopened and unmentioned, the last thing Danielle had typed earlier that day was still sitting there:

"I think I might be happy. Don't ruin it with jokes." She hadn't hit send. She might. Later. For now, it was enough to live it.

CC stood in the middle of his living room holding a candle.

It was called "Chai Bourbon Firewood"—pretentious, overpriced, and smelled like someone with a beard you trusted. He'd bought it on impulse, then lit it every night since that last date with DeMarcus.

Tonight, though, he stared at the flame like it owed him something.

The rooftop was too windy, so he stayed inside, letting the apartment stay dim and warm. A Spotify jazz mix was doing too much—horns when he needed strings, strings when he needed silence.

He didn't want music. He wanted that voice note DeMarcus had sent two days ago. The one where he didn't say anything deep— just said he'd made salmon and couscous and thought about inviting CC over, but decided against it because, quote, "I like when you miss me a little." The nerve.

CC had listened to it six times already. Tonight would make it seven.

He hit play. "—just thought about you. Not in a dramatic way. Just… you crossed my mind. And I smiled. That's all."

The fuck? Who said that? Who said that to him?

CC plopped onto the velvet couch, legs stretched out, wine in hand. He wasn't drunk, but he'd had enough to feel everything twice.

DeMarcus was not loud. Not extra. He didn't compliment CC's outfits unless asked. He didn't laugh like a performance. He didn't need anything from him—he just showed up.

And that scared the living shit out of him.

Because Church Candy had the blueprint for lust. For chaos. For getting attention. But DeMarcus didn't care about the glitter. He saw the glitter, sure—but he was looking underneath it. And that…. was new.

He pulled out his phone and hovered over the thread.

The last text was his: Next time you bring salmon and don't offer me a plate, that's violence.

DeMarcus had replied: Next time, I'll cook it while you watch.

The timestamp was yesterday. CC hadn't answered. Not because he was playing games. But because he didn't trust himself not to say too much.

Now he scrolled back, rereading everything like a teenage girl in an after-school special.

"I like you."

"You challenge me."

"I don't chase, but I don't run either "

Who was this man?

CC flopped backward and stared at the ceiling. "I don't like how much I like you."

It slipped out. Not poetic. Just honest.

He thought about their second date—days ago, but it already felt sticky in his memory. DeMarcus had taken him to a Black-owned wine tasting event where nobody gave them weird looks and the staff treated them like regulars.

At one point, DeMarcus leaned over and said, "You know why I like you?" CC had braced for a joke. A flirt. A thirst trap punchline. Instead: "Because you let people see you, even when it scares the fuck out of you."

CC had frozen. That was the exact moment he knew he was in trouble.

He called it DeMarcus Trouble in his head now. The kind that didn't make him spiral into drama—but made him clean up. He'd changed his sheets twice this week. Bought fresh flowers. Caught himself humming.

He was not a hummer. Humming was for grandparents and white sitcoms. And yet.

The wine was almost gone now. The candle had formed a little well in the center, burning low and bright. CC stared into it and did something he almost never did.

He prayed. Not for love. Not for clarity. Just for courage. To stop sabotaging what felt like peace in designer form.

He sent the message before he could overthink it: You free tonight? I'm tired of acting like I don't miss you.

Three dots appeared immediately. Then nothing. Then they came back.

Then nothing again. Then finally: Yeah. I'm free.

CC stood up and paced. He texted again: I'm not trying to be cute. I'm trying to be honest. That's new for me.

DeMarcus replied: Same. I'll see you soon?

CC typed back: Please do.

Then added: But bring that couscous. You owe me.

DeMarcus sent a laughing emoji. Then a heart. Just one.

CC blew out the candle. Not because the night was over. Because it was just starting. And for the first time in years, he didn't feel like setting anything on fire.

"You bitches better not take this seriously," Kiki announced, unrolling her canvas like she was unboxing a trap house diploma. "I didn't come here to learn. I came to drink, flirt, and paint what I think Ramon's dick looks like after leg day."

Ramon, already three sips into his first glass of rosé, raised a hand. "To be fair, my dick skips leg day. It's just vibes and one strong vein." The group howled.

The private paint-and-sip was hosted in the back of an art studio owned by a friend of Asha's. Soft lighting, good wine, Beyoncé's Cowboy Carter playing low, and a Black woman instructor who took one look at the Velour crew and said, "Y'all not gonna listen, are you?"

"Not a chance," Jean replied, sipping Pinot Noir. "But we'll tip well."

CC arrived last, wearing a matching set with one shoulder exposed and hair swept into a rainbow puff. "Don't worry," he said, pulling off his jacket. "The gay is here. We can begin."

The instructor smiled. "And you must be Church Candy."

"Only to those who survive the night."

They took their seats, each in front of a blank canvas. The sample art was an abstract silhouette of two bodies entangled under moonlight.

"See," Asha muttered, dipping her brush. "This is why I don't paint. Too many metaphors. I'm not in the mood to unpack my trauma through finger strokes."

Danielle, painting with one eye open, replied, "You're literally dating a bartender and pretending it's not serious. You're already finger-stroking your trauma."

"Excuse you," Asha shot back. "We're casually exclusive. And I am not the one bringing overnight bags with full-size lube and a maxi dress."

"Grown-woman gay," Danielle said. "We don't play."

Jamal burst through the back door ten minutes late, breathless and smiling. "My bad. Jasmine had me against the hallway mirror like I was the feature presentation."

Kiki cackled. "Good. Maybe you'll shut up for once."

He grabbed a wine glass and looked at everyone's paintings. "Why does Jean's look like a Rorschach test drawn by a sad dick?"

Jean didn't blink. "Because it is."

CC raised his glass. "To bad decisions, slow replies, and strap-ons that snap into place like vengeance."

The whole group toasted. Even the instructor raised her ginger beer.

Halfway through, the room turned philosophical the way it always did when wine hit marrow.

"Anyone else feel like they're being watched by a past version of themselves every time they do something soft?" Jean asked, not looking up from her canvas.

Danielle hummed. "Every time I let Christina rub my back without flinching, I feel like twenty-six-year-old me wants to slap the shit out of me for being so open."

"She'd lose," Jean replied.

"Only if she brought feelings to the fight," Danielle said.

Ramon said, "I still don't understand why straight people think communication is foreplay. Just say what you want."

Kiki nodded. "That's why I married him. Man told me on date three that he wanted to suck my soul out through my coochie and also pay off one of my student loans."

CC sipped slow. "A man with a financial plan and cunnilingus goals? That's love."

Jean's phone buzzed on the table. She glanced at it, then tucked it away.

"Déjà Vu?" Danielle asked.

Jean gave a smug smile. "Yes. And no, that's not his name. Y'all don't get to meet him until I decide if he's real or just really consistent."

Asha raised a brow. "What's the difference?"

Jean shrugged. "Time."

The instructor, trying to regain control, asked everyone to add gold paint to the canvas. "It's for the light source," she explained.

"Mine already got a light source," Jamal said, pointing to the vaguely erect blob on his canvas. "It's called 'Midday Wood.'"

CC leaned over and whispered, "Add veins. Make it real."

Kiki snorted her wine. "I swear y'all are a walking HR violation "

They painted. They talked. They laughed too hard. Nobody finished their canvas exactly as instructed.

Danielle's turned into a hazy dreamscape—muted tones, unfinished edges.

Jean's was precise but cold—every line deliberate, every shade calculated.

CC's had a heart hidden in the folds of a silhouette. He didn't mention it. But he saw it. And that was enough.

As they cleaned up, the instructor shook her head, smiling. "Y'all need help. But y'all tip better than God's favorite kids."

They left her a hundred in cash, a bottle of wine, and Jamal's number—uninvited.

Outside, CC pulled Jean aside. "You good?"

She nodded. "I think I might be."

"Crazy, right?"

Jean exhaled. "I don't trust it yet."

"None of us do," he replied. "But we're here anyway."

Danielle leaned over, catching the tail end. "I'll say this—if my gay ass and Jean's emotionally unavailable self can sit through a paint-and-sip without setting fire to our canvases, we might actually be healing."

CC raised his hands like praise dancers in a Baptist church. "Can I get an amen for grown folks not being a damn mess?"

Jean added, "Just don't expect me to cry at the wedding. If anyone ends up in a dress."

"Bitch, we know you'll cry," Danielle said.

"Only if the catering's good."

Later that night, Jean didn't bother undressing right away. She stepped out of her heels, dropped her bag by the chair, and poured herself one more inch of wine. It was a Friday, but it felt like a Sunday.

Déjà Vu had texted while she was still at the paint-and-sip: "Don't let the night end without telling me how you are."

Not, 'what did you do?' Not, 'send me a pic.'

Just that. 'How are you?'

She typed back: Light. I feel light. And hungry. And tired. And just fine.

He replied with a thumbs-up, then sent a follow-up: Can I say something reckless?

Jean stared at the screen: You can say anything.

A pause. Then: I like this version of you. She feels honest.

She didn't reply. Instead, she took the last sip of wine, wiped her mouth with the back of her hand, and smiled. She didn't know if he was right. But she hoped so.

Danielle folded the maxi dress neatly and placed it back in her overnight bag. She wasn't staying over tonight—Christina had an early conference call. No drama. No lingering. No weird shift in tone when they parted ways.

Christina kissed her cheek on the way out and said, "I'll call you when I'm human again."

Danielle had laughed and said, "Don't rush. I like the monster too."

She packed slow. Not dragging. Just calm. The way you do when you don't need to escape. Her mind wasn't racing. Her fingers weren't shaking. The overnight bag wasn't proof of readiness anymore—it was just what it looked like. A bag. For staying. Or leaving. Depending on the night.

She paused before zipping it shut and whispered, "So this is what trust feels like."

She didn't say it for affirmation. Just to hear it out loud.

CC sat in his kitchen, feet up on the counter, bowl of cereal in one hand and phone in the other.

DeMarcus had sent him a goodnight text an hour ago: Don't overthink today. I'm not grading you.

CC had responded: Good. Cause I'd be a solid B+ with room for tongue.

DeMarcus replied with a laughing emoji and a GIF of someone fanning themselves dramatically. That was it.

No need to dissect. No storm brewing. No crisis disguised as kink. Just peace. CC was learning to let the fire burn soft.

He looked around at his apartment—art still propped from the sip-and-paint, a single wine glass in the sink, and the same candle from earlier now burned all the way down.

He pulled out a sticky note and wrote: Stop running. You're already safe. Then stuck it on the fridge.

Ramon and Kiki were the first to pass out. Too much wine. Too much laughter. She curled into his chest like a lowercase question mark. He snored. She snored louder.

Asha and Jordan were closing the bar, texting quietly between steps behind the counter. It was smooth now. No drama. Just timing. That was enough.

Jean stood at her mirror in the dark. Not to check her face. Not to reapply anything. Just to look.

She whispered, "Okay." No performance. No armor. Just okay.

Chapter 21: I Want to Want Without Explaining Myself

Jean hadn't planned on brunch. She wasn't hungry. She wasn't sad. She wasn't trying to get cute for some impromptu sidewalk paparazzi moment. She just needed space. And the only place she could think to exist without consequence was an overpriced spot in SoHo where the mimosas were rude and the servers didn't care who you were.

She ordered a grapefruit spritz and stared at her phone.

Déjà Vu had texted three hours ago: Woke up thinking about your legs. Hope you're walking somewhere beautiful.

She hadn't replied. Not because she was playing coy—but because she was thinking about those exact legs wrapped around his back.

She sipped slow, letting the bubbles cut through her restraint. Her thumb hovered over the screen before she typed: They're walking fine. But they'd rather be over your shoulders.

She hit send before she could edit herself. Her stomach dropped. Not with fear. With appetite.

Two minutes passed. Then five.

She pretended to care about her eggs. She picked at arugula like it had insulted her in a past life. The waiter came by and asked if she wanted another spritz.

Jean didn't answer. Her phone lit up again: I'd be honored. But how do you feel about weekends away?

She blinked: Like…. out of town?

He answered: Out of town. Two nights. Just us. Good food. No pressure.

Jean put the phone facedown and took a breath. He hadn't said sex. He hadn't even said anything graphic. But something about the ease of the offer made her legs cross instinctively.

She thought about it while chewing on burnt toast.

Every man who ever tried to take her somewhere either made it sound like a reward or a trap. "Let me spoil you." "Let's see how we travel together." "You got your passport?" Always a performance. Always coded.

This didn't feel like that. It felt like…. consistency. Like someone planning not just the fuck, but the follow-through. And that scared the hell out of her.

She sent a voice note, brief and unbothered: Where?

He responded with a pin and the name of a small beach town just north of the city.

She looked it up. Not flashy. Quiet. Known for oysters, antique bookstores, and a boardwalk that had live music every Friday night. He was playing the long game. She admired that.

When the check came, she paid in cash and didn't wait for change.

Her phone buzzed again as she was walking out the door: Also, I don't snore. But I do hog pillows. You've been warned.

She replied: I don't snore either. But if the dick's good, I might hum in my sleep.

He sent back the melting emoji and a middle finger. Then another message: You're making it very hard not to fall.

She read it twice. Then typed: Don't fall. Walk. I'll walk too. We'll see where it leads.

She didn't run to the group chat. Didn't start a thread.

This wasn't that kind of story. This was the kind of moment you protected by keeping it small. Jean didn't need jokes or opinions. She didn't even need hype. She just needed to let herself want something without a backstory.

By the time she got home, she'd already started packing. Not fully. Just the little things. A new pair of earrings. Lip gloss. Panties that said, 'I thought about this trip ahead of time.' She pulled her robe tight and paused. "I'm not in love," she said out loud.

Danielle said, fingers typing too fast in the group thread: I think I have a kink.

It was late—after eleven—but CC responded within thirty seconds: Finally. Something's been off about you since you stopped dressing like a therapist who moonlights as a dominatrix.

Asha replied next: If it's toe-related, I'm leaving the group.

Danielle ignored them and kept going: No. It's worse. Christina wiped the corner of my mouth at dinner tonight. And I almost came.

Three dots. Then CC responded: So your kink is manners?

Danielle: It wasn't just that. She tucked my napkin into my lap and said 'I got you' and my whole clit lifted like it had praise privileges.

Jean popped in finally: You're a praise kink girlie. A good girl kink. It's always the cold ones.

Danielle: I'm not cold.

CC: You are a sexual winter with premium coochie under the snowpack. And apparently, all it takes is a folded napkin and a compliment to melt you.

Danielle: I wish I was kidding. She said 'that's a beautiful thought' after I shared something about my dad and my nipples hardened. Fully. In a cardigan.

Asha: You need help.

Jean: No, she needs dick with a mission statement. Somebody that calls her 'my love' and eats her out while she's still wearing pearls.

CC: Or a woman who knows how to slice a steak and bend her over a kitchen island. Honestly, I'm invested.

Danielle set her phone down and laughed, full belly, alone in her bed. Christina had already gone home. They didn't do sleepovers every night. They were grown. They had space. But the ache was still there—an ache born from sweetness, not tension.

It was new. It was working. And it terrified her.

She picked the phone back up and typed directly to Jean: I've never been turned on by soft things. That's what's scaring me. I'm used to edge. To obsession. To proving something.

Jean replied a few minutes later: Sometimes the softness is the flex. Knowing you don't need to be hurt to be seen.

Danielle read it twice. Then again. Then she whispered, "Fuck."

CC messaged her privately too. He never missed a moment to be funny, but this one came low and clear: I'm proud of you. Not because you're soft now. But because you're letting someone hold the version of you that doesn't perform toughness.

Danielle stared at it. Took a screenshot. Then deleted the screenshot before she could overanalyze her need to save it.

Back in the group thread, Jean added: This is the grownest group chat I've ever been part of. I hate it.

CC: Shut up. We're still filthy.

Jamal, who had only just chimed in, said: I got hard once just from hearing Jasmine say 'I paid the mortgage already.' That's love.

Danielle: That's debt relief. Totally different kink.

CC: Still counts. Your clit jumped from a napkin. Jamal's dick rose like Lazarus for financial stewardship. We all grown.

Asha: My turn-ons are men who apologize correctly and remember I don't like wet towels on the bed.

Jean: Mine are very tall, very well-read, and know how to shut up when I'm spiraling.

Danielle: Mine are women who say 'I'm not going anywhere' and mean it.

CC: Mine is DeMarcus. And yes, I'm saying his name tonight. I like him and I'm scared. That's my kink. Apparently, I like men who make me delete drafts and rethink my wardrobe.

Everyone sent the eye emojis.

Jamal: Look at us. One quiet-ass Friday night and suddenly everyone's healed and horny.

Danielle: We're not healed. We're just hydrated and freshly fucked. Don't jinx it.

Christina texted her a few minutes later, unprompted: Still thinking about you eating my mashed potatoes and moaning.

Danielle replied: Still thinking about how you looked when you handed me the fork.

There was a pause. Then: You're a problem.

Danielle: Only for people who don't know how to make me feel safe.

Christina didn't reply right away. When she did, it was just: Good thing I do.

Danielle went to bed horny, happy, and halfway embarrassed.

She wasn't in love. But her soul was definitely on its back, feet up. CC sat cross-legged on his bed with three candles burning and one AirPod in. Sade was playing. He had wine in his cup. His skin was oiled. His pillowcases were silk. And still, he was spiraling.

Not over DeMarcus. Over storage. Specifically: storage of the dick-ride anthology living on his phone.

He'd gone to delete one clip earlier. Just one. A blurry, poorly lit, low-angle shot from the pandemic era with a man he couldn't even name now—maybe Brandon? Braxton? Somebody with a "B" and a Benz that never really worked.

But when he tried to delete it, his thumb stalled. Because the angle was fire.

He dropped the phone on the bed, ashamed. "I have a problem," he muttered.

He opened the group thread and typed: Y'all ever try to delete old sex tapes but you can't because they're kind of cinematic?

Jean answered first: Delete the man. Keep the footage.

Danielle chimed in: Depends. Can you hear your own moans? If yes, delete. If not, keep. You deserve peace.

CC replied: Not only can you hear my moans, but you can also hear me directing. Like it's a damn studio shoot. There's lighting. Angles. Bitch, I said cut between rounds.

Asha: You're Spike Lee with a strap.

Jamal: Do y'all really record yourselves? Like camera propped and everything?

Jean: Sometimes. Other times it's POV. Depends on the vibe.

Danielle: I only record if I'm proud. Or if I know I might need evidence for the group chat.

CC: I have files. Categories. I call it The Digital D—k Museum. There's a spreadsheet with time stamps.

Asha: YOU NEED JESUS.

CC: I HAVE BEEN THE SECOND COMING FOR MANY.

He set the phone down again and pulled up his photo library. A scroll through his Private Album was like going on a historical tour of his finest sins.

There was the clip with the fireman who cried after they finished. The one with the lawyer who wore nothing but a chain and a cock ring. The short one with the flight attendant who liked it in the shower and said "more" like it was a safe word in reverse.

He had stories. He had…. footage. And now he had a boyfriend— or something like it. What the fuck was he supposed to do with this archive?

He typed back into the thread: So if you start seeing someone new, do you delete everything?

Jean: No. But I don't rewatch either. Feels like cheating in the cloud.

Danielle: I'm deleting mine this weekend. Not because Christina asked—but because I'm not that person anymore. I can't keep rewatching my pain with a good camera angle.

Asha: Archive it. Don't erase your history. Just don't live in it.

Jamal: I never record. My ass jiggles too much. Distracts from the art.

CC: Your art is finger painting. We get it.

The group was honest tonight. Nobody posturing. Just soft-core confessions.

CC added: I think I hoarded the videos because they made me feel desired. Even when I wasn't loved.

Danielle replied: That's fair. But you're loved now. So delete what makes you doubt that.

He sat with it. Then took a deep breath. And started deleting. Not all. But enough. Just enough to feel like he wasn't hiding in the past anymore.

DeMarcus texted: What are you doing right now?

CC stared at the screen for a long time before typing: Letting go of some ghosts.

A pause. Then DeMarcus replied: That's sexy. Want some company?

CC thought for three seconds. Yes. Bring snacks. I've got wine. And room.

He blew out two of the candles. The third stayed lit. Just in case.

It started with a toast. To what, no one remembered.
They were three drinks in at Velour Social, seated at their usual back table like it was a sacred altar. Jean had just returned from a facial. Danielle looked too relaxed. CC was glowing suspiciously. And Asha's cleavage looked like it had a legal team.

So naturally, the conversation turned to sex. More specifically: location.

"My wildest?" Jamal asked, like he had options. "Probably in the produce section of Whole Foods. Late night. Jasmine bent over the bananas."

Jean blinked. "In public?"

"Security footage is probably in the spank bank of some manager named Carl."

Danielle sipped her drink. "That's not a sex story. That's a crime scene."

Kiki leaned forward. "Okay, mine isn't crazy—but it was risky. Parking lot of a daycare center." Everyone groaned.

"It was Sunday!" she shouted. "The Lord's day! The kids were home!"

CC: "What was the playlist? Baby Shark?"

Ramon just lifted his glass and said, "Worth it."

Jean shook her head. "Mine was during a lightning storm in Barcelona. Rooftop terrace. I was tipsy, he was motivated, and there was one very elegant chaise lounge that is probably still haunted."

Asha blinked. "That's not wild. That's aspirational."

Danielle: "That's cinematic. The most exotic I've gotten was a hotel housekeeping closet during a wedding weekend. I was in my bridesmaid dress. She was in her server uniform. And the mop was very much watching."

Jean: "That's gay. And efficient."

CC: "Did the mop ask to join or just drip respectfully?"

Danielle: "It squeaked in support."

Asha drained her glass. "Alright. Y'all want real? Try this on." Everyone leaned in.

She continued, "Back when I was with my ex—you know the one who thought poly was short for politician—we went to a very upscale dinner party. Very Black. Very bougie. Very private."

CC: "I already like it."

"He takes me into the host's library and starts acting brand new. I'm trying to tell him no, we're guests, but he's already got his hands up my skirt."

Danielle: "Library is hot. Old books and bad decisions."

Asha: "I end up bent over a first edition copy of The Souls of Black Folk." Everyone SCREAMED.

Jamal: "Du Bois did NOT fight double consciousness for this!"

Kiki choked on her drink. "You fucked on Black history!"

Asha shrugged. "Technically, I fucked near it. The book survived."

Jean wiped tears from her eyes. "Oh my god. I'm crying. This is the best story I've ever heard."

CC stood up dramatically and bowed. "And the winner is Asha, for dick near Du Bois."

They all clapped like it was an award show. Asha took a bow. "Thank you. I'd like to thank bad decisions, strong cocktails, and the ancestors who turned their heads."

Danielle raised her glass. "To grown folks doing grown things in ridiculous places." Everyone joined in. Glasses clinked.

Jamal: "You ever think about how we're all actually nasty?"

Jean: "No, we're just old enough to admit it."

CC: "Speak for yourselves. I was born nasty. I just had better lighting by the time I turned twenty-three."

Danielle: "Honestly, I'm just glad no one here said something vanilla like 'in my bed, with my partner, under the stars'."

Asha: "Bitch, say you're boring and go."

Kiki: "My bed is exotic. Especially when Ramon does that tongue thing and I black out."

Ramon: "Allegedly."

CC looked around the table and smiled. This was the part no one understood.

People assumed this group was always deep, always processing, always healing. But this—the laughter, the filth, the way they roared and gasped and held each other accountable while drunk off truth—this was the real medicine.

The grown-up shit was nice. But the ratchet joy? That's what kept them alive.

They lingered at Velour Social longer than usual. The bar had emptied out. The music had dropped to soft background hums. Even the staff had stopped wiping things down. They knew the group would leave when they were good and ready.

Danielle leaned into Christina's last text again, rereading it like it was scripture. "Good thing I do." She hadn't replied. She didn't need to. Some things didn't require emojis or immediate cleverness. They just required acknowledgment. And space to keep becoming true.

Jean had her phone out too, scrolling through flight options. Déjà Vu hadn't followed up. He didn't need to. She'd said yes, and he believed her. That part still stunned her—being trusted without needing to prove anything.

She clicked into a hotel website and skimmed the images. The room had a soaking tub and a private terrace. That was enough. She booked it without hesitation.

Then texted: Don't overpack. Bring everything that matters. That's it.

He replied ten minutes later: I just need one thing. And she's already going.

CC watched Asha with quiet curiosity. She'd been on her phone more than usual tonight. Not typing. Just smiling. Sipping. Glancing up. Then back down again.

He waited until Jean and Danielle were debating the merits of wool coats in a post-global-warming world before leaning toward her and whispering, "You textin' my favorite bartender?"

Asha didn't even blink. "Maybe."

CC grinned. "He got a dick vein that sings, don't he?" Asha choked on her drink.

"I've never seen it," CC added quickly, "but you know I've got a gift for assessing potential."

Asha wiped her mouth, laughing. "You're not wrong. But that's not why I'm smiling."

"Then what is?" She paused. Then said, "Because he told me he missed my face. Not my body. Not my jokes. Just… my face."

CC sat back, impressed. "Damn. That's sexy as hell."

"Right?"

Minutes passed. Then Asha stood, gathered her things, and tossed cash on the table.

"You out?" Danielle asked.

Asha nodded. "He's off shift. I'm not trying to overthink it. I just want to be near him."

Jean raised an eyebrow. "No announcement?"

"Fuck no."

Danielle: "You not even gonna give us a clue?"

Asha leaned down, kissed Danielle's forehead, then whispered, "Just know, if I start bringing full-size conditioner to work, mind your business."

She walked out without another word. CC watched her go. Watched the door close. Watched the moment settle. Then said, "She gon' act like she not in love—but she ordered lingerie last week. I saw the cart."

Everyone turned. CC shrugged. "Y'all forget we shared an Amazon account once. Before she got bougie with Prime."

Danielle laughed. "This group is toxic. In the best way."

Jean added, "You know what I'm realizing?"

"What?" CC asked.

"All of us are still here. Still fucked up. Still wild. But somehow.... softer."

Danielle nodded. "That softness snuck up on us."

CC raised his glass. "To being hard when necessary, soft when earned, and nasty no matter what." They clinked glasses one last time.

Chapter 22: You're Not the Problem. But You Might Be the Pattern

Jean had her hair pulled back in a low bun and wore hoops big enough to carry groceries in. Déjà Vu was picking her up. She'd kept the outfit grown—linen slacks, a backless halter, soft gloss. It was giving intentional but unbothered.

He texted: Outside. No rush.

She checked herself in the mirror, took one last sip of sparkling water, and left before she could second-guess anything.

He looked good. Not aggressively. Just…. clean. Dark tee, wide smile, cologne that had restraint.

He hugged her tight when she slid into the passenger seat, said, "Missed your face," and didn't press for more.

Jean felt her body unclench. This man didn't need her to be entertaining. She didn't have to build a thesis just to earn a kiss.

They drove with the windows cracked. Good weather. Good silence.

But then he parked outside the restaurant, and it happened.

A woman—tall, stunning, Afro pulled into a bun that made her whole aura float—walked past and called out, "D, that you?"

He lit up. "Yo! What are you doing here?" They hugged. Full-body. Familiar.

Jean didn't move.

Déjà Vu introduced them: "Jean, this is Nia. She's an old friend from the wellness center I used to teach at."

Nia smiled. "I've heard your name."

Jean just nodded. "Hope it was flattering."

Nia laughed, said her goodbyes, and left in a swirl of sage energy.

Jean followed him into the restaurant, already fighting herself.

They ordered drinks. Déjà Vu was easy. Still calm. He didn't bring it up.

Jean did. "So…. Nia. That your ex?"

He raised an eyebrow. "No. Just a friend. One I haven't seen in months. Why?"

Jean sipped. "You lit up like she was edible."

He paused. "You mad at how I smiled? Or that I didn't edit myself to make you feel safe?"

That shut her up.

Lunch moved on. Food came. Conversation wobbled.

She nitpicked his order. Mocked his attachment to ginger beer. Asked two or three probing questions too fast—like she was looking for a crack in his calm.

Finally, he set his fork down and said, "You know this isn't the vibe, right?"

She blinked. "What vibe?"

"The one we've had every day since you texted me. Since you said yes. You're here—but you're not here."

Jean opened her mouth to object, but nothing came out. He wasn't accusing her. He was just…. honest. She hated how much it disarmed her.

Back in the car, he didn't put on music. Didn't force a joke. He drove her home and walked her to the door.

She turned toward him and said, "I'm not used to men like you."

He replied, "You don't have to be. You just have to be honest when you're scared."

She looked away. "That easy, huh?"

"No. Not at all. But worth it."

After he left, Jean sat on the couch and stared at her phone.She pulled up the group chat, typed something, then deleted it.

She opened a private message to CC instead and typed: I think I just sabotaged a good moment. I don't even know why. I can't even enjoy healthy without side-eyeing it.

CC replied almost instantly: Because healthy doesn't flirt the way trauma does. But it loves better. Don't run.

She hearted it. Didn't respond. Just sat there, wine untouched.

The part of her that used to feel powerful after these moments— the one who always made the guy chase—was…. silent. And it was the silence that scared her the most.

Danielle didn't want to go to the event. Ellie had begged. The firm was sponsoring a new mental health initiative and wanted all the top talent to show face. Christina was already attending as part of her organization's board. It should've been an easy night.

She wore the soft navy jumpsuit Christina liked. The one with the plunging neckline and gold zipper she never fully closed. She looked good. She felt good. Until they walked into the room—and there was Selena.

Not across the room. Not near the bar. Right. By. The. Sign-in table.

Of course she was on the guest list. Of course no one warned her. Of course the universe chose tonight.

Danielle didn't stop walking. Christina's hand touched her lower back lightly, and they moved in sync. Selena saw them. And smiled.

Christina clocked it immediately. "Problem?"

"No," Danielle said calmly. "Just expired food I didn't expect to see out in public."

Christina laughed under her breath. "Noted."

They made it halfway across the room before Selena intercepted. "Danielle. Wow. I didn't know you were still around."

Danielle turned. "Still employed. Still paid. Still centered. Can't say the same for everyone."

Selena's eyes narrowed just enough. "So this is her?"

Christina stepped forward without blinking. "Christina. Nice to meet you."

Selena offered her hand. Christina didn't take it. Just smiled with full lips and said, "We don't do handshakes. We do earned intimacy."

Selena chuckled like she was above it all. "Cute. Well. I hope you two enjoy the evening."

Danielle nodded slowly. "I would say I wish you well, but I think you've always gotten exactly what you go looking for—chaos, absence, distance. I'm just glad I'm no longer what you seek."

Christina turned slightly and said, "Should've worn better shoes for that exit line."

Selena's face hardened. She walked away. Not quickly. But with that stiff neck people get when they know they've lost the power dynamic and nothing they say will fix it.

Christina didn't say anything for the next ten minutes. She didn't need to. She held Danielle's hand tighter. She touched her shoulder during a long conversation with Ellie. She refilled her drink when a waiter passed by without catching Danielle's eye.

Not one act was performative. Everything was intentional. Everything was care.

They made it through the evening, back to Danielle's place, and were halfway through unzipping each other when Danielle paused. "I need to say something."

Christina stepped back, pulled the zipper up an inch. "Say it "

Danielle took a breath. "I've never had someone stand next to me like that before. Not because they were trying to prove something. Just because they knew I needed it."

Christina sat on the edge of the bed, looking at her fully. "I'm not here to compete with ghosts. I'm here to give you peace."

Danielle blinked. "That's the most dangerous thing anyone's ever said to me."

Christina: "Why?"

Danielle: "Because I might believe you."

They kissed soft, long, unhurried. There was no urgency in the way their clothes came off. No rush in the way their hands explored each other's backs and stomachs and collarbones.

It wasn't about sex. Not yet. It was about presence.

And Danielle realized—somewhere between nipple grazes and Christina's laugh against her neck—that she hadn't performed once tonight. She hadn't calculated. She hadn't run defense. She'd just… let it happen.

Later, Christina was asleep, her arm across Danielle's stomach like it was born to rest there.

Danielle stared at the ceiling. Not scared. Not overthinking. Just whispering, "Okay. Okay. Okay," like a spell she finally believed might work.

Later that night, Asha opened the door to her apartment, and there he was. Jordan. Quiet. Tired. But smiling. He stepped inside, closed the door, and just looked at her.

She didn't ask for more. She didn't need to. He cupped her cheek, kissed her once, and said, "You feel like home."

Asha didn't cry. She didn't yell. She didn't even flinch. She just said, "Oh."

Jordan had said it casually—almost offhand. "Yeah, there's this spot in Denver. Real high-end, but relaxed. They reached out. It's early, though."

They were on her couch, post-shift, postsex, halfway through their usual "watch something we'll talk through the entire time" ritual. His arm was around her. His voice soft. Nothing about the moment was threatening. Except that it was.

"Would you take it?" she asked, trying to sound nonchalant.

Jordan shrugged. "Maybe. I don't know. It'd be a big move. New vibe. New city."

"Big step."

"Right." Pause.

"You told anyone?"

"No. Just you."

Asha nodded. "Cool."

She got up like she had to pee. Stayed in the bathroom ten full minutes. Not spiraling. Just sitting. Hands in her lap. Phone facedown. Counting tiles.

He hadn't done anything wrong. But it still hit wrong.

When she came out, he was already half-asleep on the couch. She didn't say anything. Just pulled a blanket over him, kissed his forehead, and turned the lights off.

The next day, she told Jean over mid-morning matcha. Jean didn't interrupt. Didn't give advice. Just listened. "I'm not mad," Asha said. "That's the problem. I want to be mad. But I'm just…. scared. And I hate that."

Jean stirred her drink. "You care."

Asha looked away. "I didn't plan on caring."

"No one does."

A pause. Then Jean added: "He didn't say he was leaving. He said he might be tempted."

"Same difference."

"No. One's packing. The other's asking who he wants to stay for."

Asha rolled her eyes. "I'm not asking anyone to stay for me."

"Did he ask you to?"

"No."

"Then why are you fighting a war that hasn't started?"

Asha slumped back. "Because I don't know what I want. And that scares the shit out of me."

Jean leaned forward. "But you know you want something."

Asha nodded, slowly. "Yeah. I do."

That night, Asha didn't text Jordan. He didn't text her either.

The silence wasn't angry—it just sat between them like luggage no one wanted to claim.

She replayed his tone. His posture. The way he said "just you" like it mattered. She knew it did. She just didn't know what she was supposed to do with that kind of weight. Not yet.

CC stared at his phone for the third time in an hour. DeMarcus's name sat at the top of the message thread.

No new message. No dots. Just silence. And the last text? Still unopened.

It was a voice note. Sent two nights ago. CC hadn't tapped it. Not because he didn't care—but because he cared too much. It was easier to avoid sincerity than risk drowning in it.

Now, the air was different. DeMarcus wasn't following up. Wasn't nudging. Wasn't doing the sweet, low-effort checkin CC had secretly started to expect. And that terrified him.

He typed: Hey. Sorry for the delay. I got distracted. You good?

Then deleted it. Then typed again: Didn't mean to leave you hanging. Just been a lot going on.

Delete. Eventually he just wrote: Thinking of you. No reply.

CC finally tapped the voice note. DeMarcus's voice filled the room —deep, unhurried, warm. "I don't want anything tonight. Just wanted to say I miss you. Your voice. Your mind. Your whole weird way of seeing the world. That's it." Click. Silence.

CC swallowed hard. Why the fuck hadn't he listened to that before? Because he was scared of softness. Because if you don't open the door, you can pretend no one was ever knocking.

He called. Straight to voicemail.

He texted again: I listened. I'm sorry. That message deserved a better version of me. No reply.

He sat down on his bed, phone in lap, candles unlit, hair undone. No music. Just shame.

He opened a new thread to the group chat. Typed a joke. Deleted it. He wasn't in a joke mood. This wasn't funny.

He scrolled back through the thread with DeMarcus. The teasing. The fire. The slow way things built.

Then he stopped on one line DeMarcus had sent two weeks ago: I know you like control. But one day you'll realize love doesn't ask for choreography—it just wants to show up.

CC had hearted it back then. Now it felt like prophecy.

He dropped his phone on the floor. Laid back. Whispered to the ceiling, "I'm not used to being chosen without having to perform for it."

Then he added, quieter, "But I want to learn."

The phone stayed silent all night. And for the first time in weeks, CC didn't sleep well.

The table looked the same. Same corner booth. Same dim light. Same cocktails with over-the-top garnishes and dramatic names. CC's drink had a flower floating in it. Jean's looked like it could burn through glass. Asha was back on tequila. Danielle had something bourbon-based and adult.

But the vibe? Was off. Not broken. Just… thinner.

Jamal arrived last, dropped into the seat like it was a reunion. "Why y'all look like your therapists broke up with you?" Nobody laughed.

He tried again. "Is this a funeral or a fuck-it Friday?" Still nothing.

Jean finally spoke. "We're all just… in our feelings, apparently."

Danielle stirred her drink. "And apparently none of us know what to do with that."

Asha offered a weak smile. "Maybe this is the part where we realize we're not funny all the time."

CC responded, "Speak for yourself. I'm just editing the jokes before I say them now."

Jamal asked, "Why?"

CC answered, "Because I'm scared I'll say something that was true, but isn't anymore."

Jean exhaled. "I had lunch with Déjà Vu. And I almost ruined it for no reason. The man was perfect. And I got triggered by a hug."

Danielle said, "I confronted Selena in front of Christina." Everyone turned.

"And she handled it with complete grace. Which pissed me off. Because I'm not used to being that protected. Not without there being a cost."

Asha said, "Jordan might be moving. He hasn't decided. But I realized… I want him to stay. And I didn't know I felt that until I hated that I felt it."

CC added, "I left a good man on read. And now he might be gone. I've been trying to be seen without letting anyone see me."

Silence. Not heavy. Just real.

Jamal raised a hand. "I'm sorry, I thought we were still doing jokes. But now I feel like I'm at a spoken word open mic called Vulnerability & Vodka." They laughed—quiet, but real.

Jean said, "We're not broken. Just shifting."

Danielle returned with, "Growth doesn't feel good. That's why most people avoid it."

CC added, "Shit, I'd take another trauma bond and a weekend dick binge over this introspective mess."

Asha called him out. "Liar."

CC agreed. "True. But still."

They clinked glasses. The sound didn't ring as loud. But it landed.

After a beat, Jean added, "You know what scares me most?" Everyone looked up.

"That everything's technically fine. I'm not being cheated on. Nobody's lying. Nobody's ghosting. I'm just scared because there's no crisis to distract me."

Danielle: "You can't be calm because you don't know what to do with calm."

Jean nodded. "Exactly."

Asha: "We've been the fire department for our own lives so long, we don't know how to sit down without checking the walls for smoke."

Jamal finished his drink. "So what now?" No one answered right away.

Then CC raised his glass again. "To us."

Jean added. "To not falling apart."

Asha added to that. "To being present even when it's uncomfortable."

Danielle put here two cents in. "To walking toward good things without sabotaging them."

Jamal then finished the toast with, "To me staying the comedic relief, because y'all are exhausting." They laughed again. This time, it rang louder.

Chapter 23: Either You Want Me or You Want the Performance

Jean was already irritated, and she couldn't figure out why. Her hair was cooperating. Her skin looked luminous. Déjà Vu had sent a text that said "Thinking about your thighs. Also, your brain. But mostly your thighs." It was perfect. It was grown. It was filthy in all the right ways.

So why did she feel like picking a fight? She didn't have to wonder long.

He knocked lightly, holding coffee and a bag of pastries. Not from a chain—some little boutique bakery he said reminded him of her. "A little dramatic, a little expensive, but worth it."

Jean opened the door in a silk robe she hadn't even tried to tie properly. He smiled. "You always answer the door like you're about to be painted."

Jean: "Don't ask for access to the exhibit if you don't like the art."

He handed her the bag. "Fair "

They sat on her couch with no music, just the quiet hum of grown tension. Déjà Vu looked relaxed. Jean looked like a warrior disguised as a woman in leisurewear.

"So," he said, sipping, "you good "

Jean sipped too. "Define good."

"You haven't texted since the restaurant. Just wanted to check in."

She shrugged. "I figured if I needed to explain why I got quiet, then maybe you weren't as emotionally intuitive as I thought."

He blinked. "You're adorable when you weaponize logic."

Jean raised an eyebrow. "Adorable is for puppies. I'm precision."

Déjà Vu nodded. "Okay. So… precision. You still mad about Nia?"

"I wasn't mad."

"Cool. So this is just your natural Wednesday mood?"

She stood up. Pacing. "I didn't like how casual it all felt. Like you could slip into connection with anyone. Like I'm not… different."

He tilted his head. "So because I hugged someone I know, you felt replaceable?"

Jean froze. That was exactly it. She hated that he named it.

He kept going. "You know I'm not asking you to be cool with everything. But I am asking for honesty. You ghosted me the first time around. No shade—it was your right. But if you're gonna show up now, don't make me beg you to stay present."

Jean folded her arms. "You're doing a lot of assumptions right now."

He stood up, but not angry. "No. I'm doing a lot of boundaries. There's a difference."

Jean opened her mouth—ready to fire something mean and impressive—but nothing came out.

She hated that even her shade felt weak around him. He leaned in. "I didn't come back to audition for your affection. I came back because I thought you already gave it. If I was wrong, say that. But don't make me jump through hoops you didn't even know you had until I got here."

Jean whispered, "Damn. You could've just called me clingy and kept it moving."

Déjà Vu grinned. "I don't do basic insults. You're better than that."

He kissed her forehead. That was it. And left.

Jean stood in the center of her apartment like someone had unplugged her sass and left her with just… truth. She sat down. Opened the group chat. Almost typed.

Instead, she called CC directly. "Girl," he said before hello. "If this is about the man who reads books and makes you feel something, I'm busy being emotionally stunted. Call back later."

Jean exhaled hard. "You're gonna listen or I'm showing up at your place with no bra and a grudge."

"Ooh, threats. Fine. What happened?"

She told him. Everything. The forehead kiss. The emotional clarity. The part where she had nothing snarky left to deflect with. CC was quiet for a beat.

Then said, "You've met a man who's immune to bad bitch manipulation. He's grown. You're grown. It's disgusting. I love it."

Jean laughed despite herself. "I hate this," she said.

"I know," he replied. "Means it's real."

After they hung up, Jean replayed the last thing Déjà Vu said, "If I was wrong, then say that."

She wasn't ready to say anything yet. But she was ready to stop hiding behind everything else.

Christina had offered to take Danielle out. Danielle said no. Then yes. Then changed her mind again.

Eventually, Christina just showed up with Thai takeout, wine, and a stack of HBO Max options. "No pants, no plans, no pressure," she said at the door. "Just carbs and consent."

Danielle opened it in a hoodie and sleep shorts. "You're lucky you're hot."

Christina walked in, kissed her on the cheek, and replied, "You're lucky I'm patient."

They sat on the couch cross-legged, eating from the same tray, sipping wine, and talking about absolutely nothing. It was perfect.

Until Danielle started talking about Ellie's office and that turned into talking about the networking event and that turned into the Selena incident.

Christina said nothing for the first half of the story. Then quietly asked, "And how did that make you feel?"

Danielle narrowed her eyes. "Are you therapizing me right now?"

"Nope. I just want to know where your heart went in that moment."

Danielle blinked. Looked away. "It… slowed down," she said finally. "You didn't flinch. You didn't make me explain. You didn't even step in. You just stood beside me like a bodyguard with a law degree and better skincare."

Christina laughed. Danielle didn't.

"I'm not used to that."

"To what?"

"To being protected without having to earn it first."

Christina leaned in. "You don't have to perform peace for me. You don't have to earn safety. You just get to have it."

Danielle exhaled through her nose. "That sounds good. But it's terrifying."

Christina asked, "Why?"

Danielle answered, "Because if I believe it, and you leave, then I'm not just heartbroken—I'm humiliated."

There it was. Raw. Ugly. Honest.

Christina reached over and touched her wrist—not in pity, but with purpose. "I'm not here to audition either, Danielle. I want love, not applause."

Danielle whispered, "I might not know how to give that."

Christina smirked. "Well. Lucky for you, I'm patient and hot."

Danielle laughed. Loud. Finally.

They finished dinner. Watched half of a movie neither of them remembered. Ended up horizontal, tangled in each other, skin on skin, laughter laced through kisses.

It wasn't the wildest sex they'd had. But it was the most revealing. After, Christina lay behind her, arm draped around her waist, breath slow and steady.

Danielle whispered, "If I get weird again, don't let me sabotage this." Christina didn't say anything. Just kissed the back of her neck and tucked her tighter.

The next morning, Danielle texted Asha: I cried after sex. Not like deep sobs. Just a few grown-ass tears. Still counts, right?

Asha replied: Bitch that counts as an emotional baptism. Welcome.

She stared at the message and laughed to herself. Then whispered, "Okay." Then again, softer, "Okay."

CC didn't know what to wear, so naturally he wore everything. Cheetah print jacket. Tiny cowboy hat. Black mesh shirt with the nipples cut out—by design, not by damage.

He looked like he was going to seduce a gospel singer and sell incense afterward. Which, if things went well, he might.

DeMarcus was already seated when he arrived—same chill posture, same heavy ring on his finger, same smile that made CC consider therapy and a tetanus shot at the same time.

"You look…" DeMarcus began.

"Expensive? Gay? Like I run a church where everyone tithes in flavored lube?"

DeMarcus laughed. "I was gonna say 'intentional.' But all of that too."

They ordered drinks. Water for him. Whiskey for CC. He needed the burn. He took a deep breath.

"I owe you an apology. I let your message sit. I let you sit. And not because I didn't care—but because I cared so much I panicked."

DeMarcus nodded. "I know."

CC blinked. "Wait, that's it? No emotional monologue?"

"You thought I didn't know you were emotionally avoidant with killer eyebrows and a savior complex?"

CC tried not to smile. "The eyebrow thing is genetic. The avoidance is curated."

DeMarcus sipped his water. "I'm not mad. I just needed to see if your silence was a pattern or a pause."

CC sat with that. Then finally asked, "And what did you decide?"

"That you were scared, not stupid."

CC exhaled. "I am. Scared, I mean. You treat me like I'm not a circus act. And that shit feels foreign."

DeMarcus leaned in. "I treat you like someone I see. Not someone I'm trying to rescue."

CC felt his throat tighten. So naturally, he cracked a joke. "You can't be this patient and still have a dick. That has to be illegal."

DeMarcus smirked. "I assure you I do. And it's in excellent working condition."

"See, and that's what's wrong with y'all soft-spoken, spiritual niggas. You hit you with a quote, then a stroke, and suddenly I'm in love and financially reorganizing my credit."

DeMarcus laughed. "I'm not here to play you, CC. I'm here to know you."

Silence. Soft. Heavy.

CC sipped his drink and whispered, "I want to try. Like…. really try."

DeMarcus said, "Then let's try."

They left the restaurant hand-in-hand. No dramatic kiss. No violins. Just two grown men walking back to someone's place, ready to talk more… or maybe not.

CC didn't text the group chat. Didn't post. Didn't perform. He just… let it be.

Later that night, he curled up on the couch wearing one of DeMarcus's hoodies that was clearly not his size.

He FaceTimed Asha. She answered, no makeup, bonnet on, eating noodles. "You look like growth," she said.

"I feel like confusion in a good wig," CC replied.

She grinned. "Means it's working."

Jordan was waiting outside when Asha got off work. He wasn't leaning on anything. Wasn't scrolling his phone. Just standing there like a grown-ass man with clear intentions.

"Hey," he said, smiling like a secret she wasn't supposed to know yet.

"Hey," she replied, cautiously. "You okay?"

He nodded. "I turned the job down."

She blinked. "You what?"

"I turned the job down. The new place. The move. All of it."

Asha stood still. Processing. The sidewalk felt like it got louder. She could hear her heartbeat in her ears. "Why?" she asked.

Jordan shrugged. "I didn't want to leave. Not really. I just needed to know if I mattered."

Asha swallowed. "And now you do?"

"No. Now I know I always did. I was just waiting for you to realize it."

She looked down at her shoes. Then back at him. Then laughed— sharp and sudden. "You are very casual about big life decisions."

He nodded. "I'm casual with pressure. Not with you."

They started walking. She didn't say where they were going. He didn't ask. Half a block later, she said, "You want to come over?"

"Sure."

"I have wine."

"Good."

"And a new vibrator that hasn't been tested yet."

Jordan stopped. "Is this a setup?"

"No. This is me making sure you're not just turning down life opportunities for forehead kisses and dry hugs."

Jordan leaned in. "If you let me stay the night, I'll test that theory."

She laughed. "Let's go."

They didn't rush. They didn't perform. They just were. And the sex wasn't loud. It wasn't wild. But it was personal. Asha kept her eyes open the whole time. And for once, so did he.

Afterward, tangled in sheets, she asked, "Why didn't you push harder? Why didn't you say something when I kept dodging the conversation?"

Jordan looked at the ceiling. "Because I wanted to know who you were when nobody was begging you to be anything."

She turned to face him. "That's a lot of pressure for someone who just faked a cramp to pause mid-head."

He grinned. "I knew you were lying."

Asha smirked. "The lie was for both of us."

They fell asleep before midnight. No TV. No scrolling. Just breathing. And it was the most adult thing Asha had done in a long time.

In the morning, she texted CC: I think I'm happy. Like... borderline domestic. If I start looking at Pinterest countertops, pull me out.

CC replied: Bitch I already found you a backsplash. You're staying.

CC's rooftop was giving exactly what it needed to give. String lights. Plush pillows. Candles that smelled like generational wealth and emotional maturity. Two bottles of prosecco chilling in a hammered metal tub that he claimed he got from "a lesbian-owned boutique in Lisbon."

Danielle whispered to Jean, "He got that from HomeGoods."

CC turned around instantly. "I heard that. And yes, I did, but it was the section inspired by Lisbon. So I wasn't lying."

Everyone was there. Jean, Danielle, Asha, Jamal, Ramon, Kiki.

No announcements. No hard reveals. Just soft smiles and grown silence.

Asha was tucked next to Jordan on the corner couch. Jean looked suspiciously calm. CC was barefoot with a toe ring. Danielle looked happy in a way that was almost suspicious.

Jamal took one look and said, "Okay, who's dying? This energy is too…. centered."

Jean: "Shut up."

Kiki: "Yeah, shut up and pour the prosecco."

They passed glasses around. Nobody toasted right away. Then Danielle raised hers. "To fine." Everyone paused.

She clarified. "Not fine like sexy. Fine like when you say you're okay and people know you're lying, but you're trying anyway."

Jean: "To flawed."

Asha: "To trying again without pretending you forgot what happened last time."

CC: "To therapy we can't afford but are slowly becoming."

Kiki: "To dick that isn't worth our trauma, but was worth a few memorable nights."

Ramon just raised his glass silently like a man who knew better than to compete. They drank. They laughed. Then they settled.

Jean said quietly, "I almost pushed Déjà Vu away. And not with words—with my silence. I used to think silence gave me power. But now I know it just keeps people too far to love me." Nobody rushed to respond.

Danielle said, "Christina told me she's not here to audition for my trust. She wants peace, not applause. And I didn't know how to accept that without performing. I still don't."

Asha added, "Jordan didn't ask me to choose. He just chose me. And I didn't realize how loud that could be until the silence scared me more than commitment."

CC sat forward, voice softer than usual. "DeMarcus said he wasn't going to chase. And I almost let that be the end. But when I apologized, he didn't rub it in. He just… saw me. I don't think I've ever had that before."

Jamal blinked. "Okay, but can we get back to the part where we laugh and pretend we're not evolving?"

Kiki clinked her glass against his. "You're evolving too, idiot."

Jamal: "No I'm not."

Ramon: "He's been washing dishes before bed."

Jamal: "That's not growth. That's cohabitation survival." Everyone laughed.

Jean looked out over the skyline. "We've survived a lot. And we're still here. Still fucking trying."

Danielle said, "Still telling each other when the old version of us starts creeping back in."

Asha then spoke. "Still talking shit and calling it healing."

CC said, "Still wearing toe rings unironically."

Jamal shrugged. "Still me."

Kiki told him, "You're the only one I'm worried about."

They all leaned into each other as the sky dimmed and the city breathed around them. No big climax. No shocking reveal. Just the quiet joy of still showing up.

CC raised his glass one more time. "To endings that don't feel like failures."

Jean raised hers next. "And beginnings that don't ask for perfection."

Danielle said, "And people who don't need our performances."

Asha closed the toast with, "Just our presence."

They drank. And for the first time in a long time, fine didn't feel like settling. It felt like a place to begin.

Chapter 24: Wait… That's Not a Draft

Jean woke up next to him and felt something that should've terrified her: peace. Not adrenaline. Not déjà vu. Peace.

That was the wildest part—this didn't feel familiar anymore. It wasn't a ghost of something almost. It was new. Present. Alive.

The nickname no longer fit. So she rolled over, stretched against his warmth, and said for the first time: "Good morning, Moses."

No hesitation. No joke to cushion it. Just truth. He smiled without opening his eyes. "Good morning, Jean."

He was already in the kitchen later, shirtless and humming some gospel remix of SZA. There was oat milk in the fridge that she didn't buy, and he was using her skillet like he had a lease on it.

Jean didn't flinch. She smiled. That's how bad it had gotten. Peace made her smile. That's when she should've known the devil was nearby.

After he left for a conference call, Jean sat at her desk to do a little work catch-up. Email, invoices, a few saved drafts she used like a journal so she wouldn't throw shade in the group chat. She was scrolling when she saw it.

Subject: I Still Don't Trust Him

She rolled her eyes at her own dramatic ass. "Girl, that's growth adjacent," she muttered, clicking to reread it and delete the mess before anyone saw it.

Except. It wasn't in Drafts. It was in Sent. Jean stared at the screen like it had slapped her.

Not only had it gone through—but the recipient? Moses.

The message was just a couple lines:

He's patient. Kind. Smart. Beautiful even. But I don't trust it. I've dated mirrors before. They reflect what you want until they crack.

I'm scared this is another one of those. I don't want to lose him. But I don't want to lose myself either.

No greeting. No sign-off. Just vulnerability with no damn seatbelt.

Her phone buzzed ten minutes later.

Moses: Got your email. Don't worry—I'll take the hint.

No emoji. No period. Just flat. Clean. Goodbye-adjacent.

Jean stood up so fast she knocked her chair over.

She grabbed her phone, typed: Wait. That wasn't for you. It was a journal entry. I wasn't—

She stopped. Deleted it. Typed again: You weren't supposed to read that.

Then deleted that too. She needed a reset.

She texted CC: I sent it.

CC: What?

Jean: The draft. The damn draft. It went to him. Moses. The Moses. The I-wake-up-smiling-next-to-you one.

CC: Girl… no. Not that email.

Jean responded with one word: Yep.

CC replied with a meme of Viola Davis walking out with her purse and coat.

Jean wrote back: It was honest. It just wasn't… ready.

CC: So you were emotionally naked and hit send. That's called streaking.

Jean: Help.

CC: Bitch, you better put on some emotional panties and go fix it.

Jean sat back down, heart pounding. She wasn't panicking because she sent her fears. She was panicking because they were true.

Moses hadn't called. He hadn't texted back.

Jean paced the living room. Then froze. Then opened her group text app. Asha was busy. Danielle was probably mid-coffee and power lesbian cuddles. Jamal would make it worse.

She sighed. She'd been so careful for so long. Never letting anyone too close. Now one slip and she was exposed.

She texted Moses directly: I'm sorry. It wasn't meant to hurt you. But it was real. And maybe that's worse.

Then she added: You don't have to respond. I just needed you to know the difference between a fear and a warning.

She hit send. No turning back now.

Danielle was already halfway through typing her response to Jean's message when Christina walked into the kitchen.

Jean: I sent him the email. Not the funny one. The one I didn't want anyone to see. He saw it. I am not OK.

Danielle's reply had been simple: You're gonna be fine. He knows it was fear. You've got this.

Then she hit delete. Not because it was untrue. Because it was too easy.

Christina was watching her, barefoot with a coffee mug and a headwrap that could've won awards. "Everything okay?" she asked.

Danielle nodded reflexively. "Jean's spiraling. Sent the wrong email."

Christina didn't flinch. Just sipped.

Danielle added, "It happens."

Christina raised an eyebrow. "To who?"

Danielle: "Me. It's happened to me."

Christina: "And how did it feel when people told you you'd be fine?"

Danielle paused. "Like I wasn't being heard."

"Exactly."

They moved to the couch, Danielle dragging the blanket with her like a protective shield. Christina sat at the far end, angled toward her but giving her space.

"Why are you always the one who holds everyone else together?" Christina asked, casual but direct.

Danielle tried to smile. "Because I'm good at it."

"No. You're practiced at it. Different thing."

Danielle swallowed. "Somebody has to keep it together. This crew has grown but we're all still one heartbreak away from disappearing into bad decisions."

Christina nodded. "So you're the glue." Danielle didn't respond.

Christina leaned forward. "But glue dries out, babe. And nobody notices until it starts cracking."

Danielle bit the inside of her cheek. "I'm not fragile."

"I didn't say you were. I said you're not present. There's a difference."

Danielle's voice dropped. "I am present."

Christina shook her head. "You perform presence. You show up, yes. But you don't let anyone see you unless you're in control of what they get." Danielle looked down.

Christina softened. "You think I don't know how hard it is for someone like you to fall? You're measured. You're careful. You don't say things you haven't run through three simulations. But baby... falling isn't about math. It's about trust."

Danielle's voice cracked. "I don't trust it yet."

Christina nodded. "Then say that. Don't pretend you're handling me."

Danielle laughed, but it wasn't funny. "I've been handling people my whole life."

Christina: "And how's that working for your heart?" Silence.

Danielle took a breath. "You want me messy? Unfinished? Scared
"

Christina: "No. I want you real. If the fear is part of it, bring that too."

Danielle blinked slowly. "I don't know how to do that."

"You don't have to know. You just have to stop hiding behind strength."

There it was. No yelling. No drama. Just raw truth over coffee.

Danielle finally texted Jean back: You are allowed to panic. You are allowed to fear. And you're still worthy of love. Especially when you don't feel like it.

She looked over at Christina. "Thank you," she said.

"For what?"

"For not letting me get away with that neat little response I was about to send."

Christina smiled. "Strong doesn't mean available. And I don't need a superhero. I just want you."

Danielle moved closer. She didn't lean in. She didn't perform it. She just was.

Later, she texted the group: Reminder: We don't earn love. We accept it. Even when it shows up too soon or too strong.

Jean replied with one word: Noted.

Asha's manager asked if she had a minute. In bar culture, that usually meant one of three things: You messed up, someone else messed up and they're about to blame you, or… they're promoting you and want to see if you're emotionally stable enough to handle it without doing a body roll. Today, it was door number three.

"You've been solid," her manager said, leaning on the counter like he had gossip to share. "Professional, sharp, no mess. We're opening a new space uptown. I want you to run it."

Asha blinked. Not because she was surprised—she knew she was qualified. But because she wasn't sure she wanted it.

"That's a big move, she said slowly, grabbing a rag just to keep her hands busy.

"It is," he agreed. "But you're built for it. You keep things calm. You don't get rattled. People listen to you."

Asha smiled. "That's called trauma. But thanks."

He laughed. "Just think about it. You've earned the right to want more."

The moment he walked away, she pulled out her phone and texted Jean: They offered me my own bar. I think I might throw up. Also, I might say yes. Also, I might run away and start a new life in Portugal. How are you?

Jean: I'm healing from emotional streaking. Details later. Say yes to the job, idiot.

When Asha's shift ended, she didn't go home. She walked two blocks to Jordan's place, buzzed in without warning, and stood in his kitchen like she'd been there a thousand times.

He looked up from his laptop. "Everything okay?"

"No. Yes. I don't know."

She sat down. "They want me to manage the new location. More money. More pressure. More... visibility." He waited.

She said: "I don't know if I want that kind of responsibility. I've made a career out of showing up halfway so no one can blame me if I fall."

Jordan came around the counter and sat beside her. "You want me to tell you what to do?"

Asha shook her head. "I want to be brave enough to decide."

Jordan nodded. "Then I'll sit here quietly until you figure it out."

She looked at him, saw the way he didn't flinch when she hesitated.

"I'm used to preparing for failure," she said. "Not success."

Jordan looked at her. "So now you're scared of the good shit too?"

She laughed. "Terrified." He reached for her hand.

"I've seen you run. But I've also seen you stay. So whatever you choose—I believe you'll mean it."

Later that night, she stood on her balcony in gym shorts and a hoodie, staring out at nothing.

Then she texted the group: If you stay ready, you never have to feel safe. I've lived by that for years. But maybe safety isn't weakness. Maybe it's just… quiet power.

Danielle responded: It's only power if you don't weaponize it against yourself.

CC: Y'all are getting too grown for me. Somebody lie to me about their ex's dick so I feel normal again.

Jamal: Mine texted me 'wyd' today and I blocked her on three platforms out of sheer self-respect. That help?

Asha: Slightly.

She laughed to herself and whispered, "Fuck it. Let's try." Then drafted her reply to her manager. Simple. Direct. Yes. I'll take it.

Velour Social was half-empty, which was exactly how they liked it.

CC had reserved the long back table and told Jordan to bring extra napkins and even more liquor. "We're gonna get emotionally reckless tonight, he said, "and I refuse to cry into something cheap."

Jean walked in last. Danielle waved her over. "You good?"

Jean nodded too fast. Asha gave her a look. "That wasn't a real nod."

Jean slid into her seat. "I'm fine. Just recovering from hitting 'send' on an emotional suicide note."

Jamal: "Why are you like this?"

Jean sipped. "Because I've been rewarded for sounding okay after chaos. And this is my relapse."

CC passed her a shot. "Toast it, bitch."

She raised her glass. "To good dick, bad judgment, and inboxes that snitch."

Everyone clinked. Everyone drank.

Danielle was first to say it. "You didn't deserve the panic that followed. I read your message. You weren't cruel. You were scared."

Jean nodded. "And somehow, that's worse."

Asha leaned in. "You think honesty is betrayal because you're used to managing perceptions. But Moses didn't run because he saw fear. He ran because he saw your fear "

Jean looked away. "I never meant for him to read it."

Jamal: "Then don't write it in email form, ma'am. That's what the Notes app is for. Or at least a burner Gmail."

Jean tried to laugh. But it cracked in her throat. "I wanted to be ready before I told the truth. But it turns out you're never ready. You just are."

CC reached across the table and held her hand. "We're not applauding pain anymore. We're not pretending the mess is admirable."

Danielle added, "You don't have to be cleaned up to be loved."

Asha: "But you do have to stop pretending love isn't terrifying."

Jean whispered, "It is. Every single fucking time."

The group fell quiet. Not awkward. Just still.

Kiki finally broke it. "Okay, but also, can we acknowledge that the last person who made Jean feel this way was Green Smoothie, and that ended with her threatening him with a limp dick warning label?"

Jean grinned. "This one had a name. And a future. That's why it hurt more."

CC: "Growth is realizing not all pain is from being done wrong. Sometimes it's just… being seen too soon."

Jamal raised a hand. "Am I the only one who's ever sent an email, read it back, and realized I didn't even believe myself?"

Asha said, "Nope. Sent one once that said, 'Take care of yourself always.' When what I meant was 'I hope your next situationship ends with a rash'."

Danielle chimed in. "I once sent a draft to someone that ended with 'Love always,' even though I hadn't felt anything in weeks."

Jean added, "Mine was titled Closure. But it was actually Permission to Lie to Myself One More Time."

They went around the table, no longer laughing. But not crying either. Just sharing. It was probably the most honest they'd ever been.

Not because they were ready. But because not being honest had gotten too heavy.

CC lifted his glass. "To being seen. Even when we don't look our best."

Jean clinked it. "To hitting send. Even when we're not sure we should."

Danielle: "To surviving the replies."

Jamal: "Or the silence."

Asha looked around and said: "To inboxes full of lies we no longer need. And truths we're finally ready to read."

The night was winding down, but nobody was rushing to leave.

Jordan had turned the lights low. The music was soft, a slow mix of soul and R&B that wrapped around their conversation like a final warm towel at a high-end spa.

CC slid back into his seat with a fresh drink and said, "You know what's wild? We used to write emails we hoped no one would read. Now we write texts we pray they'll respond to."

Jean raised her glass. "And sometimes they do. But not until we've had a full breakdown and four glasses of prosecco."

Danielle smirked. "Or until we've edited it into something palatable."

Asha added, "Or until we send it raw, emotional, and completely inappropriate."

Jamal said, "Or until they move on and you end up performing a self-respect ritual by blocking them with sage in hand."

CC nodded, knowingly. "I once sent a message that said 'I understand' when I absolutely did not understand, forgive, or bless shit."

Danielle said to him, "That's called surviving with style."

Jean's phone buzzed. Everyone paused. She stared at it. Then read aloud:

Jean. You don't have to apologize for fear. I have it too. I read what you wrote. And while it stung a little—it didn't scare me off.

It reminded me you're real. And that maybe this is too.

So I'll wait for you to be ready. Or I'll walk with you while you figure it out. But either way, I'm here. If you want me to be.

Silence.

Jean blinked. "It's Moses."

CC whispered, "Bitch."

Danielle smiled. "And just like that, the right one replied."

Asha nodded. "Damn. He fine and emotionally literate?"

Jamal smirked. "Jesus really does save."

Jean didn't cry. She didn't panic. She just breathed. Then raised her glass. "To all the emails we wrote but never sent."

CC: "To the ones we sent, but survived anyway."

Danielle: "To the ones who read it and didn't run."

Asha: "To the ones who did—and made space for better "

Jamal: "To inboxes full of bad decisions and better edits."

Kiki: "To the drafts that kept us honest."

Ramon: "To the replies that made us grow."

CC stood up and said it loud: "To all of that—but also… No. Not that email." Everyone laughed.

Jean grinned. "And if it is that email… we face it anyway."

Danielle: "Because we meant it when we wrote it."

Asha: "And because grown love doesn't require perfect grammar."

They drank. Loud. Together.

Later that night, Jean texted Moses: Still scared. Still here. Still want this.

His reply was instant: Good. Me too.

Chapter 25: Peace Feels Like Waiting for the Other Shoe to Text

Jean woke up after Moses.

Moses was waiting on the rooftop, the city stretched out behind him in gold and shadow. A breeze tugged at Jean's hair, carrying the smell of rain even though the sky was clear.

"You're late," he said, but he was smiling like she was right on time.

Jean took the last few steps slow, not because of the heels but because… this felt like something she wanted to remember in detail.

"I had to make sure I looked like I meant it," she said.

And when he reached for her hand, the skyline turned into nothing but blur. Again.

She wasn't used to mornings without adrenaline—no silent questioning of what was left unsaid, no passive-aggressive cold shoulder, no fake stretch to gauge whether the other person wanted to leave or stay.

Just Moses. Still here. Breathing steady. Arm draped across her like he bought the rights.

She got out of bed quietly and padded into the kitchen, grabbing her phone and staring at it like it owed her an answer.

No drama in the inbox. No misread texts. No notes app confessions from the night before.

It was all… calm. That was the problem.

She sat on the edge of her couch and scrolled. Nothing upsetting. Nothing triggering. Nothing that made her heart spike or her jaw clench.

She thought, Is this what being chosen feels like? Or is this just what it feels like when someone's too stable to spark?

Then she winced—because that thought felt like a betrayal.

Moses walked in groggily, rubbing his eyes and mumbling something about needing a better pillow. He kissed her on the forehead and opened the fridge.

Jean whispered, "Good morning."

He turned, smiled, and said, "You okay?"

She nodded. "Just thinking."

He didn't press. He never did. That was another issue.

Later, after he left, she opened her laptop and pulled up a blank document titled "Maybe This is What Safe Feels Like."

She wrote:

I used to confuse love with intensity. If it wasn't urgent, it wasn't real. If it wasn't messy, it wasn't deep. And now?

Now I'm in something clean. Something quiet. And I keep waiting for it to scream. For him to disappoint me. For me to sabotage it. For the email I never meant to send to come true.

But he's still here. And I don't know if I'm holding my breath or just unused to breathing evenly.

She stared at it. Then deleted it.

Chapter 25: Peace Feels Like Waiting for the Other Shoe to Text

Jean woke up after Moses.

Moses was waiting on the rooftop, the city stretched out behind him in gold and shadow. A breeze tugged at Jean's hair, carrying the smell of rain even though the sky was clear.

"You're late," he said, but he was smiling like she was right on time.

Jean took the last few steps slow, not because of the heels but because... this felt like something she wanted to remember in detail.

"I had to make sure I looked like I meant it," she said.

And when he reached for her hand, the skyline turned into nothing but blur. Again.

She wasn't used to mornings without adrenaline—no silent questioning of what was left unsaid, no passive-aggressive cold shoulder, no fake stretch to gauge whether the other person wanted to leave or stay.

Just Moses. Still here. Breathing steady. Arm draped across her like he bought the rights.

She got out of bed quietly and padded into the kitchen, grabbing her phone and staring at it like it owed her an answer.

No drama in the inbox. No misread texts. No notes app confessions from the night before.

It was all… calm. That was the problem.

She sat on the edge of her couch and scrolled. Nothing upsetting. Nothing triggering. Nothing that made her heart spike or her jaw clench.

She thought, Is this what being chosen feels like? Or is this just what it feels like when someone's too stable to spark?

Then she winced—because that thought felt like a betrayal.

Moses walked in groggily, rubbing his eyes and mumbling something about needing a better pillow. He kissed her on the forehead and opened the fridge.

Jean whispered, "Good morning."

He turned, smiled, and said, "You okay?"

She nodded. "Just thinking."

He didn't press. He never did. That was another issue.

Later, after he left, she opened her laptop and pulled up a blank document titled "Maybe This is What Safe Feels Like."

She wrote:

I used to confuse love with intensity. If it wasn't urgent, it wasn't real. If it wasn't messy, it wasn't deep. And now?

Now I'm in something clean. Something quiet. And I keep waiting for it to scream. For him to disappoint me. For me to sabotage it. For the email I never meant to send to come true.

But he's still here. And I don't know if I'm holding my breath or just unused to breathing evenly.

She stared at it. Then deleted it.

She texted Asha: Is it possible to be this happy and still feel unsettled?

Asha: Yes. It's called unlearning. It's exhausting.

Jean: I feel like I should be running or prepping for heartbreak.

Asha: That's the old training. You're not at war anymore. But your nerves don't believe you yet.

Jean: Goddamn.

Jean called Moses. He answered immediately. "You good?"

She paused. "I need to ask you something. And it's gonna sound fucked up, but I need to know."

"Okay."

She took a breath. "Are you really this calm, or are you just avoiding rocking the boat?"

There was silence. Then he said, "I'm calm because I spent too many years trying to win people who didn't want to be kept. And when I found someone who actually wanted to be here… I figured I should make sure she knows she can trust the floor beneath her." Jean blinked.

Moses added, "But if you need noise to feel seen, I can scream real poetic if you want."

She laughed. "No. Don't ruin it."

"Then let it be quiet, baby. You earned this."

After they hung up, she laid on her couch and let that land. Maybe peace wasn't boring. Maybe it was just new. And maybe Moses wasn't the one she didn't trust. Maybe it was herself.

She texted the group:

I used to think if it didn't hurt a little, it wasn't real. But now I'm wondering if peace just feels unfamiliar to people who've survived too much intensity.

Danielle replied: Don't confuse lack of chaos with lack of love.

CC: We need that on a hoodie. Or a strap.

Jamal: Or a vibrator box.

Jean: Thank you, idiots. I love you.

Asha: We know.

CC hadn't moved for twenty minutes. Not because he was asleep. Because he didn't want to wake DeMarcus. The man was knocked out—mouth slightly open, chest rising slow and steady, with one hand resting on CC's ass like it had a permanent address there.

It was peaceful. And for CC, terrifying. He wasn't used to waking up next to someone and not performing.

No "accidental" stretches to show off his hips. No well-timed morning thirst trap selfies for the group chat. No leaving to brush his teeth and sneaking back in with breath that said minty but still nasty.

Just laying there. Breathing next to someone who didn't want more from him. Who didn't want less, either. Who just... wanted him.

He slid out of bed gently and went to the bathroom. Closed the door. Sat on the closed toilet seat in silence.

He grabbed his phone. Opened the Notes app, and typed: I think I like him more than I like being admired. He stared at it.

Then added: And that scares the absolute fuck out of me.

DeMarcus knocked on the door. "You okay?"

"Yeah," CC lied.

"You sure?"

CC paused. "Just giving you some sleep. You were snoring like God gave you a playlist "

DeMarcus laughed. "Come back. I miss the heat source."

They curled up again. This time, CC didn't fake sleep. He just laid there.

Still. Seen. Safe. That's when he realized how much he'd shrunk in the past.

He used to make himself smaller after the fun wore off. Quieter. Less bold. Less flirty. Less him. All to keep people who said things like, "You're a lot." And then left anyway.

But DeMarcus? He didn't seem to want less. In fact, CC had dialed himself down lately and DeMarcus had noticed.

"You okay?" he whispered again.

DeMarcus didn't open his eyes. "I'm great. But you're quieter lately." CC didn't respond.

DeMarcus added, "If you shrink to keep me, I'll lose interest. I fell for all of you."

CC snorted. "You sure? I got a lot of all."

DeMarcus pulled him closer. "Exactly."

They didn't say much after that. Didn't have to. But something inside CC cracked open.

Later, while DeMarcus showered, CC sat by the window in one of his kimonos and opened a journal. Not the Notes app. A real journal. Pen. Ink. Paper. He hadn't done that in over a decade.

He wrote:

I'm not afraid he'll leave. I'm afraid he'll stay and see all of me.

I'm not used to being loved gently. I'm used to being consumed. Desired. Fawned over.

But he loves like he's building something. Not burning through it. Then he texted Asha: I think I like him more than I like being admired.

She replied: That means it's real. Do you like yourself when he's around?

CC stared at the screen. Typed: Yeah. Even the soft parts.

Asha: Then don't run. Just let yourself stay.

CC got back in bed. Didn't pose. Didn't flex. Didn't crack a joke. He just laid there and let someone keep him.

Christina noticed it before Danielle did.

The way her jaw tensed when the topic shifted to vulnerability. How her shoulders stiffened when they sat too close without touching. The way she weaponized curiosity—always asking questions instead of answering them.

"You're doing it again," Christina said softly.

Danielle looked up from her phone. "Doing what?"

"Turning intimacy into a quiz I have to pass."

Danielle blinked. "I didn't realize I was doing that."

"I know," Christina said, folding her legs beneath her on the couch. "That's what makes it so dangerous."

Danielle took a breath. "I'm not trying to shut you out."

"I didn't say you were shutting me out. I'm saying you're managing me. Like a client. Like a case."

Danielle's tone sharpened. "I'm not—"

Christina held up a hand. "It's not an attack. But you asked me last week if I felt like I could be myself around you. I said yes. But now I'm asking you: do you feel like you can be yourself around me?" Danielle looked away.

Christina added: "Or are you just projecting the version you think I'll love the most?"

Silence. Not cold. Just heavy.

"I don't know," Danielle finally said. "I think I've been... performing safety. Instead of feeling it."

Christina nodded. "That makes sense."

Danielle's voice dropped. "I don't like needing people "

"I know."

"I don't like being predictable."

"I know."

"And I don't want you to feel like I'm a project."

"I never have," Christina said. "But I think you feel like you are."

Danielle didn't respond. Christina shifted slightly closer but didn't reach out. "I'm not here to fix you. I'm here to see you."

Danielle tried to speak. Couldn't.

Christina added, "And for the record, I don't want to be another woman you date by protocol. I don't want the well-packaged version. I want the scared one. The confused one. The one who's not sure she deserves it. Because that one is real."

Danielle stared at her. Then said, voice quiet but firm: "That one bites."

Christina grinned. "Good. I like teeth."

The tension broke—just a little. Not dissolved. Not resolved. But acknowledged. And for Danielle, that was big.

Later that night, she lay on the couch alone while Christina took a call in the other room.

She opened her notes app and typed:

You can't claim to be honest if all you ever show is the finished version. That's not honesty. That's curation.

And I've been curating the fuck out of my feelings.

Then she deleted it. Not because it wasn't true—but because she didn't need to archive it anymore.

She texted the group: Being seen is scary. Especially when you're not sure which version of you they're seeing. Or which one you've let them see.

Jean replied: I think I've shown Moses all of me. Even the boring parts. Still here.

CC: DeMarcus saw me asleep with my mouth open. I think that counts as nudity.

Asha: Jordan brought dinner and rubbed my feet. I didn't even clean first. Growth.

Danielle stared at their replies. Then added: I think for the first time ever… we're all seeing someone.

The chat paused. Then CC wrote: Wait… bitch, are we all finally in something at the same damn time?

Asha: Not complete. Not clear. But yeah… something.

Jean: When has that ever happened?

Danielle: Never.

Jamal popped in: Even I got someone. And she's real. Not AI. Not a filter. Swear to God.

Kiki: Wait until we all see each other again. This gon' be weird. But like… weird in a good way.

And just like that, the idea was planted.Maybe—just maybe—they were all finally somewhere. Together.

CC was already on FaceTime with Kiki before Danielle even finished the group text.

"You're telling me," CC said slowly, "that all of us—all of us—are either sleeping next to somebody, in something consistent, or actually liking the person we're talking to?"

Kiki shrugged from her kitchen. "I mean, yeah."

CC gasped. "We're in the twilight zone. Somebody check Jamal for a wire."

Danielle chimed in on audio: "It's true. Jean's seeing Moses. Asha and Jordan are getting closer. You and DeMarcus are basically husband-adjacent. And Christina saw me without earrings on and still kissed me."

Kiki raised her glass. "And I got Ramon refilling my Brita pitcher and apologizing for old gaslighting like he's on a 12-step program."

CC blinked. "I'm scared."

Danielle: "Why?"

"Because peace makes me horny and suspicious."

The group chat blew up five minutes later.

Jean: I still say this means we're in the finale episode of a drama. One of us is about to get kidnapped or propose.

Asha: No. This is just what happens when you survive enough mess to stop romanticizing it.

Jamal: Can I say something wild?

Jean: No.

Jamal: I really like her and she likes me back and I love it.

Danielle: Not wild. That's called healing.

Kiki: And she is fine, I support your journey.

Jamal: She's fine and she has edges. Real ones.

CC: Oh she a unicorn.

Danielle wrote: What if we actually did something? All of us. A gathering. Low-stakes. Not dramatic. Just us. As we are. With who we're with.

Jean: Like what, brunch?

Asha: Too much chewing. Not enough movement.

CC: Too many high-waisted pants.

Kiki: What about a rooftop thing?

CC: No. I'm calling it now. We host the first official Soft Life Cookout.

Danielle: Say more.

CC: Private backyard. Hookah optional. Music must include Toni Braxton, Floetry, and at least one remix where Beyoncé cusses.

Asha: Are children allowed?

Jean: Only if they can pass a vibe check.

Jamal: Can Jasmine come?

Kiki: If she real.

CC: She real, Jamal. But is you real?

Danielle sat back on her couch, reading the threads.

Something was happening. They weren't performing. They weren't unpacking pain. They weren't even roasting each other too hard.

They were just… showing up. Connected.

She texted Christina: I think we're finally all seeing someone. Like, at the same time. It's never happened before.

Christina: Does it feel weird?

Danielle: It feels earned. But wild.

Christina: Then I guess we're all in the wilderness now. Bring bug spray.

Later that night, CC texted Jean directly: Soft Life Cookout. I'll plan it. But it ends with a group toast. Real grown energy. Laughter. No trauma sharing.

Jean: You sure we can pull that off?

CC: No. But I believe in us. Kinda.

Danielle opened a new note: Title: No, Not That Email. Beneath it, she wrote:

Maybe for once, we aren't writing drafts we're afraid to send. Maybe this is what it feels like to live something that doesn't need editing.

She saved it. Didn't delete. Didn't overthink it. Just let it sit.

"Alright," CC said, sipping a cocktail that had no business being pink and smoky, "we need a pre-meeting."

Danielle blinked. "For what?"

CC crossed his legs. "For the Soft Life Cookout. We can't go in raw. There must be ground rules."

Asha: "You make it sound like an orgy."

Jean: "Or worse—family dinner."

They met the next night at Velour Social. Not in the main space, but the VIP back room with the plush chairs that felt like expensive therapy couches.

Everyone was there. No significant others. Just the original crew.

Kiki walked in holding Ramon's hand, then let it go like a formality. "We love y'all. But let's be clear—we still together. Ain't nobody stealing our joy tonight."

Ramon nodded. "She said what she said."

Danielle opened her notepad. "So… rules of engagement?"

CC snapped. "Rule one: no bringing up old mess. No stories that involve the phrase 'when we were toxic' or 'remember when I blocked them the first time'."

Asha: "So no emotional time travel. Got it."

Jean: "What about euphemisms? Like 'back in the day'?"

CC: "Only if it leads to growth or orgasms. If not, skip it."

Jamal raised his hand. "Can I ask a serious question?"

Danielle: "No."

Jean: "Go ahead."

Jamal: "What if someone brings up one of my old stories and Jasmine hears it and finds out about the time I accidentally sent that butt pic to the group chat?"

Asha: "Accidentally?"

CC: "Boy shut up. Next rule—every story must be about something good. Something shared. Something real."

Jean: "No performative trauma."

Kiki: "No unpacking."

Ramon: "No panel discussions."

Danielle nodded. "We're not introducing our people to the version of us that only exists in confessionals."

Asha: "This isn't an audition. It's a celebration."

CC leaned back. "Rule three: if you bring someone, you're claiming them. No 'we're just friends' energy. If they're there, they're yours. If you get dumped after, that's on you. But tonight? They yours."

Jean: "So we bringing adult love. Not play cousins."

Danielle: "Exactly."

Kiki looked around. "Y'all know what this is, right?" They all turned to her.

"It's the final email reconciliation."

Jamal: "But make it couple-friendly."

Asha: "We're adapting."

Jean: "Evolving."

Danielle: "We've spent so much time telling stories about who hurt us. Now we get to tell the ones about who stayed."

Ramon grinned. "I ain't gon' lie. I'm proud of y'all."

Kiki: "Real proud. And even more proud we don't have to lose our friends just because we're the married couple."

Ramon: "We get to do couples stuff now."

Kiki: "Like argue in the car before the event and pretend we fine when we walk in."

CC: "Like match outfits but say it was a coincidence."

Asha: "Like group vacations where somebody always ends up crying in the sand."

Jean: "Like brunch tables that need three different checks."

Danielle: "Like side-eyes that say 'you better behave' without saying a word."

They were all laughing now. Not cautious laughter. Not tiptoe joy.

Just pure, unfiltered excitement that for once—this was real.

Jamal raised his glass. "To us. Still messy. Still figuring it out. But finally seeing someone. All of us. At the same time."

CC clinked. "To the Soft Life Cookout."

Danielle: "To showing up. Fully."

Jean: "To loving out loud."

Asha: "To not fucking this up."

Kiki: "To keeping our people and our peace."

Ramon: "To being the example we didn't know we were becoming."

Danielle looked around and whispered: "Maybe this is what it looks like when you stop surviving and start living."

Jean raised her glass. "No more trauma bonding."

Asha nodded. "No more confessionals."

CC grinned. "No more lies disguised as punchlines."

Jamal smirked. "No more cheap liquor at healing events."

Everyone laughed. Then agreed.

Chapter 26: No, Not that Email!

It was the kind of weather that made you forget all your trauma for six to eight hours.

Sun just warm enough. Breeze light enough. Drinks cold enough. Music loud enough to dance, low enough to eavesdrop. The first Soft Life Cookout had officially begun.

Jean and Moses arrived first, because Jean needed to see the room before the room saw her. She wore a yellow sundress with dangerous thigh splits and sandals that could double as weapons.

Moses wore what looked like linen and divine favor.

Jean warned him: "These are my people. They love hard, roast harder. If someone brings up the word 'trauma' or a nickname from the past, you don't flinch. You just sip."

Moses kissed her hand. "If they survived loving you, I respect them already."

She smiled and muttered, "Goddamn. You're good."

Danielle and Christina arrived next—accidentally matching in cream and olive.

"I swear I didn't plan this," Danielle said.

Christina grinned. "It's okay. We look like the most well-adjusted gay couple from a lesbian drama that hasn't premiered yet."

"Speak for yourself," Danielle said. "I'm still writing notes in my phone like a trauma librarian."

Asha and Jordan followed—looking grown. She wore soft denim and a perfectly messy top bun. He wore a fitted polo and pants that said "I give good backrubs."

They held hands, no performance. Just present.

"You ready?" he asked.

"Born ready," Asha said. Then paused. "Okay, not born, but close."

Jamal and Jasmine strolled in like the Instagram couple nobody wanted to root for but had to admit…they looked happy. And yes —Jasmine was fine.

Not regular fine. The kind of fine that made you stare and forget your PIN number.

Kiki whispered, "Whew. Okay, Jamal."

Jean sipped her drink. "He brought a real person. I owe Asha five dollars."

CC arrived last, of course, wearing a sheer animal print robe, denim shorts with rhinestones, and what could only be described as "boot heels from the Book of Revelations."

DeMarcus walked beside him in all black. Calm. Delicious. He held the speaker and the Hennessy like a man fully committed.

Kiki announced loudly: "CC has entered the chat!"

CC shouted back, "I don't enter. I arrive."

The hugs were loud. The compliments were petty. The shade was subtle but omnipresent.

Danielle: "Did you do something new to your face, Jean?"

Jean: "No, just fucking someone who likes it."

Asha: "Praise be."

Kiki and Ramon had the grill going, of course. Ramon flipped ribs while holding a mimosa. "This is grown-man foreplay."

Kiki wore hoop earrings and a tee that said Soft Life, Hard Boundaries. She already had three drinks in rotation and no intentions of explaining herself.

They all took a moment. Standing there. Realizing. This was it. They were all here—with someone. Not perfect. Not filtered. Just…here.

Jean broke the silence. "You know this has never happened, right?"

Asha: "What?"

Danielle: "All of us. In something."

CC: "Girl, shut up before you jinx it."

Jamal: "Y'all acting like this is the last supper."

Kiki: "It might be. If someone says 'twin flame' I'm throwing a rib bone."

They burst out laughing. It was easy. No ice to break. Just joy, like it had been simmering and finally hit boil.

Jean leaned into Moses. "Still good?"

"Still great," he said.

"You nervous?"

"Not really. These are your people. They're part of your story."

She looked at him. "You want the whole story?"

He smiled. "I already do "

CC clinked a bottle and shouted, "Alright, bitches. The cookout has commenced. There will be games. There will be gossip. And there will be a final toast."

Danielle: "Do we know what the toast is?"

CC: "I do. But I'm waiting to see if y'all live up to it."

They didn't know what was coming. But for now? The ribs were juicy. The drinks were cold. The love was loud. And every last one of them was held.

"Game time, hoes!"

That was how CC introduced the next phase of the cookout. No preamble. No warning. Just a deck of cards he slapped onto the picnic table like they came straight from a Black auntie sex therapist who also moonlighted as a licensed medium.

Everyone groaned.

"CC…" Jean warned.

He grinned, already shuffling. "This game is called Grown Folks Only. You pull a card, you read the question, and you answer honestly. Or you take a shot of Asha's moonshine punch and risk never feeling your gums again."

First up: Jean.

She pulled a card, rolled her eyes, and read aloud: "What's something you had to unlearn in order to love someone new?"

The group immediately oohed.

Jean sipped her drink. "That calm isn't the same as disinterest. That when someone doesn't chase, it doesn't mean they're walking away. Sometimes they're just… already there."

Moses nodded next to her. Didn't say a word. Just took her hand and squeezed.

CC fanned himself. "Bitch, I'm pregnant now."

Next up: Jamal. He pulled a card and blinked. "What surprised you the most about your partner?"

Jamal said, "That she knows how to build a fire, fix a radiator, and suck soul out of body without blinking."

Jasmine choked on her mimosa. Kiki shouted, "Well damn!"

Asha: "And yet somehow I'm the aggressive one."

Asha's turn. She flipped her card. "What's one secret fear you haven't told your partner?"

The table went quiet. She glanced at Jordan, then said: "That if I get too soft, I'll forget how to fight. And if I forget how to fight, I won't survive when peace ends."

Jordan leaned in, kissed her shoulder. "Then I guess it's my job to help you remember peace can stay."

CC wiped an invisible tear. "Y'all got me out here wet."

Danielle: "A single tear counts as pre-ejaculate for Church Candy."

Danielle's turn. She flipped hers and sighed. "What scares you about loving her?"

She looked at Christina. "The fact that it's not chaos. That I actually want this. And I've spent so long narrating instead of living, I don't know if I remember how to just be with someone without turning it into a case study "

Christina smiled. "Then let's make this the first one you don't analyze."

Danielle raised her glass. "Cheers to that."

CC, of course, saved himself for last.

He pulled a card. "Who made you feel safest this year?"

He didn't flinch. "Myself. Because I finally stopped shrinking to be kept. But if I'm being honest?" He turned to DeMarcus. "This one right here. Because he didn't try to fix me, tame me, or monetize me."

Jean: "Monetize?"

CC: "You'd be surprised how many people want to turn me into merch."

DeMarcus laughed and added, "I fell for the whole circus."

CC smiled. "And I didn't have to shut it down to keep you."

The game paused. Not because anyone said stop. But because the moment landed too well to follow with jokes.

Then Jamal tried to sip and spilled punch on himself. CC stood: "Nope. That's the universe telling us we reached the emotional quota. Back to ratchet."

Kiki raised her cup. "To grown love and grown games."

Danielle: "And to people who don't weaponize your soft."

Jean: "To not checking emails we outgrew."

Asha: "To partners who don't need to read our past to write the future."

They clinked. Laughing now. Not crying. Not analyzing. Just laughing. Because somehow... they all survived enough to land here.

Kiki stood up mid-laugh, one sandal dangling from her foot like she was preaching in the middle of a potluck.

"Aight, y'all," she said, waving her plastic wine glass. "Enough games. It's time."

Everyone groaned.

Jamal: "Time for what? Dessert?"

CC: "A group massage?"

Jean: "A public apology from Jamal's nipples?"

Kiki smiled. "No. The final email reconciliation."

CC gasped. "Girl, we said no trauma tonight."

Kiki grinned. "And we meant it. But this ain't that. This version is couple-friendly. Soft life–certified."

Ramon nodded beside her. "It's one sentence. Just one. If the person you're with left tomorrow, what would you want them to remember from being with you? Not to beg them back. Not to explain. Just… what do you hope they carry?"

The group paused.

Danielle: "I hate that this is beautiful."

Jean: "And I hate that I already know mine."

They went one by one. No hesitation. No disclaimers. Just truth.

Jean stood first. Looked at Moses.

"If you ever go, I hope you remember that you never had to fix me. Just hold me steady while I did the work."

Moses nodded. Took her hand like it was the first time all over again.

Jamal cleared his throat. "If she ever left, I'd want her to remember I finally became the man I wanted to be—because she let me be it. No shaming. No training. Just room." Jasmine bit her lip. Kissed his cheek.

CC fake sobbed into a napkin. "Our little boy's all grown up."

Asha looked at Jordan and said, "If you left, I'd want you to remember that I tried. Not because I was afraid to lose you—but because I was finally brave enough to want to keep something."

Jordan pulled her close. Didn't say anything. Didn't need to.

Danielle took a sip first. "I'd want her to remember that I showed up. Not just physically. Emotionally. Completely. That for once in my life, I didn't hide behind structure or strategy. I just let myself be wanted." Christina leaned over and whispered something only Danielle could hear. Danielle smiled. Genuinely.

CC stood. Spun slowly for drama.Then looked DeMarcus in the eye. "I'd want him to remember that I loved him from the gut. Not the mask. Not the glitter. But the messy, mouthy, too-much middle of me. And I never shrank. Not once."

DeMarcus just nodded and mouthed, "I know."

CC sat down, visibly emotional. "I hate you all. This is beautiful and disgusting."

Kiki raised her glass. "I'd want him to remember that I let him see the parts of me that I used to apologize for. And that being loved out loud by him changed my bones."

Ramon wiped his eyes. "Shit. I was just gon' say I love her for letting me be corny." They laughed. They clapped. They leaned on each other like every soft thing they'd feared had just introduced itself by name.

A moment passed. Then CC snapped: "That's it. No more emotional shit. We toast at sunset. But now we eat."

Jamal: "I already ate."

CC: "You always do. Look at your plate. It's a crime scene."

Jean whispered to Moses, "They've never done this without trauma before. Never."

He kissed her shoulder. "You think this is the end?"

She shook her head. "No. This is the part where we finally start writing the good chapters."

He raised his glass. "To the inbox we don't need anymore."

As the sky dimmed from gold to bronze, the Bluetooth speaker switched to Solange like it knew a shift was happening. Not dramatic. Just… warm.

CC stood with his arms stretched out. "Y'all feel that? That's what it feels like when your nervous system stops scanning for bullshit."

Jean sipped her drink. "Or maybe that's just the tequila finally hitting."

"No," Danielle said. "It's different."

They were all scattered across lounge chairs, picnic blankets, steps, and coolers. No one standing. No one posing. Just slouched, sunk, and satisfied.

Asha looked around and said it first: "It's wild seeing all of us sitting next to somebody we actually like."

Jamal nodded. "No side pieces. No rented attention. No maybe-next-times."

Danielle smiled. "Just the now."

Jordan said, "This the most peace I've seen in one backyard."

CC added, "And the least mess. No ghost stories. No diss tracks. Just people who actually return texts and hold eye contact."

Kiki raised her hand like she was making an altar call. "Can we get a round of applause for no one needing to be saved tonight?"

They all clapped. Loud. Like they meant it.

Ramon looked up from his grill throne. "Y'all ever realize how many years it took to sit still like this? No exit plans. No backup flirting. Just… being good where you are."

Jean exhaled. "I used to be addicted to options. Now I just want one person who doesn't make me doubt."

Asha said, "Now you sound like me."

"Bitch, don't ruin it."

Danielle stood. Not dramatically—just enough to get a clear view of them all.

She laughed. "Do you know how hard it is to take a group photo where no one's cropping their partner out?"

CC shouted, "We're all in the frame, baby "

Jean: "Even Jamal?"

Jamal: "Especially me. My girl got me out here with lotion on my ankles and compliments in my lunchbox."

DeMarcus whispered something in CC's ear. Whatever it was, it made CC giggle like a child and bite his lip.

Christina traced her finger along Danielle's wrist. "How's your social battery?"

Danielle smiled. "Charged. First time in forever."

Jean watched Moses help clear plates.

Asha watched Jordan fold her sweater around her shoulders.

Kiki held Ramon's hand under the table.

CC leaned into DeMarcus's arm like he'd been waiting to do that his whole life and just now remembered he could.

There wasn't a speech. There wasn't a grand reveal. Just stillness. The kind that used to scare them. Now it felt like home.

Jean finally said what they were all thinking. "I think we're done writing old chapters."

Danielle nodded. "This time… we just live it."

CC raised his glass without standing. "To that."

Asha: "And to never shrinking to fit again."

Jamal: "And to staying in the damn picture."

Ramon: "And to the soft life actually showing up."

Kiki: "And to us not questioning it."

They clinked again. This time slower. This time deeper. This time because there was nothing left to prove. Only something to keep.

The sun dipped. Not fast. Not in a rush. Just low enough for shadows to stretch and shoulders to relax.

Someone—probably Jordan—turned the volume down on the speaker. Just a little.

Danielle stood and lifted her glass. Not performative. Not trying to be profound. Just still. Just clear. "I don't have a speech," she said. "But I have a moment." The group quieted.

"Tonight felt like a good draft. One you actually want to send. Not the kind you rewrite forty-seven times until it stops sounding like you."

Jean nodded, slow and proud. "Say that."

Danielle looked around. "I think we've all written those kinds of emails. The ones that sound brave but are really just bait. Or the ones we send knowing we'll regret them. Or the ones we don't send because we're too scared to hear silence."

Kiki raised her glass too.

"But this?" Danielle said, gesturing to the cookout—smeared plates, tangled limbs, stupid jokes, real love. "This isn't one of those."

Jamal whispered, "So what is it?"

Danielle grinned. "It's the first time we don't need the email."

CC stood slowly. "Because the story wrote back."

Jean clapped. "Bitch, that's it. Put that on a mug."

CC walked to the middle of the lawn. His robe flowing like drama incarnate. He cleared his throat. Dramatically, of course. "I was going to save this for next year," he said, "but in the spirit of soft life, group growth, and me not being a petty whore anymore…"

Laughter.

"I present to you: the final toast."

Everyone stood. Even the introverts.

CC lifted his glass like he was holding Beyoncé's first wig.

"To the inboxes we stopped refreshing.
To the drafts we didn't send.
To the people who saw us without the subject line first.
To the love that showed up before we performed for it.
To the peace we didn't have to earn.
To the friends who didn't flinch when we got soft.
And to the partners who joined us—not to fix, but to stay."

A beat of silence. Not heavy. Just… sacred.

Then Danielle added, "And if anyone ever asks if we sent one of those emails?"

Jean smiled. "If they ask if we finally wrote the one that says everything?"

Kiki held up her cup like a wand.

They danced after that.

Not choreographed. Just movement.

Jasmine twerked. Ramon grilled again. Jean made out with Moses behind a speaker. Asha slow danced with Jordan like nobody was watching—even though everyone was. Danielle whispered something in Christina's ear that made her blush and grab her ass. CC DJ'd with one hand and held DeMarcus with the other.

They weren't perfect. They weren't healed. They weren't done.

But they were in it. In the joy. In the mess. In the presence.

And for the first time, every one of them belonged there. Jean's phone buzzed. She glanced down, smiled, and, almost to herself said: 'No—not that email.'

Authors Note

Author's Note

No, Not That Email took shape around two containers: the live-table banter at Velour and the "receipts" culture of group chats. The rhythm you feel—dialogue that snaps, then a beat of quiet—comes from writing those scenes out loud, then cutting to the breath that follows. I wanted the laughs to be earned and the grief to be respected. The characters aren't composites of specific people, but the rules they live by are borrowed from very real survival strategies: audit your inbox, archive your patterns, and stop letting "maybe" invoice your peace.

Technically, the book rides three decisions:

1. **Structure**: chapters that end on choice, not cliffhanger; group chats as chorus; email snippets as pressure valves rather than plot devices.

2. **Voice**: Jean's blade, Danielle's ballast, CC's joy-as-defense, Kiki/Ramon/Asha as the stabilizers. The rule was simple—no one gets flattened for a punchline.

3. **Theme**: closure vs. boundary. We don't need to "win" the breakup. We need to stop funding it.

If you're a craft nerd: I drafted scenes in present-tense dialogue first (like stagework), layered internal beats second, and only then added prose. That kept the pages moving and prevented the jokes from choking the heart.

If you're just here for the story: thank you. You brought your own life to this book to make it work; novels are half-written by readers.

A quick note of gratitude to the real group chats that keep people alive. To friends who show up with fries, silence, or a ride home. To anyone who learned that "not replying" can be an act of profound love for yourself.

Finally, the title. It isn't an instruction to be cold; it's permission to be done. Sometimes the healthiest sentence is the one you never send.

We protect this house.

—James E. Lorraine
Crown Cipher Publishing

THANK YOU FOR READING

You just finished a story that's part of something bigger — the Crown Cipher Universe. If this book made you feel something, the next story might finish the sentence.

Join the House — Get early access, giveaways, and exclusive letters from your favorite authors.
Visit crowncipherpublishing.com/join

CONTINUE THE STORY

Every story under this crown is connected. Different voices. Same house. Protect it.

If You Loved…	Next, Read…	Author
Heavy Is the Crown	Letters in Silence	Omari Vale
Letters in Silence	The Monster Beside the Silence	Alonzo J. Crippen
No, Not That Email	No, Not That Wedding (2026)	James E. Lorraine
The Lies We Inherit	CounterFactual (Coming Soon)	Angela R. Key
We Touch Through Strangers	Heavy Is the Crown	James E. Lorraine
The Monster Beside the Silence	The Silence of the Pack (2026)	Alonzo J. Crippen

MEET THE AUTHORS

James E. Lorraine — The flagship author of Crown Cipher Publishing, architect of the Kingdom Universe, and the voice that built the House.

Angela R. Key — Author of The Lies We Inherit and CounterFactual. A master of psychological thrillers and gothic realism.

Omari Vale — The lyrical craftsman behind Letters in Silence and We Touch Through Strangers, bridging silence and connection.

Alonzo J. Crippen — The dark heart of The Wolf Gospel Series, creator of The Monster Beside the Silence.

See all titles at crowncipherpublishing.com/books

BECOME A CROWN CIPHER AMBASSADOR

Review, share, and earn rewards as part of the Royal House. Visit crowncipherpublishing.com/ambassadors

REVIEW & FOLLOW

Your words build the House. Review wherever you read.

Follow Crown Cipher Publishing on all platforms. #ProtectTheHouse #CrownCipherAuthors

We protect this F**king House.

www.ingramcontent.com/pod-product-compliance
Lightning Source LLC
Chambersburg PA
CBHW022147010726
47493CB00002B/378